Ketzia Knowles is a successful prestige property realtor. But beneath her polished facade lies a hidden power—she is a witch. Ketzia's supernatural abilities have always served her well, enabling her to manipulate energies and manifest her desires. But it's not until she meets Leon Furness, the company CEO, that she experiences the full extent of her powers.

From the moment they meet, an intense erotic connection sparks between them. As they give in to sexual desire, they awaken ancient forces that have slumbered for centuries, their passion igniting long-forgotten magic. And danger.

Together they must navigate a treacherous world where hidden adversaries seek to exploit their abilities for their own nefarious purposes. While caught in the realms of the supernatural, Ketzia's powers surge to unprecedented heights, but she realizes a relationship with Leon will be far from easy.

As they uncover the secrets of their shared past and confront the darkness surrounding them, they must face the ultimate question. Will their love and newfound powers be enough to overcome the malevolent forces that seek to destroy them?

Awakening the Goddess
Copyright © 2024 Sophie Love Marseilles
ISBN: 978-1-4874-3235-5
Cover art by Martine Jardin

Published by eXtasy Books Inc

Look for us online at:
www.eXtasybooks.com

Awakening the Goddess
The Weekend Witch 1

By

Sophie Love Marseilles

DEDICATION

This series is dedicated to all followers of the Craft. Blessed be your Awakening.

THE PROPHECY

The Prophecy as first recorded in 1168 — the Age of the Cistercians.

After the deaths of the pagan Knight and Lady at the hands of Darkness, the wheel will once again begin to turn. Seven cycles of tragedy must be borne before the God and Goddess of Night can once again take human form. Alas, their union can only result in pain and suffering for All — unless their union defies the formidable forces opposing them. If they do succeed in overthrowing the evil spirits of yore, bounteousness will be their shared reward.

CHAPTER ONE

White. *Everything is bathed in white light. It is a luminescent vastness and a cosmos of sexual energies. My spiritual sanctuary. Welcome.*

I sit upon a white throne, a dais atop a mountain of white – a mound of white crushed velvet fabric beneath me, endless reams of it. At the platform's base, a snake follows the folds of fabric upwards. It is a slow, sensual journey punctuated by a darbuka's gentle, rhythmic, hypnotic pounding. Another snake slithers into view. The two adders intertwine – briefly – before separating and continuing their respective journeys.

They reach a pair of female feet. Naked, pale, beautiful. My feet. The snakes glide over them, wrapping upwards to encircle my ankles. And now, if we were a film crew – with a camera operator – we'd move wider, pulling to soft focus on the white crushed velvet fabric of my dress, visible only from the waist down. The snakes disappear upwards, under my skirt – a hand strokes my knee. The hand belongs to a centaur. He lifts the hem of my dress and dips his head to kiss my ankles, then slowly follows the trail of the snakes. I encounter heaven at the touch of his lips. I surrender to his touch, languishing in pleasure. Other exotic supernatural creatures – angels, demons, hybrids – caress and arouse every part of my body. A leviathan teasingly sucks my left nipple while a shapeshifter who – with her long, dark hair and luminescent violet eyes – could be mistaken for my twin sister – trails its fingers up and down the softness of my stomach. Together they morph in and out of visibility, their very presence enough to tip me over the edge into an explosive orgasm, which never reaches its peak due to a sharp jab in my ribs, jolting me awake.

"Huh?" I survey my corporate—and very real—surroundings in confusion.

"You were snoring," my friend Mia whispers, pulling her elbow away from my side. It is the second day of the international annual sales conference for KX Realty Group, and so rudely pulled into this reality, I struggle to suppress a yawn. A middle-aged accountant spruiks the tax benefits of selling prestige properties off the plan. Behind him, a PowerPoint slide shows a graph charting short, medium, and long-term investment growth. It is all too boring for words, and I can stifle my yawn no more. Mia is one of the other real-estate representatives from Australia. She catches me in the act and winks. I wink back mischievously.

My name is Ketzia Knowles—at least, that's the name most people know me by. I also have another name, my witch name—but more of that later. This is the first year I have topped over ten million dollars in property sales for KX Realty Group and the first time they've invited me to this conference. The novelty of being counted as one of the elite few to attend is starting to wear off, and I am feeling the tiredness accumulated over the preceding weeks. Granted, the previous couple of days have been rather frantic. Firstly, of course, was getting to the conference. The company provided first-class travel to the resort at which it is being held this year—on Lantau Island in Hong Kong. Coming from Sydney, I'd had to adjust to a different time zone, and I'm struggling against the giddy symptoms of jet lag. Day one of the conference was yesterday. About three hundred sales reps are participating this year, which made for many meets and greets. The first networking session had left my mouth sore from smiling and my hand feeling like it was going to fall off from all the handshaking. But that is what sales is all about, and I know that to make it to the next level, I need all the international contacts I can get.

On the stage, the accountant is getting apoplectic about international tax laws, demonstrating on yet *another* pie chart how KX Realty Group takes advantage of each country's different rules and regulations to get the maximum return for its investors. It is beyond boring. My eyelids slam shut with a determination I didn't know they possessed, and I'm dragged back to my spiritual sanctuary. Sure, I need to understand the maths behind the investment scheme, at least enough to speak intelligently about it with a client. But maths has never been my forte. There's no way I would have made it to this conference, let alone sold even one hundred dollars' worth of property, if I had to rely on a good head for figures to hit my sales targets. No, my sales skills lie entirely elsewhere.

I didn't always intend to be a real estate salesperson, even a well-paid, prestige-market one. I've always wanted to be a psychologist. I did well at school and had good enough marks to enter university. Studying psychology was okay but not as profoundly fulfilling as I'd expected. While studying, I worked part-time as a receptionist at a local real estate office. Occasionally I would have to fill in for an agent and show a client around a property. I enjoyed this aspect of my job and discovered that I had a flair for interacting with the clients and making them feel like buying the places I showed them. Often potential clients want to sign on the dotted line immediately. My boss noticed the increase in sales and offered me work as a sales representative. He also offered to pay for all the study fees associated with getting a real estate agent's licence. It was an offer I couldn't refuse. So, I deferred my psychology degree indefinitely and started working full-time as a real estate agent. Something else I started doing at this time was practising witchcraft.

Before you freak out, let me assure you that I practise only good witchcraft. And because my dalliance with witchcraft is a hobby and not a full-time profession for me, I am classified as a weekend witch. A good witch — but a witch, nonetheless. It is a practice that I think I have embraced because it makes sense of the supernatural awareness that's always come naturally to me, like being able to predict the future, having extremely sensual dreams that are inspired by something otherworldly, and sometimes feeling like I have so much energy I can make things happen. Things like attract people to me. It's the thing that's made it possible for me to sell so many properties.

I don't know where this ability comes from. I don't come from a long line of witches. My mother's ancestry is Nordic, and my father is Spanish. From my mother, I have inherited pale white skin that tends to freckle and deep purple eyes. From my father, I inherited jet-black hair and a sleek, muscular frame. I wear my waist-length hair tied back in a ponytail for the conference. I'm also wearing my glasses. The glasses have clear lenses. I wear them not to protect my eyesight — which is better than twenty-twenty — but to protect other people from my hypnotic gaze. People fall under a spell when they are with me. Hypnotic vision is one of my strengths as a witch. The glasses serve as a barrier to hypnosis. They also act as a reminder to me — to only take them off if I am prepared to cast someone under my spell. Not that there's any danger of that now with the boring dude on stage and my eyes still firmly sealed shut. A round of polite applause marks the end of the session and startles me awake. Mia watches me expectantly and laughs when I join in the applause.

"You are so lucky to have slept through that one," she says, yawning exaggeratedly.

"I am so tired right now I think I could sleep for a week," I agree. "If the next person on that stage is even half as boring as that guy, they'll have to carry me out of here in a coffin."

I look around the conference room at the other participants. I notice that there are more male than female representatives. All the men wear suits. Most women are in suits, too, though some wear dresses with tailored jackets. I am wearing one of my favourite dresses, a black and white number with a discreet swirl motif, cinched at my waist with a slim, gold-buckle belt. The cowl neckline draws attention to my ample bust beautifully, while the classic cut of my black bolero jacket sets the outfit off nicely. On my feet, I wear simple black peep-toe heels and the thinnest of ankle bracelets around my ankle. I wear no jewellery or other adornments besides the obligatory conference name tag pinned to my jacket lapel. Mia wears a navy suit with a silk blouse in a caramel colour. Her bright red hair shines beneath the auditorium lights, her pixie haircut beautifully setting off her heart-shaped face. It occurs to me that seated next to each other, we make quite a striking pair. As the thought enters my head, I notice several men watching us admiringly. I half-smile at a guy sitting several rows away. He smiles back before turning his attention to the stage. The MC taps the mike, ready to announce the next part of the program. Oh well, I think. If this next session is anything as dull as the last, I can always entertain myself by checking out the rest of the delegates.

But as soon as the next presenter appears, I realise I won't need any distractions. It is Leon Furness, the global head of KX Realty. I recognise his face immediately from the company website and the corporate training videos I've watched from time to time. He always greets the screen with a dazzling smile and a down-to-earth hello. I remember his voice from the training videos. He speaks with an unusual trans-Atlantic accent, with rounded r's and an engaging lilt to his vowels.

He ambles to the podium gracefully, his medium-length brown hair shimmering beneath the stage lights, and his gaze scans the audience invitingly. He pauses to adjust the lectern before caressing the microphone with his deep, resonating voice.

"Congratulations, everyone, on making it to the KX Realty International Convention this year! Let me begin by saying that every one of you gathered here today is undeniably amazing. Invitations are only issued to salespeople amongst the top two per cent of our company internationally. You have each sold at least ten million dollars' worth of high-end realty. And that isn't easy, believe me, I know. I know from first-hand experience how difficult sales can be. Welcome to the high achievers club."

The room bursts into spontaneous applause. It isn't just his words that provoke this reaction. It is something to do with his whole being, the way he addresses the crowd and manages to make everyone in the room feel touched by his presence. He momentarily makes eye contact with me. I am seated perhaps fifty feet away from him. Yet, in that instance, I feel like I can taste the very air he breathes, smell his cologne, and feel his body heat. Then he smiles. The effect is electrifying. My mouth drops open, and I feel heat rising to my cheeks.

"Stop gaping!" Mia nudges me with that very angular elbow of hers. I smile in her direction, reluctant to let my gaze leave the enigma onstage. Leon Furness lowers his voice and confidentially continues his spiel as though talking to a trusted best friend. The room falls silent.

"When I started with this company ten years ago, I had no sales experience. I knew nothing about people. I was a geeky, shy twenty-year-old. Then one day, something changed . . ."

As he speaks, a vision appears to me. Another voice runs concurrently through my head. It tells the truth hidden behind his polished, practised speech. It is my spiritual self tapping into the telepathic energies emanating from Leon. This other voice tells the story of a childhood caught between parents battling it out in the divorce courts, of Leon having to adapt to a flurry of schools, each one more difficult than the one before. He'd travelled the world with his dilettante father, adjusting with varying degrees of success to the chain of international schools he was thrown into. Leon Furness had been subjected to bullying, racism, and every kind of social torture imaginable. Meanwhile, his father pushed the boundaries of the law further and further in every country they inhabited until he stretched them beyond breaking point and ended up . . . I'm not quite sure where—it could have been jail? But my psychic powers are unable to detect the specifics. Regardless, I sense a definite criminal element in his father.

Onstage Leon continues his spiel, sending the audience into laughter with sales anecdotes from his early, naive years in the industry. But I continue to be tuned in to the voice that tells me his life story. I still can't quite get a handle on what happened to his father, but my sixth sense tells me that after his parents' separation, Leon had reluctantly been thrown back into the custody of his mother. My paranormal abilities are finely honed, and I can work out that she had suffered from alcoholism, though I can't be sure of the extent to which it dominated her life. Leon had spent the remainder of his schooling living with her before working as a salesman. However, the fabric of his being had been stained by those merciless years spent cavorting the earth with his father. There is darkness there—immeasurable quantities of it. The witchy part of me that isn't quite so sold on purely divine energy can't get enough of it.

I catch him staring at me. Perhaps I've been projecting too much of my internal realisation into the cosmos. Maybe he has paranormal powers, too? This guy up on stage is someone I have to get closer to, and the opportunity can't come soon enough. It is as though the spirits can hear my thoughts. For the next minute, the MC is back onstage, thanking Leon. Once the applause dies down, the MC turns to the audience.

"And now I'd like to invite questions from the floor. Anyone?"

I bite my tongue as a sea of hands rises into the air. The MC hops energetically off the stage and makes his way to a woman in the third row. He pushes the microphone in her direction.

"Hi, Leon, my name's Clara," a lady with a thick mid-American drawl begins. Leon smiles at her encouragingly.

"I wanted to ask you about some techniques for closing a deal. Quite a few times, I've kept a client interested until the last sales hurdle, and then they've lost interest, chickened out, or whatever, and I don't know why. It makes the whole sales pitch leading up to it a waste of time. Do you have any ideas for preventing this from happening?"

Leon pauses before responding, smiling at the audience.

"Well, first off, Clara, you need to establish why it's happening. And at your level of sales, which by the rite of passage—seeing as you're here—must be exceedingly high, it's unusual for this kind of thing to be recurring. First, you may need to cancel out the possibility that these flaky clients aren't red herrings planted by an envious colleague who wants to waste your time." The twinkle in Leon's eye gives the game away and everyone laughs.

"Seriously, though, it's important to remember that buying something—anything—will always be based on an emotional response. These emotions can be directed towards the product, towards yourself, how the purchase is going to change the customer's life or a combination of any of these factors and many more. So, what you've got to do is analyse what's happening. Clara. Is there anything these deals that haven't come off for you have in common?"

"Well, I suppose they've been to do with sales from all different developments, so it's not like they're all to do with one development . . ." Clara stalls, thinking. Then something dawns on her. "They've actually all been really big-dollar deals. Like, I think I've pulled off one sale for more than a million dollars, but aside from that, all my other successes have been in the mid-range of properties. Maybe I just can't pull off the high-end sales." Clara looks embarrassed and seeks out Leon for reassurance. He rewards her with a warm smile.

"Clara, thank you for being so honest about that. It makes it a lot easier for me to help you. We all struggle in one or another area of our job. Maybe it's just a confidence thing for you with these high-end sales. What you've got to remember is that any purchase, every transaction ever made, involves an element of catharsis. Shopping is cathartic. Adding a couple of zeros to the end of the price tag will only make the experience even more heightened. Rather than feeling frightened by that heightened experience, I'd like to challenge you to rise to the moment and enjoy it." Clara nods her head vigorously. Leon continues his spiel.

"It sounds like you're comfortable with the early stages of the sales relationship, but then it's like you can't get past first base."

She's good at foreplay, is what you mean. But she just can't make the client come.

Leon chooses that moment to look in my direction again and a pleasant shudder passes through me. Seriously, it is as though he can read my mind. He turns his attention back to Clara and smiles.

"To put it a little crassly, if you'll excuse me, it sounds like you're great at foreplay. You're just having trouble reaching the climax. I can help you with that. Over these next few days,

I promise to teach you how to give your client the biggest, messiest orgasm ever . . ."

A shocked silence descends on the room. Leon looks momentarily confused, then alarmed.

"Sorry, did I just say that out loud?"

He did say it aloud, and I know why. This hadn't happened to me for years, but obviously, I can still channel my thoughts into someone else's energy field and influence their behaviour. I thought I had that part of my supernatural abilities under control, but maybe that's just because I hadn't met anyone to trigger that part of me for a while.

"I'm sorry, it's just because you really turn me on," Leon says, speaking my thoughts out loud. Luckily, Clara seems to be more flattered than insulted. The MC quickly grabs the mike from her and jumps back onto the stage.

"That just about concludes our question-and-answer session with Leon Furness, who can always be guaranteed to surprise us all!"

His attempt to make light of the comments seems hammy, especially considering no one in the auditorium appears to be the least bit insulted. Everyone just seems aroused. I notice the knees of a woman in the row in front of me have shifted to touch those of the man sitting beside her. People have smiles on their faces and look flushed with sexual energy. The MC seems to be the only one not affected in this way. He takes a step forward on the stage, trying to regain control of the audience as Leon smiles and waves goodbye, the MC not trusting him with another stab at the microphone.

"Light refreshments will now be served in the foyer. Go forth, network, and enjoy!" The MC follows Leon offstage, shaking his head. I lean back in my chair apprehensively. It is only then that I realise my glasses are in my hands. I must have taken them off at some point during the presentation. I'm just not exactly sure when.

CHAPTER TWO

"**W**hat the hell was that?" the MC snaps at Leon. "You were the one who wanted to open the floor to question and answer time. You have to be prepared to face the consequences," Leon replies smoothly. In the auditorium, people shuffle their way to the foyer, oblivious to Leon and the MC arguing offstage. I alone can hear them because I have tuned in to their psychic auditory pulse. Mia grins at me before grabbing her handbag off the floor.

"I am so busting for the toilet. I feel like my bladder's going to burst . . ."

"No worries." I'm keen not to break the supernatural thread connecting me to Leon. "I'll find you in the foyer later." She dashes off while I remain glued to the spot, still tuned in to the other wavelength, eavesdropping on Leon and the MC.

"Okay. But, Leon! I have hosted a lot of events. Something happened back there . . ." The MC trails off. From experience, I know what's happening. He is going through a process of slowly forgetting everything that had transpired onstage minutes earlier. Most people in the room are all going through their own method of forgetting at that moment. It is what always happens to mortals after a paranormal event.

I have an overpowering need to be close to Leon, and when he and the MC head further backstage, it's like there is an actual physical hook pulling me toward him. The auditorium is nearly empty by now, so I manage to clip up the narrow podium steps onto the stage in my high heels without being seen. I follow them through a pair of double swing doors, ignoring the *Strictly No Admittance* sign and wander up a starkly lit hallway toward what I hope are the dressing rooms. My intuition proves correct. I arrive at Leon's dressing room. The door is ajar, and I can see Leon talking on a mobile phone. Feeling every bit the groupie, I knock on the door and call out.

"Mr Furness? Hello? Mr Furness?"

He is still talking on the phone but raises his hand in my direction. Just then, a security guard rounds the corner further down the corridor. I pray for him not to notice me, but under the fluorescent halogens, that is impossible.

"Hello, ma'am?" The guard comes toward me, a severe expression on his face. He has a thick, muscular build and leathery skin.

"Mr Furness?" I call out again, ignoring the guard.

"Ma'am, this is a restricted area." The guard is almost next to me. I have one last chance.

"Leon!" I shout. The guard furrows his brow, ready to grab me by the elbow and escort me out when Leon comes to the door. He gives me a languorous once-over before allowing a deep, sexy smile to play across his face.

"Hi . . . you!" His attempt to disguise the fact that he doesn't know me doesn't fool the guard.

"Mr Furness, I'm sorry, this lady seems to have —"

"This lady?" I interrupt. "This lady happens to be Ms Ketzia Knowles, thank you very much."

Leon jumps at the lifeline.

"Ketzia is an old friend of mine. But thanks for your concern . . . Alex!" His gaze fixes on the guard's nametag before he lightly tucks his hand into the small of my back and leads me inside. I turn and give the security guard a victorious smile just before Leon closes the door behind us.

"So, Ketzia. To what do I owe the pleasure?" Even though the quaint dressing room doesn't leave much room to move around in, Leon inhabits the space with expansive ease. He lowers his frame into a plush couch, patting the empty seat beside him in invitation. As I cross the room towards him, I notice the minor details of the room — a vase of fresh flowers, a bowl of succulent-looking fruit and a laptop and tech gadgets littering the desk. Maybe I'm paying attention to these small niceties because the energy coursing between us is overwhelming. If carnal desire is pure energy. I settle into the soft couch, aware of the hem of my dress riding up as I do so.

"I just wanted to thank you for your presentation," I begin. I can feel my cheeks colouring. It seems silly, but now that I have achieved what I wanted — Leon's undivided attention — I'm not quite sure what to do with it. Up close, he is even more handsome than from afar. As if that is even possible. His eyes are a deep hazel speckled with glints of gold that shimmer beneath thick, dark eyelashes. His eyebrows are dark, too, complementing his tanned skin and framing his features beautifully. A pair of chiselled cheekbones contrasts with a splattering of boyish freckles sprinkled over his nose, below which his lips are parted just enough to reveal a row of perfect white teeth. Inside, I swoon.

"Ketzia . . . How come I've never had the pleasure of making your acquaintance before?"

"I . . . err . . . I work for KX in Australia," I stammer, feeling flustered. A deliciously hot sensation emanates from the very pit of my belly.

"Is this your first conference?" he continues.

"Yes. I've only been with the company for two years." I find myself relaxing in his company, though my senses are still on high alert.

"Wow. Congratulations, it's rare for someone to join the million-dollar club so quickly."

"Thanks." I smile. He smiles back. And that's when I see them. The diamonds. He has diamonds on his teeth.

Let me explain what I mean by that. Of course, he doesn't *literally* have jewels embedded in his tooth enamel. It is a mystical thing. Just as I have the power of hypnotic vision and can influence a person or situation through my eyes, so can a person with diamonds on their teeth affect others by smiling at them. Mostly everyone has a unique supernatural ability. They just don't know what it is. So, they don't know how to increase its power, and they don't know how to control it. They think things just happen, but most of the time, things are cause and effect. The way Leon is smiling at me suggests that he is quite aware of his impact on me. I stare back at him with my trance-inducing gaze and admit that it seems I am having just as much of an effect on him. Yes, we are both guilty of using a little cause and effect on each other.

"And now you're here, in my dressing room," Leon teases.

"Yes. It seems that I've not only made it to the million-dollar club, but I've also found its soul," I reply playfully.

"And what colour is its soul?"

That's when I see it—a flash of darkness. For a millisecond, Leon's entire being is shrouded by shadows. But then he smiles, and the crystalline force of his energy evaporates the dark cloud to light up the whole room.

"Its soul is genuinely nice," I reply, by way of supplication. The heat generating between us is becoming unbearable. It is as though a magnetic field is surrounding us, drawing us closer together. Our hands find each other first. His fingers touch mine, setting off a ripple of heat that courses through my whole body to land deep within my core in an explosion of heat.

"Who are you really?" Leon asks. His dazzling smile makes me do what I have sworn I would never do. Reveal myself to a total stranger.

"I am a witch of the Wiccan order. Ketzia is my name. Ketzia Knowles. *Knightess of the Night, Orgasmic Witch of Love, Ecstasy, Sex*."

He takes it all in. Then he rolls back his head and roars with laughter. For a moment, I think he is laughing at me. On a human level, I know, of course, that my confession sounds ludicrous. But then he lowers his face and looks deep into my eyes.

"Don't be alarmed. I am only laughing because of how extraordinary this situation is," he says. Then I hear that internal voice again, clarifying the situation. This man in front of me might be Leon Furness by name — but now he confesses to me that his true identity is *Knight of the Night*. A shock goes through my body. The Knight of the Night is my ancestral soulmate.

"I have waited an awfully long time to find you," Leon continues aloud, his hands reaching up to touch my face. His fingers stroke my cheeks, moving over my nose, brows, and chin. Delicately he traces the outline of my lips, lingering on them before travelling down to rest on my throat. The sensation of his fingers on my body is electrifying.

"I did not think it was possible for us to ever meet. I wasn't even sure if you actually existed," I reply.

"I do exist. I am real. And I am right here in front of you."

With that, I can contain myself no more. Neither can he. Our lips touch. His are smooth and moist. They press against mine, both of us pushing to explore beyond, tongues seeking each other out, shyly at first, then more persistently. I feel his hands guiding me, pulling me closer to him, and my body complies willingly. I reach my hand down to lift the skirt of my dress so that I can straddle him on the couch. Immediately I feel his hardness through the fabric of my panties, making me ache for him. His hands reach for my breasts and gently caress them. My nipples tighten beneath the constraints of my bra. My lips travel away from his, moving towards his throat. He tastes earthy, spicy, and delicious. The smell of him is divine. My lips and mouth explore his skin, moving over his collarbone, my tongue darting out to lick the sheen of sweat from his skin, gorgeous olive skin—so masculine and yet so *soft*. My fingers move to the buttons of his shirt and undo them, the fervour of my passion overtaking me so much that I rip the last ones in a rush for my hands to reach the smoothness of his chest and torso. His hands move to my waist, and he lifts me with surprising strength, so I am still straddling him but elevated slightly on my knees. He unclasps my belt and drops it to the floor. His hands brushing against the sensitivity of my stomach feels unbearably good. He lowers his hands to the hem of my dress and lifts it upwards and over my head, removing it more gracefully than I have ever been able to. He looks at me then, in my matching black panties and bra and sighs in wonder.

"By God, you're beautiful."

I savour his words, enjoying the feel of his hands as they sensuously journey to my stomach, trailing his fingers around in circles before gliding to my breasts. He pushes the fabric of my bra upwards to expose them. Then he closes his hands over my nipples and caresses them tenderly. I groan involuntarily.

"That just feels too good." I allow myself to close my eyes and completely surrender to his touch. He cups my breasts, squeezing them softly before tightening his grip. We kiss, and I lower myself to sit on him, closer. We keep kissing as I push my pussy against his groin, his erection straining at the fabric of his trousers. I want him inside me so badly—my hunger for him is raw and animal. He tugs lightly at my hard nipples before breaking our embrace and sliding his tongue down over my chin and throat to my cleavage. He presses his lips to my left nipple, squeezing the delicate tissue between his teeth and opening his mouth to suck hard.

And then, the lights go out, and the building is thrown into chaos.

CHAPTER THREE

We freeze. The sudden blackout stays our passion. Leon's hands remain on my breasts. My elbows rest on his shoulders. It seems we have been caught doing something illicit, and fate has jumped in to quell the moment. It is an outrageous position for me to be in—almost naked with a man I've only just met. Not my usual style, yet it feels so natural to be gripped by this handsome stranger, both of us so aroused we couldn't hold back. This much passion is dangerous, I think. A siren erupts, blaring through the building with a resounding echo—as though to lend validity to my train of thought.

"What on earth?" Leon says before reluctantly removing his hands from my breasts. In the darkness, I feel his body tighten, trying to work out what is going on. In the moment before the emergency lighting comes on, I fix my bra in place and slide off his lap.

"Evacuate the building. This is an emergency. Follow the emergency exit signs. Evacuate the building. This is an emergency. Follow the emergency exit signs . . ." The pre-recorded voice cycles through the commands in a grating loop. Leon and I exchange quizzical glances before hurriedly throwing on our clothes.

"We'd better get out of here," he says.

"I don't think we've got much choice," I concede, hinting that I would have preferred to continue from where we'd left off. I clip my belt on and smooth down my dress.

"Come on." Leon grabs my hand, and we head for the door together. The corridor outside is deserted. We move quickly to the emergency exit. Leon opens the door to the internal fire stairs, and we are confronted by hundreds of people rushing to escape. We join the throng, pushing our way down the concrete steps in syncopated rhythm with their panicked footsteps.

"Does anyone know what's going on?" Leon asks. But his voice is lost in the noise of the stairwell. People shout about a possible earthquake, a natural disaster, a terrorist attack, or only a fire drill. No-one knows.

It is a relief when we finally reach the emergency exit doors at the bottom of the stairwell and tumble into the afternoon light. A group of resort staff and conference organisers in hard hats and fluoro vests tries to contain the chaos of delegates spilling into the narrow laneway. They signal for us to assemble into groups of eight, to cluster in pre-arranged positions along the perimeter of the road. I stay by Leon's side. I want to make sure Leon and I make it into the same group.

"Tell me this isn't just a fire drill," I groan, all too aware that it would be much worse if it *isn't*. An official-looking person with a megaphone and an iPad is coming our way, checking off names and numbers.

"What? Didn't you feel the earth move?" Leon says, smiling at me in such a suggestive way I can't help but smile back. I realise that people are staring at us, our flippant reaction to the surrounding panic puzzling them. Maybe they can also pick up on some of the erotic energy charging between us. It is still powerful, and I can feel my whole body tingling.

"Name, please?" the official asks as he draws near.

"Leon Furness." His reply is confident and authoritative. The official glances at him briefly before scrolling through a list of names. Leon must have been marked as having special privileges as the official steps him away from the group. I

19

follow them, feeling like there is an invisible cord tethering me to Leon.

"This *is* actually just a drill," the official confides quietly to Leon, though not so quietly that I can't overhear him.

"I knew it!" I exclaim. The official glances my way warningly but chooses to ignore my outburst.

"Basically, you're free to go but — discreetly, please. The rest of the drill will take at least an hour. We foresee that this afternoon's program will be right on track to continue after the scheduled break."

"Okay," Leon replies, linking his arm with mine. "But this one's coming with me." His body is so close to mine that it sends my heart into a flutter again.

"Whatever you say, Mr Furness." The official looks me up and down. "Name please?"

"Ketzia. Ketzia Knowles."

Knightess of the Night, Orgasmic Witch of Love, Ecstasy, Sex. Leon's inner voice whispers in my mind. Hearing my title unfold from him sends my heart into another frenzy. The official nods with satisfaction when he quickly finds my mortal name on his *iPad* list.

"Thanks, Ms Knowles. You are also free to go. Please stay within the area."

"Of course," I reply, skin burning as Leon laces his fingers through mine. Together, we turn and make our way out of the laneway. On the way, I catch sight of Mia, standing with a bunch of delegates. Too late, I lower my head, hoping she won't see me.

"Ketzia?" she calls.

"Uh . . . Hi!" I stammer. Mia notices Leon urgently tugging my hand and raises her eyebrows quizzically.

"See you later," I call out, watching her expression change from surprise to comprehension to one of enlightened mischief. The wheels of the conference gossip machine will be greased by Mia this afternoon. I know it's futile, but I raise a finger to my lips, signalling a shushing gesture. She winks at me, and I wink back before turning and breaking into an exhilarated run with Leon. We hit the resort forecourt. Evacuated staff and tourists mingle around the fountain at the resort entrance, glancing curiously at us as we race past. Leon nods towards a path snaking down the side of the resort—the staff entry. We follow its course, jogging past the resort pool and tennis court and then loping over the lush green of the golf course.

"Ketzia, stop." Leon tugs my shoulder to slow me down. I stop running and face him. The naked lust in his eyes burns through me. We draw together in a passionate embrace, our lips meeting lusciously, opening to each other's needs. I hear noises coming from the direction of the resort. Several conference delegates traipse onto the golf course behind us.

"Must be another evacuation point," I signal.

"Quick, before anyone sees us."

We hold hands and continue our dash away from the resort, over the green. As we continue running, fuelled by the energy of our unspent passion, I am reminded of the tarot card I had laid out that morning—the *Lovers*. But before I can contemplate its meaning, I am distracted by the glorious vista opening before us. With the golf course behind us, Leon and I arrive at a secluded beach. I recognise it as Silver Mine Bay from the resort guide I read that morning. Giggling, we throw ourselves onto the sand, gasping to regain our breath and equilibrium.

The sun shines gloriously over the picturesque bay. Leon and I catch our breath, abandoning our shoes to sit and watch the gentle movement of boats ferrying goods and people across the water. I can't help but admire the tanned contours of his feet as he allows the sand to trickle beneath his toes.

"So, Ketzia . . ." Leon begins, his presence beside me on the beach causing my heart to pulsate erratically.

Hoping to hide his effect on me, I turn to him with a sophisticated smile.

"Is this your first escape from the drudgeries of a fire drill?"

"Certainly with a tall, handsome stranger on a secluded island," I counter, not bothering to hide my desire for him. He grins then, and I don't regret my bold admission.

"And how about you?" I reach for his hand, his fingers lacing smoothly through mine. "Have you ever escaped a fire drill with a witch before?"

He laughs, then makes a parody of pretending to look for something on the beach.

"Where did you park your broom? It might have come in handy. Particularly if you've got a tandem model."

I join in his laughter, though my mind is preoccupied with the ramifications of our shared history.

"Leon, I believe our ancestors escaped a real fire together by unifying their powers."

"Really?" He gently twists a strand of my hair.

"The thirteen-thirty-four witch trials in France . . ." I solemnly pronounce. "And again in fifteen-eighty-three in Osnabruck, Germany."

His gaze meets mine in shared sadness. It feels strange even to mention these historical atrocities, yet also inexplicably necessary. We are testing each other in a way, trying to make sure of each other's identities. The occult world is full of impostors, and you can never be too careful in choosing who to trust.

We lace our fingers together, and the heat emanating between us is overwhelming. Leon extracts his fingers from mine and traces his index finger along my lifeline, finally resting on my wrist. Then he offers his palm to me. I look deep into his eyes before inspecting it. The experience is of being transported beyond the moment, ourselves, and into a much greater context of land, sky, birth, and rebirth. I sense something momentous happening. That our coming together has repercussions beyond ourselves and the earthly world.

"Look at my palm," Leon says. Finally, I tear my gaze from his and inspect the palm of his hand judiciously. Palmistry is not one of my strong points, but I have studied enough Wiccan and Roma fortune-telling to know how to decipher the meaning of the lines. I start with his heart line. It is long and curvy, running from below his index finger towards his pinkie. At one point, it touches his lifeline, meaning his heart is easily broken. At another, it is scarred by hundreds of tiny lines crossing through it, indicating emotional trauma at some time in his life. Below the heart line lies the head line. Leon's is deep and long, signifying clear and focused thinking ability. Four crosses mark it—shrapnel from momentous decisions Leon must have made through his life so far. I can only begin to imagine what those choices entailed, but if he truly is magick, then they would have involved the fate of others. I know this from experience. My palm sports the same number of crosses, each one a burden I carry with me every day. His head line is separated from his lifeline, which travels in an arc from his thumb towards his wrist. This shows his adventurous spirit and enthusiasm for life. It is curvy, long, and deep, meaning he has plenty of energy and vitality. I examine his fate line. This is also known as the line of destiny, indicating the degree to which a person's life is affected by external circumstances beyond their control. Leon's fate line is profound. I peer closer at it, daring my eyes to contradict logic. Leon's fate line looks so profound because it is not one but literally thousands of them, layered upon each other, wrestling for the claim to his future. I have only ever seen a fate line like this on one other palm.

"Do you see?" he asks.

I nod, frightened by my observations. "The lines on our palms are identical." My palm is the one that also has various fate lines. It is a mark of my ancestry and my possible future.

"Like mirror images of each other." Then we hold our hands in the air as though they are mirrors. He takes hold of my hands and brings one to his lips. He glides his lips over each finger, not so much kissing them as caressing them with the touch of his lips. I can feel the intensity of his breath as he takes in the scent of me, and I yearn for him to explore me further. There is so much pleasure in the way he inhales the smell of my hand that I'm not sure I can cope with the excitement of further contact. But then he turns my hand over and tastes the sweat on my palm, moving the tip of his tongue to the delicate skin of my wrist, and I know that I need him more than I have ever needed anyone before. On this occasion, I will trust my instincts and surrender to the undeniable lust between us.

"Leon." I breathe his name before moving my wrist away from his mouth and pushing my lips to his. All I want is for this man to take me, to pleasure me, for me to lose myself in him.

We kiss, surrendering to the pull of each other, our mouths hungry, our hands reaching for each other's clothes, needing to feel skin on skin. Our tongues probe each other's mouths. My heart beats furiously as I stroke the smoothness of his face, the lush softness of his hair, and the solid muscles of his neck. My fingers journey beneath his collar, seeking the tenderness of his throat. I undo the top button of his shirt, feeling the delicate sprigs of his chest hair beneath my fingers as they move down his torso. Our mouths continue their exploration, our tongues stroking playfully in sensual bliss. Leon's hands stroke my hair and then glide down my back, reaching to grasp my buttocks. He lowers me onto the softness of the sand, hoisting my skirt up and pressing himself against me. I can feel his firm hardness beneath his trousers, pushing against my pubis. His fingers trace the line of my panties. His lips move to my throat. He sucks and kisses my throat while I push at the remaining buttons of his shirt, exposing his tanned, muscular chest. His stomach boasts a toned set of abs, and I have a moment of shyness, taking in the perfection of his body. But he is just as hungry for me as I am for him. He removes his hands from my panties to shrug out of his shirt sleeves but returns them there immediately once his shirt is off. He slides one finger beneath the fabric of my panties and lightly tickles his way to make contact with my clitoris. I gasp. His touch is light but so arousing, and I gasp with pleasure. He moves his finger back and forth along the bud of my womanhood before sliding the lips of my labia open to feel my wetness. I groan. He kisses me, and our tongues explore the moist sensuousness of each other's mouths as he peels my panties over my hips. He breaks from our kiss, and I moan with complaint, pulling his mouth back to mine. He pulls away again, laughing.

"Please, just let me?" he begs. And I realize what he wants is to kiss my whole body. I lean back on the sand as his mouth and hands move down my body. He lowers my panties, his lips touching me in ways that set off a cascade of shudders inside me. Then he raises his head and rests a hand on each of my thighs, pushing gently to open my legs. He looks at my pussy with hunger, and I involuntarily groan as he lowers his face to devour me, his fingers and tongue and nose seemingly in competition with each other, stroking me, sucking my juices, his tongue tracing the folds of my labia, his finger gliding down to my dark secret place, circling it. His hands push the lips of my womanhood further apart, and his face pushes into me, his teeth softly teasing me. I have never experienced such pleasure before. My back arches involuntarily, and my hands grasp the sand beneath me as I feel myself coming. He raises his head, prolonging my ecstasy and his hands move up, away from my vagina, pushing at the fabric of my dress. I help him, pulling my dress over my head and unclasping my bra while he takes off his trousers and briefs.

We are both naked. The thrill of it intensifies our overwhelming need for each other, and I wrap my legs around him, trying to bring him into me, but he resists, his tongue sliding around the tight peaks of my nipples. I am so impatient for him.

"Please, please," I murmur, pushing my pelvis up so that I can feel the tip of his penis against the entrance of my softness. My hand circles his shaft, and I try to draw him closer until he finally relents—his silky hardness throbbing against my palm. The tip of his penis pushes the lips of my vagina open before he lowers himself down and into me. I am so moist. He slides slowly and confidently in, filling me with his manhood. He gently pulls back before sliding deep inside, each rhythmic thrust sending a ripple of pleasure tingling through my whole body. I moan as our movements become syncopated, moving together to an explosive orgasm. I have never known such sweet agony. I feel myself yearning for this moment to last forever, wanting our union to be sealed by the gods, as we thunder to a shattering climax.

CHAPTER FOUR

L eon and I lie on the beach in a tangle of arms and legs. Part of me is reluctant to loosen my limbs from his, but I can feel pins and needles prickling my feet, and I have to move. Leon sighs as I pull my feet out from beneath his and stretch out.

"Please, don't ever move your body from mine," he begs, his eyes opening.

"Sorry, Leon. My feet have gone to sleep."

"Siesta for your soles . . ."

"Fiesta for my soul," I reply, not caring how corny I sound.

The sun ducks behind a cloud, and the temperature drops slightly. I feel the coolness of my skin and reluctantly pull on my panties. I like being naked around this guy.

Leon places a restraining finger on the band of lace and tuts at me. "Do you have to?"

"I'm cold. And it's getting late. We probably should think about heading back."

He shrugs his shoulders dismissively. It's his show, I suppose. He can be late if he wants to be. I shiver as a cold wind picks up off the harbour. Goosebumps appear on the flesh of my arms, and my nipples tighten. He notices.

"You're right. We'd better get dressed," he agrees, watching me hungrily as I clasp my bra and pull my dress on. He stretches into his jocks and gracefully pulls on his trousers and shirt. We lean into each other for another kiss. I can taste myself on his lips. His tongue prods at mine before we glide into each other tenderly.

"God, you're gorgeous," he says, tucking a windswept strand of my hair behind my ear. I have an urgent need to make love to him again, but the cold breeze is making me shudder. I will myself to drop my hands to my sides and lift myself to a standing position instead.

"Come on," I invite. "How much of the island have you seen?"

"The inside of the conference room, the inside of my resort suite, the inside of the lobby . . ." He stands up, and I am re-taken by his strong physique, his muscular arms, and the perfect proportions of his body.

"Surely you haven't come all the way to Hong Kong to stare at four walls?"

"I've already found the best thing this place has to offer." He smiles at me appraisingly, and I feel myself redden. "But sure, if you want someone to go sightseeing with, I'm all yours."

We head south along the beach. As we round the bay of our *private beach*, I am shocked by how exposed our love-making nest was. A medium-sized fishing village teems with a life of its own less than five hundred metres from where, only minutes earlier, Leon and I had been in the throes of naked passion. We scramble onto the busy promenade, where fishermen haul crates of fresh fish and hawkers sell food, postcards, trinkets, and mementos to the throng of tourists passing alongside us.

"Oh my Gosh." I can't hide my dismay at the mass of people.

"There we were, just the two of us . . ." Leon laughs.

"Imagine if someone saw us!" I feel giddy at the prospect.

"Don't worry, sweetness. No one saw us. Everyone is too busy looking at—that!" He raises his hand to point to a magnificent statue, visible in the distance beyond the village. It is the giant Tian Tan Buddha. I gasp as I take in the incredible vision of the world's largest seated outdoor bronze Buddha. The Buddha is perched atop over two hundred and fifty steps on a lotus throne. On each side of the staircase are statues of Buddhist saints—bodhisattvas. They are venerated for deferring heaven to help mortals reach enlightenment. I feel Leon's hand encircling mine, and I hold on gratefully. The beauty of the Buddhist symbol of purity appearing before us now, after the excitement of the afternoon, is almost too much for me. Leon notices my waning strength with concern.

"Perhaps it's a good idea if we have a rest and something to eat?" he suggests, guiding me to a small restaurant close to the foreshore. A maître d' attends to us immediately, seating us beside a giant aquarium full of live lobsters, sea urchins, squid, and fish in every colour of the rainbow. Fascinated, I watch the creatures move lazily in the water, succulent specimens of the world beneath the water. Sea life has always interested me, underwater wonders in many ways being like the world of magic. It's always there beneath the surface of the water, but we don't often see it—all the hallmarks of a mystical existence.

"Can I get you a drink?" a young waiter asks in stilted English, handing us the menus. Leon smiles at him and requests two *Yuan yang*. The waiter nods and retreats to the kitchen.

"*Yuan yang*?" I ask.

"Coffee and tea," he says.

"What? Mixed together?"

"It tastes better than it sounds."

"I hope so." Champagne seems to be more the order of the day, but when the *Yuan yang* arrives, I discover the hot drink is both fortifying and delicious.

"Here's to *Yuan yang*." Leon lifts his cup.

"Cheers." We chink mugs and grin at each other, steam wrapping delicate tendrils in the air between us.

Leon lowers his cup and reaches for my hand. "I have

another reason for ordering this drink," he begins.

I raise my eyebrow at him before he continues.

"The name *Yuan yang*, which refers to mandarin ducks, is a symbol of conjugal love in Chinese culture, as the birds usually appear in pairs and the male and female look quite different. This same connotation of a *pair* of two unlike items is used to name this drink."

"I don't think we are so very much unlike," I challenge.

"Perhaps *too much* alike."

The waiter is at our table again before I have time to ponder the meaning of his statement. We have completely neglected to look at the menu, and I rush to scan the dishes. But everything is written in Chinese.

"I guess it'll have to be a wild stab in the dark," I joke, circling my finger in the air before landing it midway down the page on a series of Chinese hieroglyphics. Leon looks across to the item I am pointing at.

"You really feel like braised ox-tongue soup?" he asks.

"Is that what it says?" I make a face. "Can you really read this?"

"What do you like to eat?"

"Meat," I reply, far too wrapped up in him to be anything other than honest. "I did have a frivolous, short-lived stint as a vegetarian, but that was doomed from the start!"

"Do you mind if I order for you?"

"I think it would be safest," I say. My mouth drops open in amazement when Leon turns to the waiter and speaks to him in what I can only surmise is fluent Cantonese. The waiter smiles and nods his head approvingly. The two of them then share a joke, and they laugh together momentarily before the waiter takes hold of our menus and retreats to the kitchen again.

"Do you speak Chinese?" I cannot hide my awe.

"I speak in tongues," Leon jokes with the touch of a grin.

Then it dawns on me. "The incantation of language . . ." I say.

The incantation of language is a magic spell used by witches and wizards since ancient times to enable communication between all beings. Traditionally, a sorcerer would use the spell to commune with plants and animals to protect the environment from volatile forces. Speaking in tongues has also been used throughout the ages to influence heads of state and to create rapport with ghosts and confused paranormal entities. It would never occur to me to use the spell for convenience.

"I guess that's easier than dragging the guidebook around with you." I try to keep it light but can't help an edge creeping into my voice. Leon taps the side of his head comically.

"I have a photographic memory. So useful for the itinerant traveller."

If he is trying to deflect responsibility for the abuse of magic, I'm not buying it. Photographic memory, my foot! I shrug, not keen to have an argument with this Adonis seated across from me.

"I have a deep respect for all spells and magic. I don't think it's something that should be used for the sake of convenience." There. I've said it. I glance up to find Leon staring at me intently.

"Sure." His expression is quizzical.

"How do you justify speaking in tongues for the sole purpose of ordering lunch? If that's not a dubious personal use of an incredible gift, I don't know what is."

"Sorry?" Leon looks utterly confused, and I feel momentarily guilty for the anger I can't hide from my words. But I charge on, nonetheless.

"What? Did you forget that I'm magick, too? Is that what you usually use to impress the ladies?"

"Ketzia, stop."

I realise I have raised my voice and look away, embarrassed. Luckily, we are the only ones seated on this side of the restaurant, and no one is paying much attention to us.

"*Ketzia,*" Leon's inner voice implores. "*I understand exactly where you're coming from. And I agree.*"

"You agree? Then how come . . ." I'm not sure if I've replied aloud or if our entire communication is now taking place on the telekinetic plane.

"*I invoked the incantation when I arrived in Hong Kong before the conference started. There was some spiritual business I needed to attend to here as well.*"

"*I see.*"

"*Look, I probably shouldn't have spoken in tongues to order our lunch, but as the spell hasn't expired yet, I couldn't see any harm in it.*"

"*I suppose not. So, what mystical element needed your attention here in Hong Kong?*" I can't shake the scepticism underlying the query, though I'm not sure what parts of the conversation are unspoken and occurring solely in my psyche. Usually, my coven keeps me well informed of any psychic activity that needs channelling. All my fellow Wiccans had known I was going on this trip. They would have let me know if any otherworldly energy needed balancing while I was here.

"*You're still not convinced,*" Leon observes.

"Up until today — apart from your figurehead role with the company — I didn't even know that you existed. By that, I mean your wizardly self . . ." I trail off.

"My wizardly self?" Leon laughs. I can't help but join in, the ludicrousness of it all knocking me off-kilter.

"Seriously. I know all the history of our antecedents. But I never read our reunification in my destiny. I didn't think it was possible."

"*It's more than possible. It's real.*" The electricity sparking between us again threatens to blow the building. That's how hot it is. But my mind is whirling, trying to make sense of the possibilities. Then it dawns on me.

"This *spiritual business* you had to take care of here — was it anything to do with me?"

"I never mix business with pleasure." His attempt to deflect me from my line of thought is simultaneously sweet and infuriating. Also illuminating.

"That's it, isn't it? You already knew about me before you came . . ." He shifts uncomfortably in his chair, and I know I'm right. "Why didn't you say something?"

"I didn't know exactly what I was looking for. Even when you came to my dressing room, *I guessed that you may have been part of the prophecy. I just didn't realise how big a part.*"

"Hang on," I interrupt. *"What prophecy?"*

"The prophecy that foretold Knight and Lady were destined to be together in this lifetime."

I reflect on my dream that morning — the Lovers card and all its connotations. I wasn't even sure if I should be trusting Leon. He leans towards me and covers my hand with his own.

"Trust me. We have always been destined to meet." His gaze penetrates my soul, the heat rising from my solar plexus testament to my attraction for him. He smiles at me, and I cannot help but smile back.

"Okay. I'll trust you."

The food arrives, and I realise how hungry I am. I haven't eaten anything since breakfast. Leon has ordered steamed prawn dumplings, shrimp with lobster sauce, crab meat sautéed with mixed Chinese vegetables — the dishes keep coming.

"Are you sure you ordered enough food?" I joke, picking up my chopsticks.

"I think we've both worked up a healthy appetite," he responds, dipping a dumpling into chilli and soy sauce. I watch him eat, fascinated by the sensual curve of his lips, his unabashed animal hunger. He catches me watching him and nods his head enthusiastically.

"Try the orange chicken," he urges.

Trying to be ladylike, I lift a piece of the delicately steamed meat and nibble. It has a tart sweetness that causes a mini-explosion on my tastebuds. My stomach rumbles in agreement, and I decide to forget about being a princess and tuck into the food as voraciously as Leon. We eat in luscious concession to our appetites and health, in servitude to our primal hunger.

"So, tell me a bit about yourself," he says casually, as though we haven't just been fornicating like animals in heat all afternoon.

"What would you like to know?"

"Oh, how about . . . everything? What's your favourite food? Where did you grow up? What kind of music are you into? What do you like to do for fun? What are your career goals?"

"This is starting to sound like a job interview," I say, enjoying the deep timbre of his laughter.

"Sorry. Bad habit. I'm just keen to get to know you better."

"Better than you already do?" The blush that spreads over his face brings an answering heat to my body. "Let's just cut the bull and ask the interesting questions, Leon."

"Such as?"

"Tell me about your childhood." The jolt that shoots through his body tells me I've hit a raw nerve.

"Plenty of time for that later. Let's just enjoy the food," he says.

I decide to let him off the hook. We completely give ourselves over to the satiation of our famished bodies. Gluttony doesn't even come close. Finally, when every plate on the table has been denuded of its contents, save a few bones from the chicken and a couple of crab claws, we lean back and sigh contentedly.

"Wow."

"That was fantastic."

The waiter arrives and clears away the plates, unable to hide his astonishment at how much food we have managed to consume. Leon catches my embarrassment at this and taps his foot against mine beneath the table.

"Ketzia, sometimes there is nothing better than giving in to our physical needs — all of them."

I smile, proud to be in the company of this mystical creature, stunned by the events of the day and full of a joy I didn't know was possible.

"All of them," I agree, leaning in for a kiss.

CHAPTER FIVE

We leave the restaurant and meander leisurely back toward the resort. The day has passed quickly, the setting sun now filtering its rays around the giant Buddha on the hilltop behind us, casting a sizable shadow on the side of the mountain. As we walk along the shoreline, the gentle lapping of the waves on the shore invites us to dip our feet. The water retains some of the warmth of the day. Ankle-deep, we wade around the bay until we are back on *our* secluded beach.

"Fancy a swim?" I invite, clutching at the excuse to see Leon as close to naked as possible again.

"As long as it's a skinny dip."

"Seeing as I didn't bring my bikini, I guess it will have to be."

No one is around, so we peel off our clothes and bundle them in a pile on the beach. Leon can't take his eyes off me as he reaches for my hand. Together we jog to the water's edge. The water is even cooler than I anticipated. My nipples tighten, my skin excited by the invigorating crispness. I dive under a wave and resurface quite a far way out. I have always been a strong swimmer and love the water. Leon is still in the shallows, and I beckon for him to join me. He ducks under a wave and reappears several moments later beside me.

"Ketzia, you're like a mermaid," he exclaims. His swimming style is laboured until he finds his footing underwater and relaxes into stillness, his shoulders and head above water. I take advantage of his position and paddle towards him. When I reach him, I straddle my legs around his body. He embraces me, his hands gliding from my back to my buttocks. We kiss, our lips hungry for the shared taste of each other. I feel his rising penis pressing against my womanhood in the water. Then he slides his fingers to open me up gently, and I slide onto his shaft effortlessly. The slipperiness of the water eases his entry. I rock onto him, allowing the gentle lapping of the waves to inform our rhythm. With my vulva tight around him, he feels immense.

"Ketzia," he moans. We kiss and push our bodies further into each other until it is impossible to tell where he begins and I end, so unified are we by sensation. I feel something pushing urgently into the small of my back, and I am momentarily confused. One of his hands supports my shoulders, and the other gently caresses my face. I cannot make sense of what part of his anatomy is pressing so persistently into my lower vertebrae, gliding downwards in a slow, sticky gliding motion.

"Leon?"

"Uh-huh?" His eyes are closed in blissed-out ecstasy. But I am sure that we are not alone in the water. There is further movement at the base of my spine, moving lower to the top of my buttocks.

"Leon, something's wrong." Finally, he is hearing me, probably because I am struggling to keep the rising panic from my voice.

"What?" He smiles, humouring me.

"I think we have company," I whisper. His eyes widen. He has felt it, too. Quietly we disentangle from each other. Something grey and eel-like breaks the ocean's surface, rushing to encircle us.

"What is it?" I scream.

"Ketzia, get back to shore," Leon shouts. The creature wraps itself around Leon's waist. I strike at it with my fist but succeed only in getting it to tighten its grip on Leon. Using both hands, I grab the snake-like sea animal and pull it as hard as possible, but it has suctioned itself to Leon's body and is impossible for me to budge. I pull harder, which causes the thing to increase its vice-like grip on his body. I stop when I realise that all I am doing is hurting Leon, his skin being pulled away from his flesh and threatening to split because of my persistent yanks. I kick underwater and am horrified to discover that the thing is not some sort of giant sea slug or eel but only the tentacle of a much larger creature, still submerged beneath the water.

"Oh no . . . this thing is massive!" I cry. Leon nods, his face pale. I wonder if he can still breathe or if the thing is squeezing his lungs so hard as to affect his oxygen intake.

"Ketzia, swim back to shore," he gasps. I shake my head, horrified at the thought of leaving him here in the grip of this thing.

"I'm not leaving you," I shout, feeling the eddying pull of the waves depriving me of choice as the undertow tugs at my body. I reach out for Leon, trying to grab him by the shoulders, but the pull of the waves is too strong and drags me away from him.

"Leon," I scream. Too late, I realise the change in the current is caused by the sea monster, churning its tentacles tempestuously beneath the surface. I fight the ocean, pushing my arms through the frothy waves, but I can't get closer to Leon. The thing has moved upwards on his body, and only his face is now visible above the grey tentacle.

"Don't worry, Leon. I'll save you," I shout. Of course, he can't hear me over the din of the choppy waves and the sound of thunder. Panic-stricken, I search the sky, amazed at the suddenness of the storm brewing directly above us. It seems an impossible coincidence. Which, I realise, is exactly what it is. An impossible coincidence. Not a coincidence at all. A reaction. A reaction to two astral bodies meeting and connecting. Somewhere something has felt very threatened by our connection. Something supernatural — taking the form of an ocean leviathan.

I summon up all my courage, take a deep breath, and duck underwater. I open my eyes but can't make out much of anything. The activity in the water is so frenetic. I come up for air only to discover that I have drifted further away from Leon. The leviathan almost entirely entraps him. I must do something quickly. Desperately I look to the shore and now curse the beach's isolation. There is no one around. There are a few rocks and boulders, but there is not much I can do with them in this time-pressured situation. No, it slowly dawns on me. The only way I can hope to save Leon will be with the use of magic. However, performing a spell in the ocean is a new challenge for me. I rack my brain for an enchantment that could work on defeating the tentacled beast and remember a spell for the conjuring of mirrors. This spell is a form of scrying, the psychic penetration of shiny surfaces such as water and mirrors. Usually, it is performed by using mirrors to deflect energy from another being, but I figure the reflective quality of the water could work as an equally good substitute.

I slow my breathing, no mean feat considering how frightened I am. I count to ten and then release my breath, exhaling through my mouth, blowing on the water's surface to create tiny ripples. It is hard not to get distracted by the storm raging above — shots of hail lash at my face and lightning flashes luridly. Fear keeps me focused on the monumental task at hand. I turn my back on Leon and the creature. They are at least fifty metres behind me. I cup a handful of water and trickle it into my other hand, trying to catch a flare of the events behind me in its cascading flow. The trick with the conjuring of mirrors is to try and capture as much of a reflection as possible of the element you are trying to influence. I keep scooping the water, peering into it, and trying to focus on the reflection of

Leon thrashing it out with the sea monster behind me. It is strenuous work, but I only need a small image to focus on. Even a tiny spot of light or shadow would be enough for me to concentrate on to springboard the spell. However, the water is so choppy all I can make out is white wave froth. I cup more water and continue to pour it in front of me, staring hard. Meanwhile, I try and think of a plan B in case I don't get anywhere with this. Finally, I catch Leon's arm and hand reflected in the water. He must have escaped the creature's clutches enough to lift them out of the water. I seize hold of the picture and burn it into my mind's eye, blocking out every other thought. Then I close my eyes and concentrate on my breathing again, slowing it down so much as to affect my pulse. Essentially, I am transcending the moment by bringing myself into a trance state. From this place of reverie, I not only can summon all my energies but can also tap into the cosmic energies surrounding us. I realize it is full of a vast, unearthly presence, unlike anything I have ever encountered. The magnitude of the force acting behind the sentient being trying to destroy Leon frightens me, but I push my fear down and concentrate on animating the visual I have of his arm and injecting it with power. I hear a shout behind me and hope it means the spell is working, but I know that to turn around now would mark the end of any chance of success I may have in defeating the sea monster. Instead, I push myself to visualize the rest of Leon's body, his face, chest, legs—his entire body and then his aura. Into all of him, I push not only my energy but every other energy force I have ever been capable of summoning. Everything reacts. The ocean calms, taking on a velvety sheen. The storm abates, and the sun makes an appearance. I swish water through my fingers, trying to create another mirror. I continue the filtering motion, only now aware of the tears on my cheeks and the shakiness of my hands. I am reluctant to turn around until I am sure the spell has worked.

"Ketzia!" Leon is almost directly behind me. His arms enfold me. Sobbing with relief, I turn around to his beautiful smiling face.

"You're all right!"

"Thanks to you. That size octopus in these waters would have to be pretty rare."

"I'm not sure that was an octopus."

"What was it then? A giant slug with eight legs?" Leon teases.

"Hardly. More like a mythical Kraken—a Chinese Kraken." I laugh with relief. My heart is still beating wildly, and I am having trouble breathing. We make our way onto the beach and reach our pile of clothes. My whole body is shaking, and I have trouble pulling my panties on.

"Whoa, Ketzia. Are you all right?" Leon rubs my arms to warm them up, but the trouble isn't that I'm cold. I'm just trying to recover from all the energy I summoned, channelled, and pushed through my celestial planes. We dress as quickly as possible, Leon helping me pull my dress over my head, his touch tender and caring. The idea that I almost lost him brings tears to my eyes again. I know we've only just met, but I feel like we have been part of each other forever.

"Ketzia, you're in shock. Let's just sit for a while."

So that is what we do. We sit side by side on the beach, Leon's arm around me. Gradually I stop shaking. My breathing returns to normal. My pulse regulates.

"You just saved my life, you know. I am forever indebted to you." His mind speaks to me.

"You tried to save me by sending me back to shore," I reply, using real words to answer him. We have arrived at a kind of unspoken understanding where all his thoughts and ideas to do with the supernatural world are communicated purely telepathically, while I can still converse in magick with him using my human voice. Maybe it's habitual for him. While engaged in the corporate world, it wouldn't be appropriate for him to flaunt his supernatural capabilities. Or perhaps he is reluctant to discuss magick openly with me for fear of attracting dark forces.

I contemplate the matter in silence.

"*Are you mortal?*" he finally asks, the question reverberating like an echo inside my skull.

"Of course, I'm mortal. We all are."

Leon looks away from me, scanning the horizon.

"Are you feeling well enough to trek back to the resort?" he asks, his voice light.

"I am," I reply. "But there is something I have to clear up first. Are you immortal?"

"Ketzia, this is an insane conversation for us to be having. I really think we should get back to the resort."

He stands up, refusing to meet my eye. Usually, I would have pursued the matter further, but the tiredness in my limbs is debilitating, and at that moment, all I want is to be back at the resort, resting. So I decide to drop the matter of Leon's mortality and the ramifications of this on our friendship. I will be returning to the subject later, though. Immortality is incredibly rare, even among paranormal beings. And if Leon is immortal, then that would complicate things between us. A mortal and an eternal being should never engage with each other intimately. Such a union could result in many unpredictable permutations in the supernatural energy sphere and unleash chaos on the human world in the form of ghosts, the living dead, and regular humans being able to tap into supernatural abilities. Perhaps that was why the dark forces had come into play today—trying to prevent our union? However, I keep these thoughts to myself as Leon helps me to my feet. We trudge along the sand to the path next to the golf course and make our way back to the resort.

Chapter Six

"Where did you disappear to?" Mia asks me pointedly at the conference dinner that night. Trust Mia to notice my absence. Leon and I had made our way back to the resort and through the crowded foyer without anyone noticing. We had then parted ways to go to our separate rooms and prepare for dinner. I'd showered, lathering my body with the deliciously perfumed hotel body wash, exfoliating salt spray off my tingling body, every pore alive with the memory of shared passion. My ankle-length crushed-velvet aubergine gown sheaths my nerve endings in enough comfort to enable everyday social discourse. Mia also wears a cocktail dress—of aqua blue. She hungrily stabs a prawn with her fork, watching me expectantly, while waiting for my answer.

"Oh, you know . . ." I reply vaguely, nodding at the waiter to refill my champagne glass.

"No. I don't. And don't for a minute think you're going to have some dirty rendezvous and not share all the details with me!" Mia threatens, jokingly.

"Okay, okay. I promise I'll tell you. But not here. Later."

"It's a promise."

I smile at Mia but groan inwardly. I'd have to be selective about what details I would share with her—certainly none of the supernatural stuff. But I could tell her about our meal and that we kissed. That couldn't hurt, surely? I take a sip of champagne, savouring its coolness. Then I start on my prawn salad, startled to discover how hungry I am again. The feast of Chinese food at the restaurant seems like a lifetime ago.

Which, in many ways, it is. Indeed, a lot has happened since then, including a very intense episode of supernatural oceanic warfare. I still can't believe the events of the day. Everything has a surreal quality about it. I look around the ballroom but can't spot Leon anywhere, not even at the speakers' table.

"He's not here," Mia confirms. Nothing gets by that chick.

"Who?" I ask innocently.

"You know who." She pokes me in the ribs. I can't help grinning. Mia always has that effect on me.

"You are so going to have to spill all the beans on that one . . ."

"Later," I confirm. A waiter clears our entree plates and re-places them with plates of delicious-looking *coq au vin*. I empty the rest of my champagne and allow the glass to be replaced by a full glass of red.

"Cheers." Mia and I clink glasses. Everyone at our table joins in, and I realise how rude I've been, showing no interest in anyone. I make up for it by conversing with an erudite American passionate about architecture. We chat, and the time passes, and before I know it, the dinner is over, and everyone is saying their farewells. I still haven't spotted Leon and am getting concerned about him. My yearning for him is physical—a palpable pain in my stomach throbs with my need for him. Mia grabs me by the elbow and guides me out of the ballroom towards the lifts.

"Tell me all about him," she commands, pushing me into an open elevator and pressing the button for the fifth floor— my floor. We are alone in the lift, and I really owe it to Mia to share the day's excitement, but I can't ignore the passionate desire mounting from my core and, as much as I feel bad about it, decide to fob her off.

"Mia, I've got a splitting headache. I'm so sorry. I'm going to have to go straight to bed."

"What?" Mia looks me over. I give her a pained expression. I'm not the greatest actor in the world, but the afternoon's events must have exhausted me enough to lend my headache excuse some credibility because she nods her head sympathetically.

"Well, you get some rest then. On one proviso — you tell all tomorrow." She holds the lift door open for me. I nod and whisper goodbye before exiting the lift. I wander up the corridor, retracing my footsteps from earlier in the day. After returning from the beach, Leon had walked me to my room, where we parted ways. I was sure the executive suite at the end of my floor was his. Without realizing that I have made a decision, I walk past my room and keep going, advancing to the executive suite. Ridiculously I feel my nerves bristling as I near the gilt-edged panelling beside Leon's door. Gold lettering inscribes the room number. *518*.

I don't want it to seem like I'm stalking him, but I figure that concern for him over his no-show at dinner is a reasonable excuse for me to come knocking. But either he's not there, or he's fast asleep or in the bathroom because he doesn't respond. I rap my knuckles against the door louder and call out his name — still nothing. I push down on the handle. The rooms in the resort all require swipe cards to open, automatically locking when closed. Leon's door is predictably locked. I'm a determined girl, but even I know when to give up. Dejectedly I turn on my heel and wander back up the corridor to my room.

When I am back in my suite, I realise I just won't be able to let it go. So, I go to the phone and dial the internal hashtag before dialling 518, his room number. I listen to it ringing, clearing my throat, rehearsing in my mind what I will say when he picks up — *Hey, Leon, it's Ketzia* — but he doesn't answer. I let the phone reach twelve rings before hanging up. I decide to have a bath, try and relax. But in the bathroom mirror, I catch sight of my reflection.

My hair is beautifully shiny, and the evening dress shows off my cleavage perfectly. I want Leon to see me like this. I'm not quite ready to give up yet. I tear off a piece of resort notepad and scribble a message on it.

Leon, I missed you at dinner. You know what room I'm in . . .

I resist the urge to scrawl a love heart around the message. Then I tiptoe down the corridor again to his room. Knock. Again—nothing. I wait a moment before dropping to my knees. Sliding the note under the door is more challenging than I anticipated. The rubber seal at the bottom acts as a vacuum seal. I swish the note left to right until it pushes against a patch of weakness and a corner slides under. The rest is easy to slide through.

Mission accomplished, I stand and straighten my dress and hair. If I really wanted, I could use a spell to gain access to the room, or at least spy through the door to see what Leon is up to in there—if indeed he is in there. But that would be against all my supernatural ethics about never using my gifts for self-serving purposes. Aside from that, it would be an uncool thing to do. After all, I don't want him to think I am desperate, slipping a note under his door in the middle of the night. Yep. I think I've got it bad. But then, he'd seemed just as keen as me earlier on. A smile crosses my lips with the memory. He has gotten under my skin. Deflated, I turn and walk back to my room.

I reluctantly remove my beautiful dress and run the bath. I've never been much of a one for polished marble. I prefer my tubs to be made of good old-fashioned porcelain. But as I lower my aching body into the pink-stained marble bath of the Lantau Island Resort, the water fizzing with jasmine salts, I think it wouldn't take much for me to get used to marble. The temperature is steaming hot, and my muscles respond by first clenching, then gently letting go of all tension. My skin reddens, dewy with warmth. I rest my head on the end of the bath and close my eyes. My mind wanders back over the extraordinary events of the day — a series of firsts for me. I have never jumped into bed with someone I've only just met — don't even know, for God's sake. I can't explain it to myself, but somehow it doesn't feel wrong at all. It feels so right.

I can't stop thinking about Leon, wishing he were here with me now, in the bath. Lightly I press my fingers to my lips, remembering his taste and the scent of his skin. My body reacts to the memory of him with a tingling sensation, emanating from the pit of my stomach. I let my fingers slide down from my mouth to brush my nipples. They are hard, peaked mounds breaking the surface of the water. I am so hungry for Leon right now. It's unbearable. I allow my hand to slide down further, feeling the strength and firmness of my stomach muscles. I imagine that it is Leon's hand that is exploring me, teasing a finger into my navel, then venturing further down to my crop of pubic hair and patting it gently before nudging my pussy. I tease myself as the soft, warm bath water laps at my womanhood. The sensation brings to mind the eroticism of the afternoon, of Leon exploring me with his mouth and hands. I wish he were here with me now. I push my finger inside and stroke my clitoris, hardening beneath my touch. Then I move my finger in deeper, entering myself, needing a release from the mounting tension. I turn around in the water to be on my hands and knees in the bath. My breasts skim the surface of the water. I lather them with soap, enjoying the velvety softness of my skin and the contrast of my tightened nipples, dipping in and out of the water. I move my knees so they are further apart and reach down to stroke my vagina and anus and the delicate skin in between. Then I raise myself so my bottom is no longer submerged in the water. I lather soap onto my hands and clean myself, inside and out, enjoying torturing myself, delaying my orgasm. My breath quickens, and I know I can't hold off for much longer. Panting, I delicately shift my weight from my knees to my feet, rocking back onto my heels until I reach a squatting position. I raise my pelvis up and down so that the surface of the water whips against my pussy and anus. I rock up and down with increasing speed, slapping the water harder and harder with my butt and vagina. Tickling my clitoris with two fingers, I finally succumb to an orgasm that releases a rush of endorphins through my entire body. A satisfied groan escapes from my lips before I relax into the bath again, satiated. I close my eyes, gently allowing my breathing to return to normal and my mind to drift off to a deep place of relaxation.

"That would have to be one of the most erotic things I've ever seen."

At first, I think I've imagined it, but when I open my eyes, I see Leon standing on the far side of the bathroom. He watches me with amusement as I come to grips with his presence.

"But how did you? When did you get here . . ." I trail off, struggling to articulate my confusion. Leon doesn't seem to share my qualms about using magic for personal gain, so entering my bathroom would have been as easy for him as clicking his fingers. I involuntarily blush as I think of him watching me masturbate, and I look away, embarrassed.

"You have got to be the most gorgeous, sexual creature I've ever had the pleasure of knowing," Leon reassures me. He perches himself on the edge of the bath and gently turns my chin so that I am facing him. My embarrassment washes away when I see the genuine lust in his eyes. My body reacts, my nipples stiffening and a gush of heat erupting from my sex. He unbuttons the cuffs of his shirt and rolls his sleeves up to the elbows. He picks up a bottle of scented oil from the bath ledge and pours a lavish amount onto his hands. Then he dips a finger into the water, seeking out the soft skin beneath my breasts, teasing me with the probing interplay of his fingertips as they move down my torso to the secret tenderness of my pussy. With his index finger and thumb, he lubricates the sides of my slit, pushing them open, using his other hand to insert a finger slowly into my depths. I arch upwards, craning my upper body towards him, my mouth wanting to meet his, but he pulls his finger out and pushes me back into the water. He keeps this hand on my breasts, holding me in place, while he uses his other hand to finger-fuck me, increasing in intensity and speed the vigorousness of his attention. He slides one finger lower to delicately penetrate the rim of my anus and carefully enter its dark sensitivity. I push my pelvis upwards, wanting more of this, more of him inside me.

"Please," I beg. "More." It is all I can say. I am so aroused that part of me thinks I couldn't cope with any more stimulation, while another more decisive part of me feels like it could handle anything.

"Stay in the bath," he says, his eyes locked onto mine as he teases his fingers over my breasts, pausing to flick each of my nipples, releasing a sharp burst of delicious pleasure-pain. He then moves this hand down to keep company with his other hand, still clutching my cunt and anus. He pushes his fingers in and out of me, using his other hand to find my clit, hard against his touch. He strokes it gently before tugging me upwards, bowing his head to meet his mouth with my bud. I squirm. I can't help it. He reacts instantly, pushing me back into the water.

"Stay still."

I nod obediently, willing myself to stay still, on the cusp of coming, needing his concentration back on my clit. He lowers his head again, his fingers vigorously fucking my anus and pussy while his tongue darts in and out, activating every cell of my clit until it throbs. Then, just when I think I can't take any more, I feel the cold hardness of his teeth biting down — just the right amount — throwing me over the edge and into a violent climax so brutal I think I'm going to die. I cry out in ecstasy, an animal sound utterly devoid of inhibition that turns into a low, exultant moan. Leon slowly withdraws his hands, smoothing them over my body. Bliss. I rest my head on the edge of the bath, my eyes closed, relishing his touch. My breathing slowly returns to normal. I open my eyes and smile at him. He smiles back, his eyes twinkling.

"Thank you," I manage.

"My pleasure." His face is flushed, and his eyes have a lustful gleam. A surge of energy courses through me, and I can feel prickles of desire rushing back greedily for more.

"Come in, Leon. Join me," I invite. He nods his head, stands up and pulls his shirt off. His torso muscles ripple, and his biceps tighten as he removes his shoes and socks. He pulls his trousers and jocks off. My breath catches in my throat as I take in his glistening hardness, his rigid phallus stirring with uncontrollable excitement. He steps into the bath and lowers his body into the tepid water. The tub is plenty big enough for both of us.

"So, would you mind repeating a little bit of what you were doing earlier?"

"With pleasure," I reply. "But first, I just need to take care of something . . ." I slide my body onto his so I am lying on top of him in the water. I can feel the hardness of his penis beneath my pubis as my lips reach his, and we kiss — a long, lingering kiss involving lots of tongue. I raise my arse out of the water, and his glans nudges the top of my inner thigh. I lower my hand into the water and stroke the shaft of his penis, holding it in position as I torment him with the promise of my pussy, already so wet and ready for him. I straddle him then, and he moans, closing his eyes in ecstasy. He pushes himself to a sitting position, deepening the position of his penis inside me so its tip reaches the nerves around my inner sanctum. It is my turn to moan. I bear down on him and rock slowly and gently back and forth, feeling his fullness inside me. He reaches for my breasts, stroking them as I quicken my movements. Then he lowers one hand to where we are joined and pushes my labia open to stroke my clitoris. Never have I felt such profound pleasure. My back arches involuntarily with mounting excitement as I reach a high of ecstasy so intense that it releases from me a rapturous scream, and I am transported from my body to a timeless interstellar state.

Vaguely I am aware of Leon exiting the bath, lifting me out, towelling me down with the plush hotel bath sheet. I observe him carrying me to the bedroom as though from far away, lifting the sheets and tucking me in delicately. I sense him slipping into bed beside me and kissing me repeatedly just before I succumb to the sweetest of sleep.

CHAPTER SEVEN

I don't know how often I've stayed in a hotel room and been woken up by the previous inhabitants' setting of the clock radio. Every time it happens, I swear to myself that next time I check in to a hotel, I will unplug the alarm clock or make sure the alarm hasn't been set. I forget to do this every time. So when I am woken by a terrible bleeping at 6 am the following day, I groan and curse myself for failing to check out the alarm clock situation the day before. That's when I recall the events of the previous evening, of fucking Leon in the bath and again, later, making love with him in the plush king-sized bed. This morning, however, he is nowhere to be seen. I suppose I should be getting used to his disappearing acts by now. He is the sign of Catalan, which renders him flighty and difficult to pin down. This knowledge doesn't prevent a wave of disappointment from washing over me, and I get dressed, hoping that he will be at breakfast but resigned to the fact that he most likely won't be.

I throw on a cream-coloured linen suit with a silky patterned blouse. The pattern on the blouse is entirely Celtic, but not in an obvious way, only in a manner evident to someone like Leon. I fix my face, carefully applying a flattering gloss of pink to my lips, and coil my hair up in a French bun. Ready, I check my mobile and find a text from Mia.

C U at breakfast buffet.

Right, she must already be down there. I grab my handbag and exit the room, happy to leave the unmade bed to room service.

People pack the buffet room. I have trouble spotting Mia but finally find her at the continental section of the breakfast bar.

"Morning, Mia," I chirp, grabbing a plate and inspecting the abundance of fruit, toast, pastries, and cheeses on display.

"Morning, Ketz," she replies, selecting a bunch of grapes and placing them on her plate.

Seeing all the food makes me realize that I am ravenous again. All the sex must be making me extra hungry. Not to mention all the supernatural energies swirling around my aura. I grab a breakfast roll and a butter pat before we edge our way to the English hot breakfast selection. Sausages, bacon, eggs, and baked beans are all displayed invitingly in a row of bains-marie.

"Look," I exclaim, pointing to a tray of hash browns incorrectly labelled *Hush Browns.*

"Something definitely lost in translation there!" Mia laughs as we each help ourselves to perfectly crispy rounds of potato cake.

"I guess we'll just have to eat them really quietly . . ." We laugh. Our plates laden with food, we find a free table and seat ourselves, waiters appearing instantly at our sides to pour steaming hot coffee into our cups.

"Okey dokey," Mia prompts. "You've been given way too much leeway when it comes to spilling the beans. What did you and Leon get up to yesterday?"

I had momentarily forgotten about him, and even mentioning his name causes a jolt of passion to rush through my body.

"Well," I begin coyly, wondering how little I can get away with sharing. "When we left the evacuation, we made our way down to the beach."

"The beach. Nice. Go on," Mia prods as my gaze wanders around the crowded room, searching for Leon. But still no sign of him.

"I admit we had a bit of a pash. I find him really hot."

"What? You kissed?" she asks incredulously. I realize I will easily get away with telling her nothing about what went on. But she is my friend, and I trust her, so I lower my voice and keep going.

"We actually ended up having sex on the beach."

Mia's reaction is priceless. She almost sprays food all over the table in shock.

"You dirty little hussy," she whispers admiringly.

"I think *he* might have called me something along those lines, too," I reply cheekily. The two of us start giggling then, like naughty schoolgirls. Another conference attendee, Aiden, makes a beeline for our table.

"Mind if I take this seat?" he asks.

"Sure, go ahead," Mia says, smiling at him flirtatiously.

With clarity, I realise that our giggling must have acted like a primitive mating call. This is how cosmic energy works. Even though Mia and I had been wholly focused on our conversation, because of its sexual content, the waves of innuendo had travelled the room and embraced everyone in a delicious mist of erotic vitality. I look around to discover several appreciative glances being thrown in our direction. Aiden sits down, placing a plateful of Chinese breakfast dumplings on the table.

"So, what are you girls giggling about?"

Luckily for us, the *Hush Browns* serve as a good excuse for our laughter, sparking a conversation where everyone at our by-now full table shares other funny travel stories. I finish my bacon and eggs methodically, keen to escape the clamour of the room, needing quiet time. When I have finished eating, I excuse myself and get up to go, but not before Mia traps me with another one of her wicked grins.

"More later," she says.

"Okay. Later," I reply. Fortunately for me, she seems pretty taken by Aiden, and the two of them resume their conversation. Perhaps she will be the one to share her sexual adventures next. I head to the lift, hoping for a few minutes alone in my room before going to the day's first conference session. My solitude is short-lived. Waiting at the lift, just before the doors open, I can feel him—sense him—before I see him. Leon.

"Ketzia." His voice is smooth and deep. He is wearing a simple streamlined grey suit with a dark maroon tie, a testament to understated elegance. He leans in to kiss me, seemingly unconcerned at this public display of affection, the mobile phone hanging from his wrist momentarily forgotten. His lips brush mine, awakening an inner trembling of desire deep within me. The lift dings its arrival. Leon places his hand against its frame, holding the doors open for me. As I enter, he raises his mobile to his ear.

"Listen, Deanne. I'm about to enter an elevator and lose reception. Please, make sure . . ." I can't make out the next part of what Leon is saying. His head is angled away from me. I wonder who Deanne is and what role she plays in his life. Probably just a business associate, though the call doesn't sound like it has anything to do with real estate.

I try to ignore the tiny flicker of jealousy splintering my innards. It's as though the idea of anyone else having any kind of licence to Leon's time is unreasonably repellent to me.

"I need him moved to a place with no valid extradition laws. It's urgent . . ." Leon flicks off his mobile and quickly pushes the *close doors* button on the lift panel to the discontent of a disgruntled-looking businessman on the ground floor.

"No extradition laws?" I say as the elevator flows upwards. Leon grimaces, sliding the phone into his pocket.

"Believe it or not, my father is an ex-con. Interpol has him on their radar. He's too old to deal with all of this, so I'm trying to help him out. Shift him to Bhutan or somewhere . . ."

"For real?" I can't believe he trusts me with this information.

"Unfortunately, yes. But I really don't want to waste time talking about that right now, while I have you so close." There is a warm ember of desire discernible in his eyes. "Ketzia, you know you have entirely robbed me of any self-control I ever possessed."

"I hope so," I reply, leaning towards him to inhale his masculine scent. He grabs my wrists, almost toppling me over in his eagerness. He pushes my wrists back, pinning me against the lift wall, sliding his tongue into my mouth while pushing his body against mine. I can feel the tightness of his penis pressing against me, the linen fabric of his suit doing nothing to disguise its hardness. I surrender completely to his touch, revelling in the joy of his adoration. Our lips meet — briefly — before he breathes his mouth back down to the delicate skin of my throat and collarbone. My body responds to his, pushing against him, wanting to be closer.

The lift pings, announcing our arrival on the fifth floor. A nice-looking couple in matching calico shorts, presumably tourists, are waiting to enter the lift. The woman smiles at me, and I smile back, running a self-conscious hand through my dishevelled hair before exiting the lift with Leon.

CHAPTER EIGHT

This time we go to his room. I was right about him having the executive suite. Where my room is comfortable and luxurious, his is obscenely opulent. Everything — the wallpaper, the furnishings, the fittings — is inlaid with gold. From the vast bay window in the living area, the view stretches beyond the beach we made love on yesterday to the far horizon.

"I was kind of sad when I woke up to find you missing this morning. You keep disappearing on me," I say as he shuts the door behind us.

"Sorry. Had business I had to attend to. But I'm totally here with you right now." He pulls me into him and presses his lips to mine. I willingly comply with a torrid kiss that leaves me in no doubt about the depth of his passion. Still kissing, we move to the oversized couch piled high with cushions of a softness I have never encountered before.

Before I know it, my jacket is discarded, and our kisses graduate to something else. Leon's body is muscled and masculine, and he smells sweetly of musky aftershave. He nibbles on the region of my throat just below my ear, his tongue and lips taking it in turns to tantalise and tease me. I kiss his throat, my hands moving to the back of his neck, stroking the fine hairs there. It feels so good to be making out with him. My tongue finds his, and we pash, a hot, heady mix of tongues, lips, and sensuality. We can't keep our hands off each other. The temperature in the room is heating up. Leon grabs my waist and pulls me onto his lap. I can feel the hardness of his erection straining against the fabric of his trousers.

I straddle him and thrust my pelvis forwards and backwards over the stiffness of his erection. He pushes me onto my back and tears my blouse off me while I feverishly undo the buttons of his shirt and glide my hands over his firm chest, lingering to squeeze his nipples before following suit with my tongue. I move my fingers over the smoothness of his body, dipping my index finger into the crevice of his navel before sliding it further down to tug at the waistband of his trousers.

He unclasps my bra and circles his thumbs around my areolas before leaning in to bite the stiff peaks of my nipples, first one, then the other. His hands move down to my hips, roughly positioning me beneath him, before unclasping my belt buckle. My linen suit trousers slide off me effortlessly. The sight of my scanty G-string fuels his hunger for me, and he pulls it down forcefully, yanking it over my knees and over my ankles to free my body from its lacy constraint. He smooths his hands up over the backs of my legs until they reach my buttocks. He squeezes my butt cheeks with longing, murmuring with pleasure at their softness. I undo his belt buckle and unzip his fly, then push his trousers down and his jocks with them. His penis rises stiffly, a ramrod shaft dying for attention. I oblige, wrapping my lips around the circumference of his cock, sucking on the swollen head of his penis. Leon slides out of his pants and jocks completely. We are finally both naked. His hands are still on my arse cheeks, and he uses them to guide me around, positioning me so that I am on all fours above him with his penis in my mouth and my pussy hovering above his face. I almost die when I feel the tip of his tongue slide inside me to taste my wetness. It just feels too god damned erotic. Then he uses his fingers to stroke my lips apart so that he can suck on my clitoris. His tongue is incredibly agile, titillating me by sliding up and down the inner sides of my trim. He is turning me on. His penis hardens even more, so I keep sucking, enjoying the power I have over him and that he has over me. I lick his prick up and down, sliding my tongue along his shaft, tasting the saltiness of the pre-cum oozing out. I am wet now. Leon starts finger-fucking me while darting his tongue in and out thirstily. He pinches my clitoris and I almost completely lose control. My tits are incredibly tender, resting lightly on his lower torso as I keep sucking his cock.

"You're going to have to stop doing that," Leon warns. "I'm going to come." He pushes himself up and positions himself behind me, never letting go of my snatch once. Then I feel the head of his cock opening me up and pushing into my deepness. He guides my arse forwards and backwards, rocking me in an increasing rhythm. I move faster and faster until I am fucking him so fast and so hard that we are thrown simultaneously into a messy and highly satisfying orgasm.

We recover together, our sweat-drenched bodies glistening. I lie on top of him on the couch, my body quivering. He caresses me tenderly, sweetly kissing my face.

"You are so beautiful," he whispers.

"You, too," I whisper back, kissing him gently.

We rise slowly, slightly disorientated from our lovemaking, collecting our clothes and dressing. I pick up his shirt and pause to breathe in its delicious scent before passing it to him. He grabs my G-string from the couch and buries his nose in it before handing it back to me. We smile at each other, suddenly shy in each other's presence. Then a sudden rush courses through my body. Afterglow. I can't resist the urge to raise my hand above my head and stretch my whole body out. The endorphins whooshing through my body threaten to throw me into another orgasm.

"I feel fantastic!" I can't help but yell it aloud. So incredible is the heavenly buzz emanating from deep within my pussy and now spreading to my fingertips and toes. Leon grins at me, suddenly aware of how aroused I still am. My excitement arouses him, and he pushes me back onto the couch. We go crazy, kissing each other, grabbing hold of each other's bodies, not caring about anything other than the pure joy of sensation, the white heat of lovemaking pushing our bodies into another frenzy. We are half-dressed, but Leon finds a way to enter me again, trousers loose around his knees. We are like animals, driven by intense need. I push my hips up to meet his as he slams into me. I grab hold of his arms and clench my fingers around his biceps. We screw each other with blatant lust, fucking with pure desire. We continue pushing each other to the limit, testing the boundaries of our connection. He slides his tongue hungrily down my entire shape, pausing to suck on my toes before travelling back up again, his hands never losing contact with my skin, gliding over my body in a motion simultaneously sensuously soft yet rough in its greed and need for me. I also can't get enough of *his* body. I stroke him, enjoying his armpits' warm hollows, his arms' smooth tanned skin, and the rugged, chiselled contours of his jawline. He enters me again in a tangle of arms and legs, and we ride the wave of our lovemaking, peaking together in a hot sticky climax earth-shattering in its pleasure.

After a long while, we recover our breath, and he slides out of me. The emptiness he leaves behind is almost unbearable.

"Ketzia," he sighs. "That was amazing."

Indeed. Oh, yes, indeed it was. I smile.

A beeping that sounds like it comes from another universe invades our post-coital bliss — Leon's phone.

"Fuck," he swears before lifting himself off the couch and reaching for his mobile, vibrating crazily on the coffee table.

"Hello," he answers. Whoever's on the other end of the line speaks loudly and seemingly without pausing for breath.

"Just give me a second. I'll call you back." Leon hangs up, sorts through the jumble of clothes on the floor and starts dressing.

"You're wasting your time," I breathe, my voice husky from exertion.

"Huh?" he replies.

"You're only going to have to take them back off again," I say, languorously stretching out on the couch.

"Sorry, Ketzia. I would love to spend the whole day with you, but I really have to return this call — work." His eyes have a faraway look, and I realise any attempt to seduce him further would be futile.

"Okay," I say. I'm very satisfied, even though I am secretly cursing his phone — and his work — for taking his attention away from me. He hands me my clothes, and I quickly get dressed. His mobile starts buzzing again.

"See you soon?" he asks hopefully, phone in hand.

"If you like."

"Oh, I more than like," he replies before he answers it. We quickly kiss before I leave, the sound of his sultry voice as he answers his mobile resounding in my head as I make my way back down the hotel corridor to my room.

CHAPTER NINE

The rest of the conference disappears in a haze for me. Partly because I've had more sex in the space of 24 hours than I have had all year or maybe even my whole life, and partly because Leon is called away to oversee some big project in London on the second day. So I am left alone, with Mia, of course, for company, but nothing and no one to fill the void left by Leon. A few of the guys try it on with me but soon realise that my dreamy stare is all about the man who is missing and that I am incapable of registering interest in them, and they quickly give up.

On the last night of the conference, I skip the closing drinks party, preferring to be alone in my hotel room. I numbly channel-surf the hotel's dubious offering of international porn and heavily censored media, hoping to stumble on something to take my mind off my misery. I don't understand what has happened to me, but it's as though I have become utterly obsessed with Leon and anything other than him holds no interest for me.

I am back in Sydney a few days later, working the daily real-estate grind and still desperately missing Leon. He hasn't responded to any of my emails or Skype requests. All my messages to him have only been met with silence. Maybe I was just nothing more than a fling for him. I try to play it cool, but the guy managed to get under my skin, and I struggle to forget about him. I try to think of our time at the conference as a fun, one-off sexy experience, but I ache with the memory of Leon's body. More than anything, I yearn to kiss him and see and touch his handsome face. Mia and my other work-mates notice that I'm glum but don't know why, though Mia suspects, I'm sure. She tries to cheer me up by inviting me to go for a lunchtime manicure, but I don't feel up to talking about how much I miss him and tell her that I have an appointment to show a client property. Because really, there is nothing anyone can do to save me from my unhappiness — except maybe magically divine Leon.

At the end of my first week back, I knock off work early and allow my intuition to guide my steps to my old Wiccan headquarters in Castanna Street. Meredith, a Wiccan priestess and the closest thing I have to an earthmother, greets me at the door. Immediately upon opening the ornate wooden door, she envelops me in an immensely warming, comforting hug.

I can smell incense, aromatic herbs, and myrtle oil through the layers of her shawls and the draperies of her dress. She guides me inside, and before I know it, I am seated in a plush woven armchair with lavender pouches pressed gently to my eyes while two other members of my clan knead my hands, gently incanting soothing vespers. Their energy is powerfully healing, and I feel my strength returning. I had not realised how significantly depleted I'd been, but Meredith had known what I needed the minute she laid eyes on me. That is her rare talent and gift.

"Thank you," I whisper when the ceremony is complete and the lavender pouches have gently been removed from my eyes. A cup of rich, ambrosial tea is handed to me, and I sip at the brew greedily. It has been too long since I drank of the seed of nasturtium. I feel momentarily guilty about how I have neglected my needs and my Wiccan practice, but Meredith calms me with a level stare.

"Why don't you tell us what's been going on with you?" she suggests, passing me a bag of chocolate-coated figs. She remembered my weakness for unusual sweets. I pluck one from the bag and place it on the tip of my tongue. An explosion of taste erupts in my mouth. I smile involuntarily. Velveteen Slips, the chef at the Wiccan centre, handmakes the figs. I'm sure she puts something exotic in the delicacy—for the warming, comforting sensation tingling through my whole body suggests more than a sugar high. I smile. Meredith smiles back.

"Nice to finally see you with a smile on your face," she says.

"Yes, well, things have been pretty . . . extreme lately." I then tell her the whole story about the conference and meeting Leon, our shared ancestral history, our lovemaking, and my final sad and lonely conclusion that he is no longer interested in me. I don't leave anything out, even telling Meredith about the supernatural sea creature that hunted us in the ocean. Meredith listens patiently, nodding encouragingly, whenever I struggle to tell the tale. Finally, I am done. Meredith stares at me intently before speaking.

"You need to make a decision. Either you decide to let Leon go, or you do everything within your power to bring him back."

I don't need much time to mull it over. I already know that a life without Leon is no life for me. Something about my expression gives me away, for Meredith speaks again.

"I see you have already made up your mind. Before we go any further, I want to make sure you know exactly what you are getting yourself into."

I feel a swell of butterflies somersaulting in my stomach. Meredith has never spoken to me in this way before. She is warning me, but she is also conversing with me as an equal and not as a teacher to a student. The whole experience is highly unsettling.

"I don't understand," I say, responding as much to her words as to the cyclonic energy generated from her being. She takes me by the hand and guides me down the hall to the library.

The Wiccan library is everything a good library should be. It has no windows and is covered with floor-to-ceiling bookshelves housing everything from ancient tomes on paganism to modern collections on psychiatry and everyday philosophy. Meredith balances on a stepladder and pulls down an ancient-looking grimoire from the uppermost shelf. A grimoire is a sort of textbook for spells, with instructions on how to use magic. Dust covers the grimoire. She places it reverently on the paua-inlaid coffee table and wipes it clean with a cloth before settling another one of those intense stares on me.

"This grimoire traces the lineage of our clan through several millennia. I don't know how much in touch you are with your past lives . . ."

"A little," I say with a flicker of my hand. History has never been my forte.

"Well then, let me give you a condensed version of your former selves."

Meredith tells me that throughout time every occurrence of my and Leon's paths intersecting has been met with tragedy. I feel a lump form in my throat as she recounts a seemingly endless cycle of sadness, of the pagan knight and knightess having their love thwarted by spirits. One of the spirits was a sea serpent, and chills run down my spine with the tale's familiarity. In the 12th century, the incarnations of the knighthood were destroyed by rituals that demonised love and sexuality. Over time, it seemed, my path and that of Leon had been continuously blighted. I wondered if it would be possible to change the course of history within my lifetime. Meredith says, "It is possible to put an end to this cycle of destruction, but first we need to make sure it's what Leon wants, too."

Meredith closes the book and returns it to its place on the shelf, and I feel something inside me break down.

"I just don't know." I swipe at the tears falling down my cheeks. "When we were together, everything seemed so wonderful and simple. But now he won't return my calls, my emails. Nothing. I haven't heard from him since the conference."

"In that case, the first thing we need to do is to make sure that he is not in danger."

I feel my throat constrict. Amid feeling rejected, this is one thing that had never occurred to me—that Leon may have met with foul play because of his union with me. Meredith gently pats my shoulder, sensing my alarm.

"Don't worry. It will take me only a moment to find out." She places her hands on her temples, closes her eyes, starts humming, and gently rocks on the spot.

She is astral travelling, finding Leon's soul-self somewhere in the universe. I wait in painful anticipation. She stops rocking and humming, drops her hands to her sides, opens her eyes, and smiles.

"The good news is that your lover is unharmed."

A breath of air slowly seeps out of me in relief.

"What else?" I am almost too afraid to ask.

"He is just as scared as you are. He has been keeping his distance because he understands, all too well, the ramifications of a union with you. The only way you're going to convince him that such a union is possible will, ironically enough, be with the use of a little magic."

Meredith's eyes light up at the prospect. She likes nothing better than being able to use her gifts of witchcraft.

"But your union will involve risk—have no delusions about that."

"I understand." I make a momentous decision. "I am prepared to risk everything for this man. I want him. I need him."

Meredith nods her head. Gently pulls me to her.

"Come back tomorrow night," she says, kissing my forehead. "We will incite his spirit to come to you using the Spell of Orgiastic Love. It is the only spell to be used in these circumstances."

I gasp. The Spell of Orgiastic Love is one of the most advanced and secret of the Wiccan rituals. I have never partaken in it, nor do I know of anyone else who has. Meredith smiles at me.

"It is a beautiful ritual. Go home. Relax. Tomorrow is Saturday and a full moon—a good time for magic. Bathe. Please use pure oils in your bath. And then return here tomorrow night just before midnight."

She walks me to the front door of the Wiccan headquarters, and we embrace before I take my leave, my head buzzing. The Spell of Orgiastic Love! I can't believe Meredith is prepared to entrust me with such a sacred rite. I've hardly been a model student of witchcraft, particularly of late. My commitment to the craft has always been haphazard at best, especially compared to some of my clan's other more dedicated members. I've often missed my fortnightly witch meetings—esbats— due to sheer laziness or the temptation of frivolous social events I've been invited to. I also can't believe that she's taking my affair with Leon seriously enough to want to invoke this powerful spell. The gravity of the situation hits home. This *thing* I share with him must really be playing it out on the supernatural field as much as on the purely physical and emotional level. Part of me feels immensely privileged to be counted as ready for this rite. Another aspect of me feels nervous. The enormity of my affair weighs heavily on me as I leave the familiar comfort of the headquarters.

CHAPTER TEN

On my way out of the Wiccan headquarters, I bump into my old friend, Charles Aynsley, a master theurgist of his own order and fellow Castanna Street Wiccan chapter member.

"Hey, Charles." He has probably just finished attending a class and is seemingly oblivious to my serious discussions with Meredith.

"Ketzia." He gives me a soft peck on the cheek. We amble down the front steps together, pleased to see each other.

"I haven't seen you in a lifetime," he says, always prone to exaggeration.

"I've just come back from a work trip overseas," I say, thankful for the excuse for not showing up at the Wiccan headquarters more often.

"Well, it's so good to see you again. Hey, what are you doing now? Do you want to catch up for a drink? There's a great bar I know just a couple of blocks away."

I hesitate for a moment, but his enthusiasm is contagious.

"Sure, thanks." A drink with an old friend might be just what I need to let go of all the stress of the last couple of days. "I suppose it's not too early in the day for a drink."

"Never too early for a drink — or some magic!" Charles exclaims.

We walk a couple of blocks to the bar — a downstairs establishment lushly furnished in red velvet drapery, complete with a set of gargoyles hanging over the bar. I can see why Charles likes this place. It has Gothic written all over it.

"What's your poison?" he asks once we're seated in a matching set of Louis XV boudoir chairs.

"Surprise me," I say, giving him a big grin.

I am feeling much more positive about my situation with the action plan for tomorrow night in place. It is good to catch up with an old friend, too. Charles goes to the bar to order our drinks, and I reminisce about the first time I met him—at a re-enactment Wiccan course I'd undertaken a couple of years ago. At first, I remember, I hadn't liked him. With his tall, gangly frame and shock of prematurely white hair, I had initially found him a little creepy. Over the course, however, we'd been partnered for a few reconnection exercises, and I'd overcome my initial wariness of him and discovered him to be a fun and lively guy, though sometimes a little too gushy in his enthusiasm for everything witchcraft related. Charles runs a consulting business specialising in healing and life pathway exploration. He also serves as a *corporate shaman* to the boards of several Fortune 500 companies. His resume would be an engrossing read. His enthusiasm for witchcraft also spills over into other areas of his life, including herbology and potion mastery.

"This is going to be a definite surprise for your tastebuds," he announces, placing a substantial multi-coloured cocktail in my hand.

"It looks like all the wonders of the universe in one glass— what on earth is it?" I ask, taking in the effervescent swirls of green, blue, yellow and red.

"Just try it. Reserve your judgement!" he replies, taking a sip of his matching iridescent concoction.

"Okay." I take a sip, and a burst of sweet and sour assaults my taste buds. The flavour is intense but delicious.

"This is good," I say.

"Of course," Charles says. We sit and enjoy our drinks for a moment in silence.

"So, what were you doing at Castanna Street tonight? A class or something?" I ask. Charles's eyes cloud over for a moment before answering, and I hope I haven't said anything wrong.

"I had a meeting with the head Wiccans," he says. "They've decided to expel me from the senior council."

"What?" I lower my glass in disbelief. "But you're a master theurgist. You have all these skills . . ."

"You're telling me."

"But that's terrible," I exclaim, indignant on his behalf. "Why would they do something like that?" Charles just shrugs his shoulders casually.

"What can I say? It was a political decision—no need for you to get upset about it. I'm philosophical about the whole thing. Besides, it will free up some of my time for more noble pursuits . . . Like drinking cocktails with pretty ladies." He winks at me flirtatiously, and I can't resist winking back.

"I'll drink to that." We chink glasses again and spend the next hour talking magic, discussing everything from a recent dream conference Charles went on to gossip about celebrity witches and fad groups sweeping the internet. It is the most relaxed I have felt in ages. When we finish our cocktails, my mood is the best it's been since I last saw Leon in Hong Kong.

"Ketzia, it's been too long between drinks," Charles says. We've never been for drinks together before, but I don't want to burst his bubble by reminding him of that.

"Let's extend to dinner. I know a great place not too far from here . . ."

My first impulse is to decline his invitation—after all, I don't want to send him the wrong message about my interest in him or anything. He senses my hesitation and leans forward reassuringly to place his hand on my arm.

"Just dinner. I promise. Please tell me we live in a world where two friends with a common interest can partake of a meal together without it causing World War Three?" Charles sure knows how to win me over. Besides, it's a good point. I can't help but laugh and nod my head.

"Great!" Charles says.

"But on one condition," I say, raising a finger.

"Go ahead," Charles replies seriously, almost as though awaiting his execution.

"You paid for the cocktails, so I insist that I am going to pay for dinner."

"Ah, lucky for me then that I'm going to take you to the most expensive restaurant in town."

We arrive at Alfredo's, and I can tell it will not be the most expensive place in the world. Plastic red-and-white checked gingham tablecloths cover the tables. The menu is scrawled on a chalkboard above the bistro-style servery. There are no suave waiters in pedigree suits, only an old Italian man in a tracksuit behind a counter taking orders. Charles watches me take it all in.

"Okay—it might not win any prizes in the best interior decorating awards. But the food here is unbeatable."

"That's great," I say, deciding on the homemade gnocchi with three-cheese sauce. Charles goes up to the counter and orders a lasagne for himself and a bottle of red for the table.

"Hey, I don't know how much of that I'm going to be able to drink," I protest when the sparkling bottle of Lambrusco arrives.

"Leave what you don't want to me," Charles says easily.

The food is indeed delicious, and we pass the rest of the evening in playful banter. Charles asked me what I was doing at the Wiccan headquarters. I say I was just there touching base, seeing as I'd neglected the place for so long. I feel the need to keep private everything about my discussions with Meredith about Leon, my ancestry, and the Wiccan rite scheduled for tomorrow night. Thankfully, Charles seems satisfied with my answer.

"Are you still working in real estate?" he asks.

"Yes," I say, surprised that he has remembered this detail.

"What's the name of the company you work for?"

"KX Realty. We specialise in high-end property. Portfolios of the rich and famous."

"Hey, I might swing by one time, get you to show me around some places? I could use another investment."

Startled, I nod my head. I had heard a rumour once that Charles came from inherited wealth. Maybe it was true.

"Corporate shamanism doing well?" I ask, choosing to stick to a known ground. Charles grins at me, a sprig of parsley caught between his front teeth.

"Very well. I'm one of the few people doing it, and there's a real demand. I can charge pretty much anything I like."

"But what do you actually *do*?"

He laughs again, his tongue darting out and removing the offending piece of garnish with a quick, scissor-like motion.

"It varies from client to client. Essentially, I identify the faults and weaknesses embedded deeply in the CEO's subconscious or the organisation itself. Those hidden evils manifest in little everyday failures or huge corporate collapses that no one else can see. And then I get rid of them before they turn into big — or bigger — problems."

"What kind of evils?" I ask, fascinated and a little frightened at the same time.

"Sometimes, the head of a company may have unknowingly allowed their soul to be hijacked by a destructive supernatural force. When you're capable of traversing several or many realms of consciousness, or connectedness — like you or I are, then you can tap into all of that and influence it."

"So what do you do? Perform an exorcism or something on them?"

"No. I'd never get away with that. These people are generally cerebral, numbers-driven operators who don't believe in the cosmic or the divine. Lucky for me, I have a business degree and a PhD in mathematics, so I'm capable of reducing metaphysical concepts to algorithmic formulae they can understand and relate to."

"That's pretty advanced."

"Then I wrap it all up in some new age namby-pamby or some such tosh to engage their subconscious mind before hypnotising them."

It's my turn to laugh.

"It's so deliciously manipulative. Don't they ever suspect what you're doing?"

"Never. I give them concrete life-coach kind of tasks to complete as homework, like exercise, diet, and breathing meditation. Things start to improve for them, and they equate it to that."

"Sounds like you're providing a valuable service."

"I don't pretend to be an altruist. My business ventures are purely driven by money. And power."

"Power?"

"Imagine the rush of influencing some of this country's top decision-makers without them even being aware of it."

I feel a warning nudge again of something like terror. Why is he telling me all of this? Why does he trust me with all these details? My speculations are answered when he says, "I trust you, Ketzia. Apart from anything else, think about it. Who would believe you if you told them?"

"True." I must concede the point. "They'd think I was bonkers."

Charles raises his glass.

"Here's to bonkers."

"Bonkers!" We chink glasses.

After polishing off much more of the wine than I'd intended, I finally fare him well and head home.

CHAPTER ELEVEN

The following morning I am decidedly hungover — probably not the best state to be in for someone about to embark on the most intense spiritual ritual of her life. My mobile beeps with an incoming message alert, and my heart jumps into my mouth at the thought that it could be Leon. But no, it's only Charles, sending me a message thanking me for our dinner last night. He has signed it off with a kiss. Uh-oh. I don't want him to get the wrong impression, but it would be rude not to reply. So I send a benign message.

thx. was fun. c u at castanna st again some time.

I mooch around the house for a while before finally pulling on a pair of tracksuit pants and jogging down to the local shops. I grab a paper at the newsagent and head to a cafe. Several cafe lattes later, my head is decidedly clearer, and I head back home to tackle the housework. My house is a pretty, quaint little terrace with window boxes under all the windows. It is two storeys, but small. Upstairs has just one big loft bedroom and an ensuite bathroom. I vacuum the entire house, throw on a couple of loads of washing, fertilise the pot plants, and before I know it, strands of silvery sunlight seeping through the blinds alert me that it's already afternoon. I follow Meredith's instructions and take a long leisurely bath before consuming a microwaved TV dinner in front of the box. There is an old re-run of a Colombo detective show playing, and I watch that until it's time to go.

At night Castanna Street is decidedly dark. As I round the corner by the train station, I realise I have never been in the primarily industrial neighbourhood outside daylight hours. Sure, I've taken a few evening classes in the finer points of Wiccan philosophy — but that was during summer when the daylight hours extended until later at night. My heeled boots echo on the concrete footpath, and I wonder if it wouldn't have been wiser for me to drive over rather than using public transport. But then I reach the steps leading up to the headquarters, and a gush of warm, welcoming energy greets me and sweeps aside all my worries.

Meredith opens the door before I even get to pull on the old brass knocker. She has her cloak of mystery on. I smile shyly at her, wishing I'd worn something more interesting than my jeans and winter overcoat.

"Ketzia," she greets, guiding me inside. "Did you walk?'

"I caught the train," I say. "I didn't realise quite how lonely this neighbourhood gets after dark."

Meredith merely nods, then turns her attention behind me as a towering blonde woman I have never met enters the building. Something about her is vaguely familiar. She is covered head to toe in jewellery. I avert my eyes, her intense gaze too strong for me to meet. Then it comes to me. The blonde woman is Countess Gretha, one of the highest order of Wiccans in the southern hemisphere. I have seen photos of her before in Wiccan magazines. She is quite a celebrity in supernatural circles. That she has come here tonight, specifically for my purposes only, becomes apparent when she addresses me directly, her voice a clear resonance of reason.

"You must be Ketzia," she says, reaching out a long spindly hand covered in rings knitted together by a swathe of golden chains. "I am Gretha."

I take her hand and feel a direct surge of pure crystalline energy course through my entire body. If ever I felt out of my element, now is the time. My tongue is so dry it is stuck to the roof of my mouth, and I am rendered speechless. Thankfully,

Meredith steps in, leading us up the long internal hallway of the headquarters.

"We will be using the Celestial chamber tonight. It is ready."

I have only been privy to the Celestial chamber once before, on a guided tour of the building. Then, it had seemed a spartan, windowless room in the centre of the building. It is filled with thousands of candles tonight, and for the first time, I notice the small candleholders protruding from the walls at different heights to encase the entire room in a glorious, circular glow. There are already three other people in the room. They are seated on the floor, on plush floor cushions, meditating. Meredith leaves Gretha in the room and pulls me gently into the corridor outside.

"Come with me," she says, ushering me into her office. Meredith's office is a small room with a simple office desk and chair in it. Folded over the chair is a terry-towelling robe.

"Please undress and put the robe on. Then we will be ready to begin. I'll wait just outside."

"Should I take everything off?" I ask, suddenly feeling shy.

"Yes, please. Don't worry. No one will be looking at you, merely channelling energy through your chakras," Meredith reassures me. Feeling slightly better, I take my coat off as she leaves.

Moments later, she taps on the door again. I step out of the room, and she leads me back down the corridor to the Celestial chamber. I am wearing the robe and a pair of fluffy disposable slippers that have also been provided for me. Meredith opens the door, and I am overwhelmed by the eruption of pure, white light energy that pours out. Everyone is humming at different pitches, the variety of timbres producing a rich kaleidoscope of sound. The volume increases, heralding my entrance. Instantly I feel as though my entire body is charged — every cell rendered alive and full of potent energy.

Meredith guides me to the centre of the floor, where a soft hessian mat is laid out. Words are not necessary to communicate what is required of me. It is as though the reverberations of sound carry enough meaning that I intrinsically know what to do. Meredith helps me out of my robe, and I lie on the mat, naked.

Meredith kneels on the floor beside my right shoulder, completing the symmetry of the four other Wiccans positioned in a perfect circle around me. The humming ceases in a simultaneous, unpremeditated way. Within the ensuing silence, I feel warmth spreading through my entire body, as though heat is pushing its way through my fingertips, toes, and the very strands of hair on my head. The sensation is giddying yet grounding. I tune in to the sounds of breathing. Each Wiccan is blowing exhalations of energetic breath into my being. My whole body reacts. Then — a gentle touch. Soft fingertip taps on my extremities, gently moving closer to my core chakras. It feels beautiful — like getting a deep tissue massage but with only the most delicate pressure. I hear a voice. It is Gretha. She speaks with a rich consonance.

"Spirits of Earth, Fire, Air, Water, bring your energies to this astral body so that it can draw the goodness to it that is its due."

She repeats the incantation several times, and then everyone joins in gentle humming once more. Hands caress my body, smoothing over the contours of my wrists, ankles, knees, and hips. Everyone's hands move in a glorious, unified rhythm, arousing the life force present in every cell of my being.

"Breathe, my friend. Breathe," Gretha instructs. I realise I have been holding my breath in anticipation. She cups her graceful hands on my solar plexus, and I breathe into them. I breathe deeply and consciously, allowing myself to surrender to the moment completely.

"Good, that is exceptionally good," Gretha says. "Now we are going to drizzle you with the salt of the earth, a symbolic and natural gesture." The hands leave my body. Light, fluffy grains of salt are scattered over my shoulders, showered down my thighs, and sprinkled over my throat. Usually, I would associate salt with a hard substance but the way it is being dusted over me—like a velveteen blanket of snow—opens me to the experience of salt as an ephemeral mineral of a multi-hued quality. It also tickles me slightly, and a little smile creases the corners of my mouth. The Wiccans commence their humming again, getting louder this time until their voices erupt into the air in open-mouthed vowel sounds. Their hands trail over my body again, the salt acting as an exfoliant, a paranormal metaphor for the skin of this world being discarded. I feel like a snake shedding its skin. As though in sympathy with my thoughts, Gretha unwraps a boa constrictor from a hook on the wall. I can't believe it. I hadn't even noticed the snake when I came into the room, and now it is slowly moving its head from side to side as Gretha holds it over my body. She hisses at it soothingly before lowering it onto my feet. The boundaries of my trust are being tested. Meredith smiles at me reassuringly and nods her head.

"Relax. Let the power of the serpent energise your being," she says. I find it pretty hard to relax with the snake slithering up my leg, but then I notice that everyone is touching the snake with their fingers as it journeys up my body, and I realise they are committing just as much trust to this exercise as I am. After all, if the snake was to bite someone, it is far more likely to be one of them than me, especially if I lie still. So I freeze over entirely and shut my eyes. I pretend that the malleable, hard, yet slippery being moving over my body is not a snake, just an inanimate object like a stocking filled with rice or something. My visualisation works enough to relax me just enough not to scream. Then something strange and wonderful happens. The snake wraps itself into a coil on my midriff and rests. It lies there, still, as though it were basking in the sun on a hot summer's day. The Wiccans remove their hands from the snake and start to chant.

"Snake Woman, shedding her skin,
Shedding, shedding, shedding her skin
Bird Woman taking flight . . .
Star Woman shining bright . . .
Moon Woman riding the night . . .
Blossom Woman opening wide . . ."

I am cast into a place of freedom like never before. I feel that anything is possible. The Wiccans keep chanting. The snake starts to slide over my body, but now I am enjoying it. I am at one with the snake, as I am at one with the whole universe.

"Snake Woman, shedding her skin,
Shedding, shedding, shedding her skin
Bird Woman taking flight . . .
Star Woman shining bright . . .
Moon Woman riding the night . . .
Blossom Woman opening wide . . ."

I join in the chant, I can't help myself, and something incredible happens. I start to levitate. I only realise that I have lifted off the ground when I feel the smooth scales of the snake caressing my back, creeping up my spine, swirling around my torso. I open my mouth and cry, "I am the Knightess of the Night, Orgasmic Witch of Love, Ecstasy, Sex." I repeat it several times, truly owning my birthright for the first time and finally relieved to experience the extent of my potential. Rays of light course through my body, and I am finally free to be me.

The witches draw closer, hands outstretched beneath my floating body, not physically touching me but embracing me energetically with a warm, pulsating force. They resume their humming, a deep, resonant embodiment of femininity. The muscles of my body feel as though they have turned to liquid, and the very bones of my skeleton morphed into molten matter. The witches all cease their pulsating harmonies simultaneously, replacing the voluminous sound with short pants of breath, changing the air temperature in the room. As though from far away, I hear a voice.

"Breathe." It is Gretha. She is summoning me back from the brink of possibilities. Obediently I inhale, the oxygen filling my lungs acting as a kind of salve, a gentle pre-emptive coating to shelter me from the shock of returning to normality. I continue breathing deeply and slowly, each exhalation releasing me downwards towards the floor until I am no longer suspended in the air and my body contacts the mat. The snake coils its way back onto my stomach during my descent. It rests in a neat curl around my belly button. I feel a deep affection for it, for what it has enabled me to experience.

Lightly I raise my hand and stroke its scaly softness, wanting to communicate my gratitude to it. The snake lifts its head. Its dark, glassy eyes peer into mine. I am mesmerised by its puissant stare. A stream of images flows through my consciousness. Through the snake's eyes, I see the spirit of the ocean serpent responsible for the death of my ancestors centuries ago. I transgress my chi, using the snake to embody the spirit of the ocean serpent, willing myself to understand why the serpent felt the need to destroy them. Instantly I sense an icy channel of fear. Something had made the serpent frightened of these early incarnations of Leon and me. I struggle to discern what it could have been. Through the miasma, I can finally decipher something black lurking at the edge of their midst. *This* is the threat, not the man and woman at the forefront of the picture. I cannot define any identifying features in the ominous presence. I do not even know if it has a human shape. What I do know is that the serpent's wrath was misdirected. Inhabiting its body, I feel its regret at the discovery, its impossible wish to redact its actions.

I return to the room, the snake's gaze sadly latched onto mine, our shared experience forging a deep bond between myself and the creature.

"I think he likes you," Meredith teases, breaking the spell. Giggles erupt around the room, a lively effervescence replacing the intensity of the ritual. Gretha places a hand on my shoulder, her jewellery chiming.

"How do you feel?" she asks.

"I feel . . ." Where do I begin? How can I describe the enormity of what I am feeling? The journey of the ritual was so profound and intense. I feel like a different person. No, I feel like more of the same person. I don't know where to begin.

"I feel wonderful," I finally settle for and am greeted with a roomful of smiles.

"Well done," Gretha says, and her praise bathes me in confidence, a deep sense of accomplishment washing over me. Carefully I lift the snake from my belly and pass it to Gretha. Slowly I rise from the floor, flexing my wrists and ankles, returning to earth. The others are busy closing the circle, snuffing out candles and incense, and whispering individual supplications to end the ritual. Meredith holds my robe open for me, and I tie it around my waist. Reverently we leave the Celestial chamber together, unified by our collective mystical covenant.

"Everyone, meet for tea in the library," Meredith says, guiding me to her office to get dressed.

Five minutes later, I am back in my jeans and t-shirt, seated in an exceedingly comfortable ikat upholstered Chesterfield in the library. As I sip herbal tea and eat chocolate periwinkle cookies, the experience of the ritual takes on an other-worldly, unrealistic quality. The logician in me is reluctant to believe the exultant knowledge that Leon and I have only ever been forced apart due to misinterpreting an encroaching source of evil. I'd kill to find out what the evil element is all about — particularly as it seems to have followed us through the ages — but I am quietly satisfied with the wisdom I have attained. Especially as it means I can now trust Leon and pursue him wholeheartedly.

A burst of laughter breaks my train of thought. Meredith has been telling everyone a story about how she *accidentally* cast a binding spell on her dog, which consequently developed a fetish for her mobile phone. It kept burying it in the backyard until she realised she had inadvertently interchanged the dog's understanding of the word *phone* with *bone*. Peals of laughter scatter around the room. Gretha has a braying, infectious laugh and I instinctively lean toward her. The snake still wrapped around her arm slithers onto the floor, gliding over the carpet to arrive at my ankle. It lifts its head as though seeking permission from me before journeying up my leg.

"Oh, how cute," one of the witches remarks. I smile as the snake slides over my torso, draping its body in a hug about my neck. Its cold sturdiness around my shoulders feels like the most natural thing in the world.

Gretha observes the snake's movements silently. Then she says, "He's bonded with you."

"It's a boy?" I reply, locking eyes with the creature. A deep current of understanding travels between us.

"Take him home with you," Gretha says.

"Huh?" I can't have a snake. I wouldn't know the first thing about how to look after it. "But he's yours," I say to Gretha.

"He belongs with you now," Gretha replies firmly. She clasps my knee affectionately as she rises. "Besides, I have others."

I watch as she exits the room, everyone bowing their heads in deferential farewell tokens as she leaves. My new friend slithers forwards from my shoulders, craning around to look back at me. I stare with astonishment into his eyes. One of them shuts in a mischievous wink for the briefest of moments.

CHAPTER TWELVE

R ed. Everything's red. Everything is bathed in a patina of russet hues – a shiny blood-red vastness. A cosmos of sexual energies swirl around my spiritual sanctuary.

I sit upon a red throne, a dais atop a mountain of red. A mound of red crushed-velvet fabric spreads out beneath me, endless reams of it. At the platform's base, a snake follows the folds of fabric upwards. It is a slow, sensual journey, punctuated by the gentle, rhythmic, hypnotic pounding of a darbuka. Another snake slithers into view. The two adders intertwine – briefly – before separating and continuing their respective journeys.

They reach a pair of female feet. Naked, pale, beautiful. My feet. The snakes glide over them, wrapping upwards to encircle my ankles. And now, if we were filming, we'd move the camera wider, soft on the red crushed-velvet fabric of my dress, visible only from the waist down. The snakes disappear upwards, under my skirt – a hand strokes my knee. The hand belongs to a centaur. He lifts the hem of my dress and dips his head to kiss my ankles, then slowly follows the trail of the snakes. I encounter heaven at the touch of his lips. I surrender to his touch, languishing in pleasure. Other exotic supernatural creatures – angels, demons, hybrids – caress and arouse every part of my body. A Leviathan teasingly darts his tongue over my left nipple while a shapeshifter who – with her long, dark hair and luminescent violet eyes – could be mistaken for my twin sister – trails its fingers up and down the length of my torso. Together they morph in and out of visibility, awakening me to the presence seated on the matching throne beside mine. I instantly recognised the distinctive jawline, luscious lips, and golden twinkling eyes. Leon. Just seeing *him releases a gush of wetness between my thighs, enough to tip me over the edge into a colossal climax that startles me awake.*

I lie in bed, staring at the ceiling, panting. I recover slowly from my fabulous dream, bathed in sweat. I roll onto my side lazily, and I scream. Lying on the pillow beside me is the snake, coiled in a neat pile. I had forgotten all about him. He stares at me sleepily, and I overcome my returning squeamishness to stroke him gently along the ridge of his spine. If snakes even have a spine. I know absolutely nothing about snakes.

"Good morning, my friend." He looks at me, expressing something distinctly resembling love in his eyes. I realise that I do not know his name. If he even has one? Gretha never mentioned it, and I never thought to ask.

"What's your name?" I ask him. He continues his placid stare back at me. Was I expecting him to speak? The magic ritual last night must have done my head in. Now I'm thinking I'm Dr Doolittle or something. I slightly chuckle as I push back the sheets and get out of bed. I need to pee, and my teeth could use some toothpaste. My snake friend remains on the bed as I head to the ensuite. I attend to my business, brush my teeth and splash some cold water on my face. I inspect my face in the mirror. I look different, somehow, to what I did yesterday. My skin has an almost luminescent quality, the whites of my eyes are astonishingly clear, and I have a sparkly quality to my whole being. Who knew magic could be so good for your health and your looks?

A pleasant surprise awaits me when I come out of the ensuite. My snake has twisted himself into the shape of a heart on the bed. It can't be a coincidence.

"Oh, you're so sweet." I plant a kiss on the top of his flat head. I have to come up with a name for him, even a temporary one. I can only think of a book I remember reading as a child about a boa constrictor called Bo. Quite a nice name, and synonymous with the word *beau*, which I think my new friend would be pretty pleased about.

"Bo. Shall I call you Bo?" He raises his head a little, which I interpret as a nod.

"All right. Bo, it is." I scratch his scaly skin gently. He rolls over for me to tickle his belly, exposing an elaborate patterning of scales. Each plate is a different colour, creating a mandala-like swirl on the underside of his body. Very pretty.

"Now—Bo, are you hungry?" He lifts his head up and down. He's probably ravenous. But what on earth do snakes eat? Mice? Eggs? Time to get out the laptop. Do some Googling. I head downstairs to my computer on my kitchen table, calling out, "Come on, Bo," as though he is a dog or something. I really must have gone completely nuts, I think to myself, just before hearing the thud of his body landing on the bedroom floor. His head pokes around the door of the bedroom. Then he rolls himself into a ball and bounces downstairs to arrive at the bottom before me. Wow. I don't know what the average intelligence of a snake is, but Bo appears blessed with a high IQ. I've got a lot of research to do.

I turn on my laptop and click on the kettle while waiting for it to boot up. I'm hanging for a coffee, but it's probably more urgent to figure out what to feed Bo for breakfast. I type *what do snakes eat* into the search engine. Instantly millions of responses pop up. Oh, the miracle of the internet. I sift through the most credible entries. Snakes can eat almost anything, including pigs and small mammals—eek!—but they prefer to consume their food whole. They also like eggs. I'm sure I've got a half-carton of eggs in the fridge. I get up from the table and check. Bingo! I take out an egg and place it on a plate on the floor. Hopefully, Bo will know what to do with it. He is watching me from the base of the stairs, slithering over to the egg, his little tongue flickering in and out in excited licks. He reaches the egg and puts his lips on the top of the egg. Then he unhinges his jaw and swallows it whole before slithering away under the kitchen table, presumably to finish digesting it. I also place a little water bowl on the floor if he's thirsty. Seeing he's satisfied, I take time to brew myself a pot of coffee before resuming my snake research. Somehow, I think many of the facts I'm discovering about snakes won't apply to him. For example, he's so independent I don't think he'd like to be boxed in a terrarium. I think he'd probably prefer free rein of my house. However, I decide to go to the pet shop and buy some live mice to feed him and gather some rocks for him to rest under. One of the websites suggests creating a toilet for your pet snake out of wood shavings and old newspapers. The matter of toileting hadn't occurred to me up until this point. I look at Bo.

"Do you need to go to the toilet?" He gives me a quizzical stare. Then I remembered that the previous owners of my terrace had put a dog flap in the laundry door. I pick Bo up and carry him out to the laundry. I place him gently on the floor and show him how the swinging mechanism of the dog flap works. He observes me with his usual silent reverence. I just hope that if he needs to poop, he'll go outside and take care of business in my little backyard.

The rest of the day passes by in a kind of a blur. Luckily, it's Sunday, and I don't have to go to work or do anything strenuous. I potter around the house for a while, then catch up on some reading—I've half-finished a romantic fiction about a couple on a cruise ship. It makes me think of how much I miss Leon, and I hope that the spells of the night before will soon start to work their magic! I give my mum a call. She is retired and lives in a remote part of the New South Wales south coast, so I don't get to see her very often. We catch up on each other's weeks, though I don't tell her about Leon or the Wiccan circle. She tells me about her garden and how she has successfully grown a complete winter harvest of vegetables — potatoes, silver beets, and even mushrooms. She has five chooks, too, and has names for them all. I hear about how Margo has been laying two eggs a day, but Doreen has been ill, lost a few feathers, and stopped laying altogether.

It is a great catch-up, but something in my voice must have given me away, for, at the end of our conversation, she says, "Men are great, but everything you need is within you."

She's always a bit cryptic like that. I think it comes from spending too much time on her own. After the conversation with my mum, I pull on my runners and go for a jog. My neighbourhood is full of old liquidambar trees. They are deciduous, and their shed, dried leaves cover the pavement. I collect some rocks for Bo and then jog home. It's good to build up a sweat, and I hit the shower as soon as I get in the door. After my shower, I create a tower of the rocks I collected in the corner of the living room. Bo watches with interest before falling asleep on the couch. Snakes sleep a lot, I'm learning.

I'm an organised person, so I spend the rest of Sunday night getting ready for the week ahead — ironing shirts for work, polishing my shoes, and stocking up on healthy snacks for my handbag at the local grocery store. The pet shop isn't open on Sundays, so I don't buy any mice for Bo, settling on some raw chicken wings from *Coles* that I will feed to him whole over the next couple of days. Nighttime arrives quickly, and I am so tired that I hit the sack early, with Bo curled up on the pillow beside me.

The following morning I almost sleep through my alarm. I dress for work hurriedly, letting Bo wrap himself around my waist as I make the bed, carefully placing him on top of the quilt when I am done. I replace his water bowl with fresh water and put two of the raw chicken wings on a plate on the floor downstairs for him. Then I leave the house.

After my peaceful Sunday, I am expecting more of the same at work on Monday. However, as soon as I show up, I can tell the day will pan out quite differently than expected.

First, a dozen red long-stemmed roses await me at my desk. Mia sits next to me and sticks her nose in one of them, enjoying the scent.

"Who's been a naughty girl all weekend, then?" she asks with a wink. I just grin at her. I can't believe how gorgeous the flowers are. No card is attached, but I know they could only be from one person. Leon. The spell must have worked! Our boss, Ron, chooses that moment to walk past my desk, stopping in his tracks with a dramatic double-take.

"Nice flowers!" He whistles.

"Thanks," I murmur, embarrassed. I don't want the whole office to be privy to my love life. I switch on my computer, trying to look professional. My inbox is flooded with emails. Every sale I have been working on for the last couple of months is finally coming to fruition. Everyone I've been trying to sell properties to suddenly wants to buy.

"Hey, Ketz." Mia leans back in her chair to get around the blind of our desk partition.

"Yeah," I reply distractedly, still scanning emails. The red light on my desk phone also needs attention, flashing luridly to signal a full box of voice messages.

"Can we get together today to discuss tomorrow's presentation?"

With everything going on, I'd completely forgotten that Mia and I are meant to be doing a corporate investment presentation the next day.

"Sure," I say, pressing play on my machine. There are over twelve messages from prospective clients wanting me to show them properties. I can't believe it. This phenomenon can only be explained as a ripple effect caused by the spell on Saturday night.

"Maybe when you're not so busy, maybe we can talk about it?" Her voice betrays only a little of the frustration she must be feeling with me. Mia has patiently waited for me to finish listening to my messages so we can focus on our talk.

"Shit, sorry," I apologise. I give her my full attention as we review the PowerPoint slides we'll be using and plan our speaking slots. When we're done, I return to my computer. I sift through my emails, trying to see if I can find any from Leon, but there is still no word from the man. Oh well, he has sent me the flowers, an impressive gesture—I should be content with that.

I am swamped with work and barely have time for a coffee, let alone any more hunting for word from Leon. But then, just after midday, the Skype function on my laptop alerts me to a message. It is Leon. Finally.

Hey, Ketzia. Sorry I've been unavailable.

That's okay.

What are you up to?

Swamped with work.

That's good.

Where are you? I bite my lip expectantly. There is a delay in his response. Then—

I'm at Brisbane airport, about to board a flight to Sydney. Can I take you out for dinner tonight?

Of course.

I'll call you once I land. xxx

The connection drops out then, and I am left with burning cheeks and a ball of hot anticipation in my stomach.

The rest of the afternoon passes in a haze. Thankfully I am so busy the rest of the day getting back to my clients—and signing off on a personal, record-breaking number of contracts—that I don't have too much time on my hands to think about Leon and my feelings for him. Part of me is hurt that he hasn't been in touch for so long, but another, bigger part of me is happy to be catching up with him again. Admittedly I'm a little nervous, too. I hope his feelings for me are as hot as mine are for him.

Five o'clock ticks around, and I shut down my computer. I bundle the roses and pop them in a bag to take home. I want to enjoy their beautiful scent in my house. Mia raises her eyes at me as I dash out.

"You're in a bit of a hurry — where are you off to?" she asks. I smile at her but shake my head.

"I'll tell you all about it tomorrow." I leave Mia impatiently waiting for the details. She should be getting used to this by now.

I arrive home and plonk the roses in my most oversized vase, carefully filling it with water. I note that the chicken wings have disappeared. Good. Bo must have been hungry. A quick scan of the room reveals that he is resting on the tower of rocks I built for him.

"Hi, Bo," I say. He opens one eye sleepily.

I head to the bathroom for a shower. I want to look — and feel — perfect tonight. I douse my skin with essential oils, thinking of Leon as I languorously scrub my body. My breasts tingle with anticipation, yearning for his touch. I trace my finger along the delicate skin on the underside of my breasts, my nipples unbearably taut. Then I allow my hand to glide down my stomach to my pussy. Gently I open the lips of my labia and slide my finger along their moistness. My clitoris is a hard jewel, protruding just enough to make it easy for my thumb to gently stroke it. I am so aroused. I push my body against the hardness of the shower screen, flattening my breasts against the glass. Then I feel myself coming in a slow, languorous orgasm that ripples through my whole body. I turn the jets to cold, needing to calm myself down, enjoying the icy prickles of water cascading down my body.

I step out of the shower and towel myself before inspecting myself in the mirror. My body looks great. The long muscular curvature of my thighs perfectly sets off the roundness of my hips. My breasts are full and pert. My skin is glowing. I head to my wardrobe to decide what to wear. My closet is full of corporate clothes for work and tracksuits for bumming around the house. However, I also do have two or three lovely dresses that I save up for special occasions. Tonight is going to be one of them. I hold a magenta wrap-around to my body and inspect my reflection in the mirror. No. Not that one. I place it back on the rack and pull out the red halter-neck dress that I've owned for years but only worn occasionally. It will look good with my little brown fur-trimmed jacket. I have a smashing pair of red heels to kick off the outfit. Decided, I pull on a tiny red lace G-string and a red lacy halter-neck bra designed to push my breasts up, amplifying my already generous cleavage. I opt for a pair of sheer pull-up pantyhose. I slide the stockings on, pointing my toes so as not to ladder them, smoothing the delicate silk over my skin, sending another surge of pleasure through my body. My endorphins are working overtime. All I can think about is Leon and sex, sex, sex. The clock is ticking, so I don't indulge my senses anymore and pull on the red dress hurriedly. I step into the ensuite again to put on my makeup. Carefully I apply eyeliner and mascara before choosing a red lipstick that matches the dress's colour. Then I coil my hair up into a sophisticated chignon. I clip on a pair of pearl drop earrings my mother gave me and a delicate pearl necklace to match. Then it's time for my killer heels and one final inspection in the mirror. I have to admit it to myself. I look amazing. Good enough to eat. Hopefully, Leon will think so, too.

CHAPTER THIRTEEN

Leon has texted me the address of the city's swankiest new restaurant, Vue de Monde. I Uber it there, enjoying the appraising glance of the driver as he checks me out in my hot red dress. Vue de Monde has a discreet entrance behind a historic sandstone arch, and Leon is waiting for me beneath the archway. He gives me a leisurely once-over as I high-heel my way towards him. It is as though he has undressed me with his eyes, and I feel the heat rising to my cheeks. He smiles at me, leaning in to kiss me. Our lips meet, and instantly I feel the deep connection of our sojourn in Hong Kong.

"You look stunning," he says.

"Thanks." I struggle to find words now that I'm finally with him again. He takes me by the elbow and gently guides me into the restaurant. The maître d' escorts us to a window table lit romantically with candles and a delicate arrangement of roses. Once seated, Leon takes a breath and looks deep into my eyes as though searching for something.

"First," he begins, "I owe you an apology."

I smile at him reassuringly.

"Go on," I say.

"I'm so sorry for disappearing on you. My father was taken ill, and I had to go and visit him. It's so complicated. I can never disclose the location of my father, and so I have to abandon all my media devices before I see him."

I nod. I'm, of course, already somewhat aware of his father's chequered past and understand the need for secrecy.

Surely, Leon could at least have sent me a message before he left.

As though reading my mind, he continues, "I know I should have let you know first, but the truth is I was also scared about the passion we unleashed. I didn't want either of us to get hurt . . ." He trails off, and in the silence, I telepathically hear him say *and knowing the historical ramifications of our union,* before he resumes the train of thought out loud. "I feel like a bit of a coward, but I just wasn't sure if I wanted to chance it."

"So, what made you change your mind?" I ask. My voice is soft, but the challenge is still there. I'm not going to let him off lightly.

"In a word? You," he says, checking my reaction shyly. "I just couldn't stop thinking about you, needing you . . ." He reaches for my hand. His touch is electric. "And I thought, hell, life is for living. I think it's worth the risk — to be together with you."

His words fill me with profound happiness. He's put a lot of thought into this.

"I agree," I say. "I know it could be risky — our union. But I'm not averse to a bit of danger . . ." I trail off. A waiter appears at the table, ready to take our orders. The menu is a soothing mix of modern international cuisine. I order a duck confit with a gratin of vegetables, and Leon orders a wagyu steak, medium-rare. Our glasses are filled with excellent wine. The waiter disappears to the kitchen, and I raise my glass.

"Here's to the danger of passion."

"Danger," he replies. We chink glasses. I savour the full-bodied red, allowing it to rest in my mouth before swallowing.

"I believe congratulations are in order, too," Leon says.

"Oh?" I haven't the faintest idea what he's talking about.

"You've totally exceeded your sales targets this past week. Seems like you're on fire!"

"Been keeping tabs on me, have you?" I try not to betray my delight in his praise. Also, I know the real reason for the increase in my sales quota, and I don't want to reveal anything about my recent use of magic to him.

"I get sent all the sales data of every employee. Outstanding sales agents are usually highlighted. Today there was just one . . ."

I smile, unable to contain my delight any longer. "So, how long will you be in town for?" I ask.

"I bought an open-ended ticket. I can manage international affairs from pretty much anywhere. And now I have a pressing need to be right here — with you."

His intense gaze sets off a flurry of butterflies in my stomach. God, he's gorgeous. The idea that he has come here to be close to me makes me swoon.

Our meals arrive. The duck is moist and rich, basted in a piquant cranberry sauce. It melts in my mouth. I watch as Leon slices into his steak and delicately places a bite in his mouth. I catch a glimpse of his tongue and imagine it tracing lines over my body. He has a tiny dimple to one side of his mouth that creases endearingly as he chews.

"This is delicious," I say. "How's your steak?"

"Perfect," he replies. We eat in companionable silence for a few moments. Then I take another sip of wine. It is such a smooth, velvety drop I feel like I could drink it all night. I lower my glass to the table and realise Leon has been watching me.

"I can't wait for my mouth to be on those gorgeous lips of yours," he says. My insides shudder in anticipation.

"Hopefully, that's not the only place they'll be," I say.

"My hotel is just around the corner," Leon continues, reaching for my hand and trailing his fingers sensuously over the top of my hand before wrapping them around my wrist. "Tonight, I'm going to take you back to my hotel room, and I'm going to fuck you. All night long."

He says it quietly so that no one else in the restaurant can hear, but I hear him loud and clear. It's as though my whole body can hear him because it starts tingling with excitement and throbbing pulses deep inside my vagina.

"Be warned, I plan to fuck you back," I say, just as sexily. The energy coursing between us is insane — electric. The lighting in the restaurant flickers.

"Uh-oh," I exclaim, "we're doing it again." The restaurant is plunged into darkness, the only light coming from the candles on the tables and the streetlamps shining through the window. From the kitchen can be heard crashing pots and chefs swearing. I extract my hand from Leon's grip. The lights come back on. Leon glances around the restaurant leisurely, watching order being restored. I can't believe how nonchalant he is about us causing another blackout. Finally, his gaze returns to mine. I stare at him levelly.

"Well?"

"Ketzia, the restaurant had a small power failure — so what? I'm sure it happens all the time."

"You don't expect me to believe that you think that was just a coincidence?" I ask. Leon merely shrugs his shoulders and reaches over to refill my wine glass.

"Drink up," he says. "You may need the fortification."

We spend the remainder of the meal engaged in light conversation — about work, world affairs, the weather. It is as though we have an unspoken agreement not to discuss anything to do with magick. The subject sits at the periphery of our words, silently. I can't help but wonder, however, at the possibilities of our union. We can have so much of an impact on the world without even trying. Imagine what we could do if we set our minds to it.

CHAPTER FOURTEEN

On entering Leon's hotel, we are greeted by several people in the lobby, who all address him formally as *Mr Furness*. A bellboy shows us to the lift and is about to enter with us when Leon gently places a fiver in his palm and says, "I'll take it from here."

The elevator doors close, and Leon turns to me with a look of such ferocious hunger the floor drops away beneath me.

"Ketzia," he says, stroking my cheek with his finger and letting it rest on my lips. Then he trails his finger down my throat, running it beneath my necklace.

"There are so many things I want to do to you," he says. His eyes are dark, and I feel, for a moment, that this man is capable of anything. The current of danger sparking from his being frightens me a little bit but excites me even more. After all, didn't we make a toast to danger tonight? Isn't this what I have secretly been yearning for?

The elevator dings its arrival at Leon's floor. Silently he guides me along the elegantly furnished corridor to the presidential suite. The breathtaking harbour view is the first thing that grabs me as I step inside. It is as though the Sydney Opera House and Harbour Bridge have been positioned exclusively for my viewing pleasure. The vast suite itself is tastefully elegant and decorated luxuriously. Most of the time, I forget how wealthy Leon must be, but here in his opulent hotel room, it is impossible to overlook his riches.

"Wow," I exclaim, wondering what he would think if he ever came over to my modest little townhouse.

"Nice room, nice view, I agree," Leon says, popping a bottle of champagne waiting for us on the coffee table. "But meaningless without you here to share it with."

I smile at him, accepting the glass of champagne.

"Well, cheers." We chink glasses. The champagne is deliciously crisp and nutty in flavour. Leon downs his glass in a swooping motion while I sip at mine delicately. He puts his glass on the table, his eyes dark and full of erotic energy. I place my half-drunk glass beside his on the table. We face each other, and a swirl of mist weaves around our bodies like smoke. I'm not sure precisely what Leon wants to do to me, but I'm enjoying the sensation of the mist and his longing gaze raking over my body.

"Sit down, Ketzia." I lower myself onto the plush couch. Leon slowly drops to his knees and removes one of my shoes first, then the other. His hands slide up my legs to the top of my pantyhose. He glides one stocking off, pausing to kiss the skin of my inner thigh, sliding his fingers down the underside of my knees, over my calf muscle and ankle. Then he removes the other stocking and pushes the hem of my dress so it is bunched around my waist. He leans forward and pushes his face into my panties, inhaling deeply. Sighing, he stays in that position, breathing me in, the heat of his breath unleashing something inside me. I ruffle his hair and push my pelvis upwards, wanting more. He obliges, hooking a finger into my G-string and lowering it over my legs and off. Then he leans in, using both of his hands to open me up before licking me deep inside, his tongue moving in and out, his breath hot on my clitoris, his fingers moving down to trace the outline of my anus. His lips join in with his tongue, and his fingers move in and out of me, and I am so wet and horny that all I want is more. The mist is still swirling around us, becoming denser and denser. Leon's head is still buried in my pussy, his tongue and lips bringing me to an ecstasy of pleasure as a ripple of an orgasm travels through my body, making me shudder. Leon looks up and smiles at me. I smile back. His hands travel up my body.

"Take your dress off." I turn around on the couch so that he can unzip me. Then I lower the straps of my dress, stand up and step out. Leon also stands up, expertly unclasping my bra and letting it drop to the ground. He lowers his lips to my left nipple and teases it with his tongue, then takes the peak into his mouth and sucks hard. I unbutton his shirt and let it drop to the ground. He flicks his shoes off and unties his belt. He stops sucking on my breast for a moment to undo his trousers and let them drop to the ground. He pulls his jocks off next. He is incredibly hard and big. I want him inside me. We tumble onto the floor. He pins my hands above my head with his hands and kisses and bites my taut, aroused nipples. I can feel the head of his penis nudging against my upper thighs, and I open my legs wide, desperate to have him inside me, but he is determined to prolong the agony of my desire and lifts himself so that his manhood rests on the top of my pubis. His cock pulses against my skin, the length of his silken shaft throbbing with readiness. He continues to suck my tits. They are so hard they feel like tiny pebbles under the smooth surface of his tongue.

The excitement coursing through my body becomes so unbearable that I forcibly push myself upwards, using all my strength to topple him sideways and onto his back. Straddling him now, I lift my hips and slide onto his shaft. The impact of his cock engulfing me, the head of his penis contacting the deepest part of me, unleashes a cry of pleasure from my lips, and I feel myself come instantly. I sit on top of him, gently rocking myself up and down his rock-hard mast, saturated in my juices, wanting this moment to last forever. He joins in the rhythm until we are both rocking, panting deeply, feeling every part of each other's pleasure and desire. I raise myself on my heels and slide up and down his member. He clasps my buttocks and helps push me along, fingering my entire pubic area until we finally peak in simultaneous ecstasy.

I rest my head on his chest for a moment, listening to the thudding of his heart. We are both drenched in sweat. Leon absently strokes my spine, his fingertips sending a rush of sweet coolness along my skin. A fluttering sensation also envelops my legs, and I am confused for a moment as to the source of the pleasure. Then I realise the mist still surrounding us is wrapping tendrils around both of our bodies.

"Leon?" I raise myself on my elbows and look into his eyes. "I think something's happening."

"Something certainly just did." Leon raises his shoulders off the ground, and I roll off him. Then he sees what I see. In amazement, we survey the translucent vapour weaving intricate patterns in the air. The smoky haze thickens, transforming into an almost human spectre. It is a female form, an elegant, willowy woman in a floor-length velvet robe. She has long, golden hair, delicately arched eyebrows, and dark lashes framing mysterious, ebony eyes that twinkle at me seductively. She is the most beautiful woman I have ever laid eyes on. Fingers of fog swirl beside her, orbiting into the shape of a man—a long-haired gentleman dressed in a flowing peasant-style shirt and long trousers. He has similarly chiselled cheekbones to Leon, with a cute dimple on one cheek and plush lips that smile at me beckoningly. His body's muscularity is visible through his shirt's fine silk. He is—in a word—hot. As gorgeous as the couple is, I cannot help feeling frightened by the apparition, and I impulsively reach for Leon's hand.

"Don't be afraid," the woman says. Her voice has a beautiful melodic quality.

"You have summoned us. We are your ancestors," the man continues, smiling encouragingly at us. I am completely lost for words, so I feel incredibly grateful when Leon clears his throat and telekinetically addresses the pair.

"We did not intentionally call on you. Thank you for your visit, but . . ." He trails off, unsure of how to continue. The spectres smile at us.

"My name is Edana," the woman says, moving closer to me.

"And I am Dimitri." The man introduces himself, moving closer to Leon. The names are familiar to me, being from Wiccan mythology. Edana refers to passion, and Dimitri means lover of the earth.

"We are here to elevate your passion to new heights," Edana says, her long fingers weaving in and out of transparent form. They morph into tendrils of smoke that delicately rest on my naked body, sending little sparks of dynamite into my system. I look at Leon and see that he is also wrapped in the fine mist. His eyes reveal the excitement this gives him. He meets my gaze, and we reach an unspoken mutual agreement. We are going to let these two creatures take us to heaven.

Edana and Dimitri head in the direction of the bedroom, and Leon and I pick ourselves up off the floor and follow them. The bedroom is even more luxurious than the rest of the suite, the enormous king-sized bed covered in the finest silks. Edana lays her beautiful body on the bed and pats the sheets beside her. Obediently I slide into place and allow her to run her fingers over my body while the men watch from the side of the bed. Her touch is playfully erotic and sensual, her fingers awakening a depth of arousal I didn't know I could experience. It is as though everywhere she touches — the curve of my shoulder, the dip between my collarbones, the undulating swell of my breasts — becomes ignited, sparking into a white-hot display of sexual fireworks. Unwittingly I arch my back on the bed and moan. Edana continues her journey over my body, breathing life into every particle of me, making my whole body hum with throbbing need.

I faintly register Dimitri shrouding Leon in a column of smoke and gently guiding him onto the bed beside me. Leon's eyes gleam with catlike animalism as he moves onto his hands and knees on top of me. My desire is so intense my body lifts from the bed to contact his, my hands clutching his shoulders, stroking his hair, touching his lips. He lowers his face and kisses me, a kiss so intense and so erotically charged it threatens to remove me entirely from my senses and transport me to a state of pure bliss. Dimitri and Edana envelop us with their spiritual energies, guiding us and pushing our stimulation to this other level.

Then Leon enters me. We both gasp with shock, simultaneously experiencing the deep core of energy connecting all sentient beings to the future and the past, the earth's pull, and the stars' magic. Dimitri pulls on Leon's hips, and futilely I try to hold onto him as he draws out of me. I never want him to leave my body. I want to keep this connection forever. But then it is okay because he is entering me again, even deeper this time, and Dimitri helps him to establish a thrusting rhythm as Edana glides her hands over the sides of my body. I never knew a missionary position could feel this good. Leon's thrusting increases in speed and I raise myself to meet him, our lovemaking an ode to the pantheon of time, a journey beyond the self. We reach a climax together, and both cry out, Dimitri and Edana joining in, our voices a chorus of exultation in the luxury of the presidential suite of the best hotel in town. And then, as mysteriously as they appeared, Dimitri and Edana vanish, leaving behind only a tiny residue of fog that quickly dissipates. Leon and I turn to look at each other, both of us still recovering from the intensity of the experience.

"Wow." Any word seems hopelessly inadequate to communicate the profundity of what we have just experienced. I lie back on the bed.

"Wow," Leon agrees. We lie on our backs beside each other in silence for a moment. Then a bubble of laughter erupts from my belly, and Leon starts laughing, too, and we laugh together uproariously, like crazy people after they have just escaped a near-death experience, dancing on the edge of hysteria. Finally, we calm down, and Leon takes me in his arms, stroking me softly until I drift off to sleep.

CHAPTER FIFTEEN

At first, I think I am dreaming or have changed form — turning into a raven or a hawk because I have a bird's eye view. I am looking down from above, looking down on Leon asleep on the bed with a dark-haired woman nestled protectively in his arms. A gasp. Then I realise the dark-haired woman is me. Then, who am I? A spectre of myself — my back plastered to the hotel ceiling, unruly strands of my hair sticking to the white plasterboard behind me as though pulled by some invisible electrokinetic force. I am magnetised to the ceiling while lying on the bed with Leon. I panic for a moment at the impossibility of this duality. Then it dawns on me that I am having an out-of-body experience. In Wiccan philosophy, such an occurrence is regarded as a gift, an opportunity to receive wisdom. I relax into it, allowing myself simply to observe.

Leon and I are wrapped into each other in a sleepy caress. I must be hot, for I push the sheets down in my sleep, so they are gathered at our waists. It is strange to see my own body in the flesh. Mirrors never actually give us an accurate idea of what we look like. I've always bemoaned my slightly masculine shoulders, but now that I can see them three-dimensionally, I realise they are actually in perfect proportion to the rest of my body and set off the narrowness of my waist beautifully. Still cemented to the ceiling, I watch as Leon turns to me in sleep and starts kissing me. I respond, kissing back, my hand gliding to his cheek, stroking it absently before gliding down his muscular torso to its destination beneath the sheets.

It is surreal watching myself this way — kind of like watching a movie of yourself in real-time. Leon and I kiss passionately. His hands move to my breasts, my leg slides over his, and the sheets drop off the bed with the motion.

I watch, transfixed, as our lovemaking becomes more and more rhythmic. Then, at the periphery of my vision, I notice something else. Surges of dark and light energy ripple outwards from the bed as though it has been dropped into a sea of hot lava. Fiery red energy battles waves of white light in a metaphysical contest between good and evil. I start to understand the purpose of this out-of-body experience. It will make me more fully comprehend the ramifications of a union with Leon. We cannot connect, it seems, without it impacting and awakening both dark and light cosmic energies. The Spell of Orgiastic Love taught me that we are not responsible for any maliciousness threatening our union. However, something about our partnering still threatens to disturb the delicate balance of the paranormal realm. Fear shrouds me in its cold clutches as I contemplate the possible outcomes of such a disturbance.

I am a voyeur of both planes of existence. The red energy deepens in colour as Leon and I engage in mutual masturbation. Then I raise myself in bed and position myself so that my pussy rests on his mouth while I lick his penis, my tongue trailing up and down his ramrod shaft before taking him into my mouth completely. Leon licks my pussy, his hands and fingers getting involved, opening me up to drink my wetness. From my vantage point above, the waves of red and white energy are getting more and more frenzied. I feel a cool knot of dread grip me as I watch it shade to pure ebony. This is bad. Really bad. Just as I register the thought, something happens, and I am thrown back into my hot, sweaty self on the bed. Bam! It takes me a moment to recover from the shock of being psychically thrown around. I roll off Leon gasping for breath.

"Hey, what's going on?" Leon looks me over with concern and the urgency of interrupted desire.

"Don't ask," I say. Cautiously I peer over the edge of the bed. My gaze meets with the plush cream carpet, the hotel insignia discreetly embroidered into the pattern—no red or black or white tsunami of energy approaching from anywhere. But it was here before, so where did it disappear to? Or maybe it's still there but not visible to me anymore now that I am back in my body. I fearfully dip my finger into the air beside the bed, testing for, I don't know, heat or some other indication of the psychic energy I witnessed. But the air feels completely normal.

"Ketzia?" Leon urges, his hand resting lightly on my shoulder. I turn to face him, sliding my body along the sheets to be closer to him.

"Leon." I choose my words carefully. "Do you think that maybe our being together is somehow not a good thing?"

"Not at all." He smiles, and I can see it will take me a bit more work to get him to take me seriously about this.

"What if you found out that making love to me had a negative impact on the rest of the universe? That our union has an impact on the rest of the world that extends beyond ourselves?"

Leon is still grinning at me, so I know he's not taking this seriously. With his index finger, he traces a line around my areola.

"I would say"—he speaks precisely—"that the rest of the world can go to hell."

Then it happens. Sheets of white light flash around me. A disorientating and sickening wave of emotions engulfs me. I am transported to a space beyond time or place, connecting with everything past — present — future. I push my hands to my mouth, frightened that I will be sick.

"Ketzia? Ketzia, are you all right?" Leon calls out to me as I rush to the bathroom, the cosmic burden of my birthright too much for me to bear. I hear Leon following close behind but manage to shut the bathroom door behind me before he can make his way in. There is no way I want him to see me like this.

I clang the lid of the toilet seat up just in time. I hurl a copious amount of greenish liquid into the toilet bowl, my mind racing feverishly. I still don't quite understand why I am having such a violent physical reaction to my out-of-body experience and, of course, the dark energy I witnessed, but it frightens me no end.

"Ketzia? Are you all right?" Leon calls out from the other side of the door.

"I'll be right there," I call out, flushing the toilet, keen to get rid of the sick smell in the room. I turn on the faucet, splash cold water on my face, rinse my mouth out, and find a hotel-issue small toothbrush and toothpaste on the vanity. The minty flavour helps erase the bad taste in my mouth and the bad feeling in my blood.

"Ketzia. You don't have to hide from me. I just want to make sure you're all right."

I rinse my mouth again, dry myself off with a towel and open the door. Leon is waiting for me, a hand on one hip, a concerned expression on his face.

"I'm fine," I tell him. "Just a bit of indigestion."

"That seemed like more than just a bit of indigestion to me." He watches me closely as though he is studying me. Not knowing what to say, I shrug and smile.

"You're not pregnant, are you?" A plausible deduction, I suppose, but so off track, I can't help but chuckle.

"Unless I belong to the point-zero-one per cent of the population that can actually still fall pregnant while taking the pill—then no. And I take it religiously, so don't worry about that. Probably just too much champagne . . . and possibly too much sex."

At the mention of the word, Leon draws me into his arms again.

"On the contrary, perhaps it's caused by not enough sex," he whispers into my ear.

We tumble into bed again, our passion reignited, and I forget about the red and black energy, the white sheets of light, and everything paranormal. Instead, I concentrate on the muscular curvature of his biceps, the firm roundness of his shoulders, and the tapered leanness of his torso. He enters me, and we fuck hungrily like animals in heat, his manhood touching the secret softness of my femininity with each thrust, my nerves tingling, sending me into deeper and deeper throes of ecstasy. I look deep into Leon's eyes, and it is as though I can see right into him, into the core of his being. A shadow flitters across Leon's eyes, and his pupils expand until their blackness fills his irises, bleeding into the whites.

A vivid red miasma of supernatural energy shrouds his being, his hands growing claw-like talons with which he pins my wrists down onto the bed, and I am terrified of what he is turning into. I whimper as he roars, a rush of demonic heat coursing through my body as he ejaculates inside me, a heat so intense and dry I feel as though I have been burnt, scorched alive, internally combusted. And then it is over.

Leon collapses on the bed beside me. I dare myself to look at him. The talons have disappeared from his fingers. The red energy field around him has dissipated. And when he turns to look at me, his eyes have returned to normal and are full of kindness.

"Ketzia, that was wonderful." He gently presses his lips to my cheek, only then noticing the tears silently trickling down. Alarmed, he raises himself on one elbow.

"Ketzia, are you all right? What's wrong? Did I hurt you?"

I sit up in bed, the burning sensation still inside my body but less intense now, less frightening. I am unsure of how much to tell him. The truth could be the demise of the ungodly spirit that inhabited his body only moments previously, or it could be the catalyst for an even darker upsurging in the supernatural realm. I decide to play it safe.

"It was just a very intense experience for me, Leon," I say. "You didn't do anything wrong. I'm just a bit emotional — that's all."

"Oh, sweetie," he says, stroking my back. "I'm sorry."

"Nothing to be sorry about," I say. Usually, I would enjoy his hand on my back and his sweet caresses, but now his fingers feel almost as though they are made of razor blades, so sensitive is my skin. I give him a quick, reassuring peck on the cheek before hopping out of bed.

"I'm just going to have a shower," I say, heading to the bathroom. I can feel Leon watching me as I cross the room, so I turn and smile at him reassuringly.

"Okay." He smiles at me before resting his head on the pillows and shutting his eyes.

I enter the bathroom and turn the shower on, pushing the dial of the shower jets to icy. The cold water streaming over my burning body calms me down, and I feel my breathing returning to normal. I hadn't realised how terrified I'd been by this occurrence, but now that I'm alone in the shower and have had a chance to collect myself, I can't deny it. The paranormal energies I'd witnessed during my out-of-body experience and Leon's shape-shifting during our lovemaking have left me feeling rattled and scorched. Gently I lather my body in the hotel body wash, a delicate and no doubt expensive mix of aromatic jasmine and essential oils. I finally turn off the shower and exit the cubicle, wrapping myself in the soft plushness of the cream-coloured hotel towel, the insignia embroidered on the edge in gold. I dry myself off and then moisturise my entire body with the hotel body lotion, a rich cream with the same delicious jasmine scent as the body wash. My skin feels soft and supple, and the burning sensation has disappeared. I feel better than I have in ages, every pore of my being extraordinarily awakened and alive.

I cloak my invigorated body in the hotel bathrobe and return to the bedroom. Leon is fast asleep. I lower myself to the edge of the bed and take a moment to just look at him. Asleep, he is just as handsome as he is awake. His dark hair is tousled messily on the pillows. A shadow of stubble emphasises the masculinity of his jawline. Long lashes shutter his closed eyes. He breathes quietly through slightly parted lips, giving him an angelic demeanour. I can almost completely shrug off his demonic image emblazoned on my memory of our lovemaking session earlier. I just don't know how to make sense of it. Nothing Leon has done or said has ever made me feel uncomfortable — so why this nagging suspicion that not everything is as it seems?

I shrug. Maybe it is all just a product of my imagination, a warped message from my subconscious that has more to do with my innermost fears and hang-ups than any kind of supernatural reality. Perhaps it is best to view the experience as a kind of dream that needs to be interpreted on a symbolic level. The red and black energy could represent my unwillingness to abandon myself to the pleasures this outrageously handsome man is able to provide me with. His taking on demonic features while we were fucking may have been merely a manifestation of my lust for darkness. Because I must admit, I have always been drawn to black power, as much as I try to channel that curiosity into lighter pathways. Or maybe it is something unrelated to either of us. But if that is the case, it could mean that we are both in danger, unwitting targets of an unseen force.

Leon murmurs something in his sleep. I lower my head so my ear is close to his mouth. If he's sleep-talking, I want to listen to what he has to say! His words are mainly incoherent, though I distinctly hear him say the word *delicious*. Maybe he's dreaming about food. The thought of food alerts me to a deep rumbling in my tummy. I'm ravenous. My gaze strays to the clock on the bedside table. Six AM. Too early for the breakfast buffet? Leon rolls over and mutters something else. I lean in again, closer, to hear what he has to say.

"Delicious arse . . ." Yep. I heard right. He must be dreaming about sex. He murmurs something else. I lean in closer to listen to him, and that's when he grabs me in a bear hug while calling out, "Ketzia, you have the most delicious arse."

"You trickster!" I squeal. As we laugh, I notice him hardening beneath the sheets, and I am full of desire for him once more. Breakfast will have to wait.

CHAPTER SIXTEEN

The breakfast buffet is an abundance of fresh fruit, yo-ghurts, muesli, pastries, gourmet bread and jams, eggs any way you please, sausages, bacon and not a *hush* brown in sight—the hotel kitchen prefers to display its culinary prow-ess with potatoes on a tray of perfectly shaped miniature tart-lets. The label advises me that the delicious-looking morsels originate from Savoy, France, and their main ingredients are potatoes, reblochon, lardons, and onions. There is more pre-tentious spiel following this, but I don't bother reading it. I slither one onto my already full plate before heading back to the table where Leon is halfway through a cantaloupe, his mo-bile phone stuck to his ear, madly scrolling through his iPad, nestled between his plate and his coffee cup. He looks at me and mouths a *sorry – work*. Ho-hum. I nod, suddenly self-con-scious about the amount of food on my plate. I don't want him to think I'm a pig. I'm still wearing my red dress from last night. I hadn't brought an overnight bag or anything. I can still feel the sweaty aftermath of our sex and yearn for some-thing cooler and less clingy to wear.

A waiter appears next to me and pours coffee into my cup. I murmur thanks and take a sip. The steamy black liquid gives me an instant caffeine hit, further triggering my hunger. Leon is still immersed in his business dealings, so I tuck in unabat-edly. I pierce the skin of a slow-roasted tomato and manage to courier it to my mouth without spilling any of the juices streaming out of it—a sweet and sour blend of spices that is heaven on my tastebuds. Next, I sample my soft poached egg with a sliver of salmon. Finally, I take a bite of the tartlet, its buttery moreish crispiness unlike anything I've ever eaten.

"Good, huh?" Leon grins at me, his phone finally off, and I realise he has been watching me the whole time. Embarrassed, I smile through a mouthful and nod. I prong another bite of tartlet onto my fork and hover it over to Leon.

"Here, try this."

Obediently he opens his mouth. Chews. Smiles. "Almost as delicious as you."

I blush. God, I can't believe the effect he has on me. It's like all the sophistication of my adult years has been stripped away, and I am transparent and vulnerable before him. Ridiculous. Ridiculous and wonderful all at once.

"Busy day planned?" I ask, clutching at this mundane lifeline back to normality. Leon sighs, glancing at his phone and his iPad again. Both beep like neglected children demanding attention.

"It never stops."

I wish I hadn't asked him about work, as his attention pulls away from me and focuses back on his phone, now buzzing insistently on the table. He looks at the screen, picks it up with an apologetic expression, and answers.

"Doreen," he says, "what's up?" Even in the crowded breakfast dining room, I can hear the high-pitched gabbling of *Doreen* through the phone. I wonder who she is and if she's even remotely worth the little spark of jealousy worming its way through my veins.

"Doreen." Leon speaks calmly, evenly into the phone, interrupting her flow of whatever. "All you need to do is to call Jeff Ridgeway. He and I discussed the arrangement in detail last week. There is no caveat on the property anymore. It has been removed. So that doesn't need to be written into the contract. Also . . ."

I tune out. It's all work stuff, and none of it has anything to do with me and my comparatively small-scale real-estate sales. Leon operates in a completely different league to me. He is, after all, the top dog of KX Realty.

Slightly deflated, I reach for my phone, deep in the depths of my handbag. The battery is almost dead, but I can see one missed call from an unknown number and a text message from Mia at the office, wondering where I am. Shit. We're meant to be doing that presentation this morning for the rest of the staff and investors, and I had completely forgotten about it. I quickly message her back, a guilty *on my way*. Sure, she'll be thrilled to learn I've spent the night with Leon but mighty pissed if she has to start the presentation independently. She gets nervous about public speaking.

Leon is still engrossed in conversation with Doreen, so I lean over and peck him on the cheek in farewell. He covers the mouthpiece of his phone with one hand.

"You're leaving?"

"I have to go," I say. "Sorry." He sighs, shrugs, nods, reaches for my hand and won't let go.

"Doreen?" he says into the phone, his gaze never leaving mine. "Something's come up. I'll call you back shortly." Then he clicks his phone off, dumps it on the table, and pulls me close. He kisses me.

"Leon," I whisper. Other people are watching us with interest. Public displays of affection are obviously a rare occurrence here.

"Ketzia. Come back tonight. Let's have dinner together. We could see a show. Go to a concert. Whatever you like . . ."

"Sounds promising," I say, distracted by his phone going nuts on the damask tablecloth again.

"Thank you," he says.

"What for?"

"Last night. This morning. For being you. Everything."

We kiss with deep, sensual longing, and this time, I don't give a damn how many people witness it. However, they won't be able to see too much as the lights start flickering before plunging the place into darkness—another blackout. A maître d' responds quickly by opening the blinds to let in natural light before the lights flash and return to normal. Spooky. This blackout thing seems to be a regular occurrence whenever Leon and I are together. A coincidence? I'm not sure. Unless there's trouble with the electricity stations that I haven't read or heard about. Whatever the case, there's nothing I can do about it, so I turn and leave, blowing Leon a final parting kiss on my way out. He sends me a return kiss, back on the phone again, his iPad taking a hammering from his impatient fingers. But as I step out of the breakfast dining room and into the lobby, I get a distinct sense of being watched. I turn one last time and catch a fleeting shadow of movement in the corner of the room. But then my phone beeps again. It's Mia with another text message, wondering where the hell I am and sounding a bit desperate. So I hotfoot it to a taxi, the concierge elegantly opening the door for me, and I am off to work.

CHAPTER SEVENTEEN

"In summary, the project will require a team of at least six of our best sales staff just to manage the daily queries as well as taking potential clients on tours of our completed apartment complexes at Darling Harbour." Mia clicks a button, and the PowerPoint presentation slides to a finish. I have slipped quietly into the back of the room, grossly late. Our manager, Ron, takes the floor.

"Thanks, everyone, for joining us today. I think we'll all agree that was a wonderful presentation. Thank you, Mia." Everyone claps politely. Mia smiles, though the strain of doing the presentation on her lonesome is painfully evident to me. I join in the applause self-consciously. Mia's eyes meet mine and shoot daggers at me. I will have to devise a rather good excuse for being late. I'm still dressed in my cocktail gown from the night before, so it's bleeding obvious that my reasons can only be fun, which will probably worsen things with Mia. Many sales reps and investors are keen to talk further with Mia, which is a great sign but probably not one she'll be eager to acknowledge with me, now that I am her temporary Judas. They take her attention while I use the opportunity to quietly slip out of the room to the relative safety of my desk.

I flick on my computer. Plenty of emails greet me, all investors keen to purchase more properties. I sift through them, methodically answering the most urgent ones, relegating the more speculative to a folder entitled *prospects*. I have at least fifty sales waiting to be closed. Keen buyers, all of them. Super keen. It's a miracle rendered possible by the ramifications of my attraction spell for Leon. I finish clearing my inbox to the sound of Ron's jovial voice farewelling the presentation attendees and showing them out to the lift. He re-enters the office and makes a beeline for my desk. I decide the best tactic is to get in first.

"Ron," I begin. "I'm so sorry I was late this morning. I have no good excuse to offer. I just completely forgot about the presentation meeting . . ."

"Hey, hey—" Ron cuts me off. He smiles at me. "If you weren't our top sales rep who has slammed not only national sales records but also some major international ones this week, I might be annoyed. But you have single-handedly put this little office on the map. I'm fielding calls from people I never even dreamed would want to talk to me. It's exciting. And we've all got you to thank for it. So maybe, if it weren't for all that, I might just be the teensiest bit annoyed about you being late for work today. But as it is, right now, I'm ready to bow down and kiss your pretty little toes . . ." Ron laughs.

Of course, Mia chooses just that moment to walk past behind him. I've just let her down significantly, and then she has to listen to the boss praising me. Not good. Ron catches me watching her with concern as she makes her way to the ladies' toilets.

"Oh. Yeah. You might have to smooth things over with Mia. She's kind of ropeable. She's not that great at public speaking, you know."

"I thought she did well," I respond defensively.

"Yeah, like a canary on steroids." Ron laughs at his joke. Admittedly, Mia tends to speed up a bit when she's nervous. But his stupid quip only makes me feel ten times worse and even more determined to make things up to her. I stand, offer Ron a polite *excuse,* and head for the ladies'.

Mia is washing her hands when I finally corner her in the ladies' toilets.

"Mia, I am so, so sorry about being late this morning. I don't know how, but I promise I'll make it up to you."

Mia is so angry she's shaking.

"I suppose now that you've slammed the sales targets of the whole team and since you've been slammed personally by the head of the whole organisation, the usual rules don't apply to you anymore." Mia, in a rage, is a sight to be seen. Her eyes spark volumes of unrestrained emotion. I try to calm her down and stop her from saying things she'll regret later.

"Mia, please . . ."

"What? It's true, isn't it? Unfortunately, the rest of us still have to play by the rules and show up to work on time, not wearing a — what the fuck is that thing? A glamour gown."

"Mia, I understand why you're angry at me." My attempts to pacify her sound lame even to my ears. But she's my friend, and I will try my hardest to win her over.

"I let you down. In a big way. But it looks to me like you did well in there. The investors loved your presentation. Ron thought it was great . . ." I figure a little white lie won't hurt in this situation. "You should be proud of yourself."

Mia sticks her hands under the hand dryer, the noise of it effectively blocking out any further attempts from me to calm her down. However, I notice that her shoulders are not so rigid anymore, so maybe she is starting to relax a little. Her gaze meets mine in the mirror. I give her my most earnest and pathetic puppy-dog face. Mia can't resist it. She withdraws her hands from the dryer.

"Okay," she mumbles.

"I'm sorry."

"It's okay." We hug then, and I feel relieved. Then she pulls away and looks me sharply in the eye.

"But you'd better tell me what's been going on. All of it. And I mean every last juicy detail."

I laugh. The woman loves gossip with a passion.

"All right. I'll tell you." Just then, the door to the toilets swings open and Myrna, the receptionist, comes in. She's a skinny older woman with a mess of curls always pinned to the top of her head with a pair of pens.

"Morning, girls." Myrna smiles at us before going into a cubicle.

"Let's do lunch," I suggest to Mia.

"Great. Your shout. Even *one* of your recent bonuses will be worth more than my whole pay packet for the month."

"You're such an opportunist." I grin. "It's a deal."

"And you will be spilling the beans on everything," Mia reminds as we head out of the toilets.

"Do you think it will be too obvious if I go home and change first?" I whisper as we head back to our desks. Mia gives me a once-over, the twinkle back in her eye.

"You want to slip into something more comfortable?" she suggests cheekily. "Can't imagine why . . ."

I shove my mobile into my handbag and switch my computer to sleep mode.

"Back soon," I promise. Mia nods, her attention back to work. The phone on her desk is ringing, and her computer is beeping at her with new messages. It looks like she could be enjoying a busy day now, too. I head out of the office as inconspicuously as possible, keen for another shower and desperate for a fresh change of clothes.

Chapter Eighteen

I'm still wearing my teetering heels and very elegant, though ridiculously impractical, evening gown, so I decide to get an Uber rather than battle out the journey home on public transport.

The driver gives me a quick once-over as I slide into the backseat of his car, but thankfully doesn't seem to be much of a one for small talk. I give him a winning smile, which he catches and returns in the rear-vision mirror. He whistles the theme song from The Simpsons before pulling into the mid-morning traffic. My phone jangles discordantly in my hand-bag. I grope around in its depths before pulling it out and reading the caller display. It's Leon.

"Hi, you," I answer.

"Ketzia," he says. His voice sounds strained.

"Is everything okay?" I ask.

"Listen. Everything's just going kind of crazy with the company now. I'm going to have to go overseas again."

"Oh, really? When?"

He pauses before answering. "This afternoon, actually."

"Oh no." The words escape from my mouth, deflated. His news makes me feel like I have been kicked in the guts.

"I'm really sorry," he continues. "I really want to see you again before I go, but I just can't leave the office right now. Listen, is there any chance you can swing by here?"

"When?" I ask. "Now?"

"It's kind of our only chance."

"Okay. I'm on my way. Where's your office?"

"Head Office." Of course. I'd been there once for an induction seminar when I joined KX Realty.

"I know where it is. I'll be there soon." I click my phone off, tap the driver on the shoulder, and give him the change of directions. He hangs a swift right and steers us up William Street towards the CBD and the towering skyscraper that Leon's empire graciously inhabits. On the way, I muse over how eagerly I'd responded to Leon's request. It was pathetic, about as opposite of playing hard-to-get as it was possible to be. I decide that in the future, I'll be more restrained in running to his beck and call. After all, I want him to think I'm sophisticated and desired. Also, as much as I've been enjoying the purely sexual nature of our liaison, I can't help but wonder where it will lead. Does he want a relationship? Does he want us to be monogamous? Does he love me?

I sigh — so many unanswered questions. I will have to find some way to raise these questions with him. Meanwhile, I can't wait to be in his company. A rush of heat courses into my sex just at the thought of him. Oh, I've got it bad. Real bad.

I tip the driver generously before exiting the car, and he rewards me with a huge grin and a *thank you, ma'am*. I think I've spent more on Ubers and taxis in the last week than I usually do in a whole year, but my new sales commission growth should more than cover the expense.

I enter the foyer of the KX International offices and head straight to the reception desk, my clingy red dress attracting a few barely veiled glances of lust from the business folk mingling in the lobby. The receptionist's steely gaze only compounds my self-consciousness about being inappropriately dressed for this conservative, high-end business environment. Ignoring the hint of disapproval in her manner, I remove my glasses and direct my attention onto her.

"I'm here to see Leon Furness," I announce, the confidence in my voice betraying none of the nerves jangling around inside me.

"Your name, please?" she asks.

"Ketzia Knowles."

Her manner changes instantly the moment she hears my name. Leon must have told her to expect me.

"Certainly," she replies politely, pushing a button on the console behind the desk. "One moment, please."

I patiently wait as she converses with someone via the reception phone, receiving and relaying some instructions. Then she gets up from behind the desk and walks me over to an elevator on the far side of the foyer. She pushes the button for the lift, holding the doors open for me. Once inside, she enters a code into a keypad recessed in the panel board and then presses the button for the top floor.

"This will take you straight to his office," she says before exiting the lift.

"Thanks." My voice is swallowed by the doors sliding shut, removing her from my existence in a single sliding motion.

I barely have time to check my face in the elevator mirrors before a ding signals my arrival at the top floor. The lift doors slide open, and I am instantly dazzled by the panoramic view from the floor-to-ceiling windows encasing the entire floor. Sydney Harbour sparkles in the morning light, the water a mass of twinkling diamonds dotted with ferries and cruisers. The peaked shells of the Opera House roof add their shimmer to the vista at the far end of Circular Quay.

I take a few steps into the room. It would have to be the ritziest office environment I've ever been in. An ornate marble drinks cabinet is recessed into the wall behind me, while a spectacular granite boardroom table flanked by twelve hyper-modern stark white chairs boasts a huge glass vase overflowing with meticulously arranged white orchids and lilies. Everything appears made of glass or marble and carries the professionally styled look only an interior designer can create. A far cry from the mess of used takeaway containers, dirty coffee cups, and overflowing desks and disorder that is the KX office I usually work in. My eyes slowly adjust to the brightness, and it takes me a moment before I spot Leon, seated in a low-slung mahogany recliner behind a vast, glass-topped office desk. He has a headset on and signals to me that he can't talk yet, whispering a *sorry* and blowing me a kiss.

Three screens are running simultaneously on the desk in front of him. One has the ungainly face of Sean Shottler, the New York office board chairman. Another has Christine Ho's serious face staring at him from the Asia Pacific head office in Jakarta, while a third screen projects the harried countenance of Rowena Bennett, the head of KX Realty's British office. All inhabit different time zones and come to Leon with various demands. One thing they have in common — they are all in the throes of various corporate and construction emergencies. In Jakarta, one of KX Realty's almost complete skyscrapers has collapsed due to faulty pylons being used during the first phase of construction. In London, a consortium group KX Realty is a part of is threatening a lawsuit against the government due to a prime piece of public land they were counting on buying being sold to other investors without going to tender. While in New York, the share price of their latest off-the-plan architectural release has plummeted — for no apparent reason. Leon runs his fingers through his hair before addressing them all.

"Sean, Christine, Rowena. These are all serious issues, and please understand that they are difficult for me to address remotely. I will arrange to meet with you, and any related parties, in person over the next couple of days. The itinerary will commence in Jakarta, then on to London, followed by New

York. I'll have my secretary fill you in on all the details of my availability."

Leon presses the *end call* function on his tablet, throws the headset onto the table, reaches for my hand, and pulls me towards him.

"Sounds busy," I say, feeling sorry for him. With all the glitz and glam of the external trappings of his success, it hadn't occurred to me how much pressure the guy must constantly be under.

"It's a bit of a mess," he agrees dismissively, focusing entirely on me. Or, to be more precise, on my breasts. His fingers lightly caress their roundness, releasing a rush of endorphins that travel through my entire body.

"Listen, Leon," I begin.

"Hmm?" he responds, lowering his hand to lift the skirt of my dress and slide up under it.

"I was kind of hoping we could talk." His hand continues its journey up my dress, teasing its way up my thigh.

"Of course." He smiles at me, dazzling me with that infectious grin of his.

"I need to know . . ." I'm finding it hard to concentrate with his fingers now edging away the seams of my G-string to tickle my pussy. But I continue. "I need to know what we are."

"Well, I believe you're the sexiest woman I've ever encountered, and I'm the lucky guy who gets to know you. Intimately." He teases his fingers over my pussy, stroking me. He is so not taking this seriously. I pull away. I need to know what to expect from our — whatever it is — affair?

"Leon." I falter. "I really like you."

"I really like you, too, babe," he replies, stepping in to plant a kiss on my lips. I surrender — momentarily — to his touch, breathing in the spicy scent of his cologne.

"It's just . . ." He half-smiles at me as I try to continue my train of thought. "It's like we've gone about the whole thing in reverse. I mean, we hardly know each other . . ."

"Is that how you feel?" His gaze penetrates mine, probing for an answer. "Or is it what you think?" I shake my head, uncertain of the difference.

"The way I feel . . . I feel as though I've known you forever. But the reality is we've only just met . . . and shared all these incredibly intimate, passionate experiences . . . but . . . I don't know . . ."

Leon pulls away from me, turning away to face the magnificent view. I hope my words haven't somehow upset him. Surely he must have wondered where we're headed, too? Finally, still turned away from me, he speaks.

"Ketzia. I'm not going to lie to you. I've never been good at relationships—if that's what you're trying to tell me that you want. I prefer to keep things uncomplicated. Simple."

"Simple? How can you say that? *Nothing* about our being together was ever going to be simple. Listen, I'm not saying I want a relationship . . . necessarily . . ." I falter, unsure of exactly what I'm trying to say. Leon turns around to face me.

"So what *do* you want?" he asks.

With his words, I realise that I don't know. I want to be with him. I want to spend more time with him. I want to get to know him better, beyond the purely sexual and the spiritual. I smile hopelessly.

"I just wish you didn't have to go away. I wish we could spend more time together."

"I'm sorry, Ketzia. I wish that, too. I really do. And we will. As soon as I get back from overseas. I promise you."

Maybe it was best just to leave it at that—for now.

"I'll look forward to that," I say, trying to sound casual, but the words catch in my throat. A series of electronic pips from Leon's desk signals more work that needs to be attended to.

A screen lights up with another employee's face demanding attention from elsewhere in the world — a timely distraction. Leon throws a swift glare at the rabble of technology.

"It's all right," I say, sounding braver than I feel. "The rest of the world needs you."

He laughs at this and visibly relaxes. Then we kiss, the most tender of kisses. I feel his entire being merging with mine, our collective energies trapped within the universe of our lips and mouths. I wish it could last forever. Another series of electronic pips from his desk puts an end to it. Leon lifts my chin and looks deep into my eyes.

"I'll be gone for less than a week," he promises.

"It's all right," I say. Irritatingly I feel the pricking of tears threatening to spill out of me.

"Goodbye, princess," he says.

"Goodbye." I smile and head straight for the elevator, determined not to cry in front of him. I catch the kiss he blows me from behind his desk and the full impact of his expression of longing as his gaze trails over my entire body, igniting a fire of passion. The doors slide shut. And then, I am gone.

The impact of our meeting hits me full force as the lift zooms down to the ground floor, and I start crying uncontrollably. I realise it is the first time we have even attempted to discuss what our relationship — if you can even call it that — means. Leon had been receptive to the discussion, but he had also seemed a little relieved that his work commitments forced us to abandon it. Perhaps all he is after is a sexual liaison? Perhaps there is nothing emotional in this for him at all? Maybe he fears a deeper relationship with me because of our shared Wiccan histories? Meanwhile, my heart breaks with longing.

The lift progresses down through the floors, and I realise something else. This is the first time we have met and not made love. A series of firsts, then. I wonder if the two are related — our talk about the future and our not having sex. Have I fallen for a relationship-phobic man?

Before the lift doors open on the ground floor, I wipe my tears and straighten my hair. I'm probably just overthinking things, emotional from the manic break from routine, and needing sleep. I plaster on a smile and stride across the reception floor with determination. I have Mia to think about now. I need to get home and change for our lunch. Almost as an afterthought, I remember that I also have a pet snake to attend to, and a genuine smile replaces my fake one as I look forward to seeing Bo again.

Chapter Nineteen

It feels strangely disheartening to return to my humble terrace after the corporate majesty of Leon's office. I kick off my shoes and give my feet a quick rub. Heels that high are not designed to be worn for that many hours straight. I cross my lounge room and register that the house has a sharp acrid smell, and I sniff around to locate the source of the pungent aroma. Bo? He is curled on top of the stack of rocks I built for him, looking extremely content. I lean in to kiss the top of his cute head. He smells wonderful. So the bad smell is not coming from him.

I go into the kitchen and pour myself a glass of water. Its coolness refreshes my parched throat, and I gulp it down in one motion. I place the glass on the counter and finally discover the source of the bad smell. Leon's roses. They droop in their vase on the kitchen bench, sadly wilted. The water is grungy. They didn't last long, I think to myself.

Reluctantly I pull the bunch out of the vase to toss the dead flowers in the bin, a thorn tearing a strip of skin off the inside of my thumb in the process. Damn. I stick my thumb in my mouth to ebb the flow of blood. The thorn has pierced my skin deeply, and the wound releases a hot gush of leaden-tasting blood. I turn the tap on and run cool water over the cut before wrapping it in a tea towel. My first aid kit is somewhere in the laundry cupboard, and it takes me a bit of hunting before I finally find the Band-Aids wedged behind a stack of towels. I stick two on for good measure and then return to the kitchen, where I tip the boggy-smelling flower water down the drain and scrub the vase. It's not good to have dead things in the house.

I dash upstairs to get changed. My front doorbell chimes — a honkytonk sound I usually find amusing but is downright annoying to hear just now when I'm in such a rush. I run back downstairs and peer through the spy hole of the front door. It's Charles. How does he even know where I live? Then I remember the impromptu gathering I'd had at my place last year one night after a meditation session at Castanna Street. Charles had been part of the group I'd invited back. It had been a pleasant evening of Bohemian folk music, wine, and Wiccan discussions about the tarot, astrology, ancient herbs, and wisdom. I open the door.

"Charles!" I exclaim.

"Ketzia." He smiles shyly. "I was in the neighbourhood and thought I'd pop in for a visit."

"I'm kind of on my way to work," I say. I don't have time for him right now. Charles looks me over, and I feel like a kid with her hand caught in the cookie jar because I'm still wearing my evening dress.

"Fancy job." He laughs. I've got no choice. I'm going to have to invite him in.

"Yeah, well." I smile guiltily. "Come in."

"Thanks." Charles steps inside. He's wearing a black business suit with a silver tie and a leather backpack strapped to his back.

"Cuppa?" I offer as he follows me into the kitchen.

"That would be great. Thanks, Ketzia." He manoeuvres the backpack off his shoulders, drops it to the floor, and perches himself on one of the kitchen counter barstools. Oh dear. It looks like he's settling in.

"So, what brings you to the neighbourhood?" I ask, filling the kettle.

"Private client," he replies. Hence the flashy suit, I guess. The kettle boils. I put a couple of teaspoons of instant in a cup.

"How do you have your coffee?" I ask.

"Black, no sugar. Thanks."

I pour hot water into the cup, stir it, and slide it over the bench to him.

"Aren't you having one?" he asks, slightly put out.

"No, I've already had a coffee this morning." If I don't join him for a cup, I figure he might take the hint and get going faster. I hate being rude, but I need to get changed and head back to the office for my lunch with Mia. I can imagine how she'd react if I were late for her a second time in one day. Charles takes a sip of his coffee.

"This is great."

"It's only instant. Sorry."

"It's fine." Charles stares at me intensely. Enough to make me feel just a little bit uncomfortable.

"Nice of you to dress up for me," he says, undressing me with his eyes.

"I didn't know you were coming," I reply, shocked and a little defensive.

"You're a witch. Of course, you knew I was coming," he replies with a suggestive laugh as though we exclusively share the secrets of magick. As much as I don't want to hurt his feelings, I will have to find some way to get rid of him.

"Charles, I'm sorry, but I really do have to get ready for work. I'm kind of running late as it is. Can we maybe arrange to do this some other time?"

"Do what?" he asks, lowering his cup to the bench. He steps towards me, and I feel a tiny flicker of fear pass through me, a premonition heralding something dark and unsavoury.

"Do what, Ketzia?" he repeats, inching closer towards me. I take a step back.

"Charles," I begin, retreating yet another step as he comes closer. "Charles, I think you may have the wrong idea."

My back is against the wall. Charles draws even closer.

"Ketzia, I love you," he says.

"What?" My exclamation is a shrill testament to shock. What is this guy on?

"You and I belong together."

"Charles, what's gotten into you?"

"You. You have gotten into me and made me see what I should have seen long ago. And you're right. We deserve each other." As he is saying this, he has a crazy glint in his eye, and I am starting to feel scared. Has he been stalking me or something?

"I'm sorry, but you're going to have to leave," I say before his outstretched fingers reach my wrists and encircle them roughly.

"You're so beautiful." His voice has a dreamy, dangerous quality.

"Charles, let go of me." I'm almost shouting, trying to get through to him. But my words only have the opposite effect as he tightens his grip on my wrists.

"You're hurting me, Charles. Let go." He grins and leans closer, pushing his body against mine in forced intimacy. When he tries to kiss me, I lose control.

"Get off me," I shriek, lifting my leg to knee him in the balls. He is one step ahead of me, however, twisting to the side just before I make impact. The movement throws me off balance, and I topple over, landing on all fours on the floor. He grabs me by my hair and yanks it back so I am facing upwards, staring at his leering face. I claw at his trousers, trying to latch on to one of his legs to throw him off balance, but he kicks my hands away like they're made of tissue paper.

"Help!" I scream at the top of my lungs. Charles lets go of my hair, and for a second, I think he is coming to his senses, but it's only to free his hands so he can slap me — hard — across the face.

"Quiet," he commands through gritted teeth.

"Help!" I scream out again, even louder this time. I'm hoping old Mrs Jones next door has her hearing aids switched on, or that the postman's coming past, that anyone will hear me, but I know my chances are slim. Charles slaps me again, even harder. My cheek smarts painfully, and my eyes well with tears.

"I mean it," he says. "Be quiet." That's when I see it. The knife. He is holding a knife.

"I don't want to have to use this," he warns, and he is so creepily calm about it that I feel even more terrified.

"Stand up," he commands.

I obey, pulling myself off the floor in an awkward movement that I hope doesn't betray my terror. He places the blade of the knife to my throat. His other hand encircles my waist.

"Ketzia, I'm really sorry that it's come to this. I was hoping you would have entered a more evolved mode of being."

I almost guffaw. What the hell is he on about? The knife at my throat silences me. I'll have to try another tack.

"Charles," I whisper. "I'm sorry I was so ... so rude. I just ... Can you put the knife down? Please?"

He considers for a moment. He removes the knife from my jugular but keeps it in front of him threateningly. Then he shoves me into a chair, my comfy Incan-upholstered sitting chair that I usually use for meditation. After this, it won't be any use for that anymore, I think. Then an afterthought — how can I even be thinking about my chair when my life is so obviously in danger? Crazy how the mind works. Charles watches me unflinchingly as he puts the knife down on the kitchen counter and grabs for his backpack. Alarmed, I watch as he zips it open, reaches inside, and pulls out a small brown bottle and a scarf, his gaze never leaving its guard on me for even a second. His fingers struggle to twist open the lid of the bottle. It looks like it contains a potion or brew. I watch, terrified, hoping for the chance to escape. The cap appears to be screwed on tightly because Charles has no luck getting it off. He wraps the scarf around the lid to give him more grip, and his gaze finally strays from mine to get a better handle on what he is doing.

This is my chance. I take it and bolt. One step, two steps, three steps, and four, I'm almost at the front door when I feel his wretched nails scrape my scalp and his fists clench around my hair. For once, I curse my long tresses as he yanks and drags me backwards. The pressure is unbearable. It feels like he is scalping me. My feet kick against the floor, but it's no use. Charles hauls me back to the kitchen, where he picks the knife up off the bench, presses it to my throat, and pushes it in. I feel the trickle of blood before I register the sharp pain where he cut me.

"Get down. Kneel down," he shouts.

I drop to my knees in fear, like a well-trained dog. My body is shaking so hard I'm almost convulsing. I try to say anything to snap him out of this insanity, but my mouth is parched and incapable of speech. I sense tears flowing down my cheeks as though from far away. A dry, raspy noise spills from my throat as I struggle to breathe. I don't want to give up. I want to fight. But as Charles pushes the scarf—now tainted with the contents of the bottle, which he has finally managed to open—over my mouth and nose and I inhale the poisonous tincture, all of my willpower seeps out of my body as I unwillingly yield to the intoxicating calm of unconsciousness.

CHAPTER TWENTY

Cramping. That's the first thing I'm aware of. Cramping in my calf muscles, I straighten my legs, and pain shoots through them, an avalanche of pins and needles. Something clunks around my ankles. I try to open my eyes, but my eyelids are so heavy. I take a deep breath, push through my exhaustion, and open my eyes. I am in a dark place. It seems foggy. Certainly gloomy. I try to sit up, but chains that anchor my wrists to my sides pin me down. I lift my head to get a better idea of where I am. There is a mattress beneath me — an unfamiliar mattress on an ornate four-poster bed, Jacobean by the look of it. I swallow, and my throat flares with pain, making me croak. My breath makes small involuntary whimpering sounds with each exhalation. Partly it's fear. I have no idea where I am.

"Oh, you're awake." The voice, so delighted and warm, almost dissipates my fear. Its friendliness belies the flood of memories washing over me. The memory of Charles hitting me, hurting me, capturing me. He grins at me innocently now, and I stare back at him — helpless, confused, and utterly terrified.

"Water." The effort it takes to spit out the word almost sends me spiralling back into unconsciousness. Charles disappears, leaving me staring at the dark ceiling, shiny with residue. There are so many giddying questions floating around my head. What does Charles want from me? Where has he taken me? Why? But they are all reduced to the need to alleviate my throat's searing shards of glasslike dryness.

Charles returns with a glass of water, a bendable drinking straw aimed at my mouth. I take a sip, immeasurably grateful to him for bringing it to me, before remembering that he is the cause of my pain and discomfort. Isn't this what they call Stockholm syndrome? The irrational empathy of a hostage with their captor? I angle my head and see that the room has cave-like proportions, empty of furniture beside the bed I am shackled to. A plethora of multi-coloured candles lights the room. It is a prison, and I am his hostage. I have no idea how dangerous he is, but I'm also determined not to become his victim.

I finish the glass of water, the straw making little gurgling sounds as it scrapes the empty base of the glass. It's such an ordinary sound—a noise associated with high school dates in cheesy neighbourhood milk bars, so discomfiting in this cave-like room with its absence of natural light.

"Thanks." I smile falsely, testing the waters. Charles takes the glass and walks over to a small sink recessed into a kitchenette in the furthermost wall of the room. My eyes have adjusted to the eerie half-light of the place, and I take in the Spartan surroundings with mounting trepidation.

I am in a kind of cellar or basement. Perhaps it is a dungeon? The exposed sandstone bricks of the walls are almost black in places, the result no doubt of years of mould and damp taking their toll. The only light in the area comes from the candles flickering around the room's circumference, their glow imbuing not cosiness but a shadowy ominousness. Near the kitchenette is a thick wooden door with hard metal buttressing. I notice it with interest, identifying it as a possible avenue of escape. A large tapestry hangs on the opposite wall, depicting a medieval torture scene—knights in battle on horses, naked maidens tied to posts, serpents twined around their bodies. Something about the image magnifies my fear. A cold knot of terror settles deep within me.

I must be careful and very clever. Who knows what Charles is capable of? He stands at the kitchenette with his back to me, whistling softly. I decide to take the plunge.

"Charles?" My voice comes out loud and brittle, a croaky exhalation of sound that does nothing to disguise my fear.

"Ketzia . . ." But he still has his back to me. I can't gauge his mood.

"How long have I been here?" I figure it's a neutral question. Besides, it's one that I would like to know the answer to. Finally, he turns around and faces me. In his hands, he holds a mortar and pestle. His long, silvery fingers busily grind its contents.

"Sometimes to discover our true purpose, the essence of our inner soul, we need to remove ourselves from the distractions of the superficial, capitalist way we lead our modern lives."

He doesn't look at me directly as he speaks, still busy with the mortar and pestle. Intermittently he turns back to the kitchenette bench and adds more of one thing or another to the bowl.

It is too dark for me to make out the ingredients. There is something strangely casual about our exchange. It feels almost like the regular domestic banter of a couple discussing life's trivialities while cooking dinner. However, there's nothing trivial about this situation whatsoever. I close my eyes, trying to find the best tactic for getting out of here. Maybe I should play into his hands as best as I can. Pretending being with him is everything I've always wanted—something like that. I open my eyes and scream. Charles is standing right beside me. I don't know how he does it, but it's like he can move without making a sound, a catlike skill of speed and agility. I force myself to smile at him. He doesn't smile back.

"Open your mouth." The command is delivered in a cool monotone, his fingers clasped like talons around the handle of the spoon that he dips into the mortar and then positions in front of my mouth. The pungent smell of the tincture makes me gag. I have no idea what it is, though I can identify the overpowering scent of aniseed.

"Open," he repeats. I open my mouth. What else can I do? Charles places the spoon in my mouth and deposits the contents. The taste of the potion is not all that bad. I swirl the liquid around my mouth, trying to ascertain the ingredients. Perhaps if I can figure out what he is feeding me, I will have a greater chance of overpowering its effects. Unless, of course, it is poison. Maybe he just wants to kill me? But the sharp tanginess of the liquid has a velvety smoothness, too, so I don't think that's the case. Besides, if he just wanted to kill me, he already had plenty of opportunities to do so. Among the conflicting mix of flavours attacking my taste buds, I can identify mugwort's bitterness and acacia's astringency, tempered by the sweetness of apricot nectar.

Even though I hate Charles more than I've ever hated anyone at this moment, I can't help but admire his mastery of herbology, even in these diabolical circumstances. I swallow, and Charles immediately positions a second spoonful of the liquid in front of my mouth. Obediently I allow him to push the spoon into my mouth while racking my brain, trying to remember what mugwort and acacia are usually used for. A lesson I took on Wiccan herbology ages ago comes to my mind, and I draw on my dusty knowledge to aid my assessment. They are both stimulants. I remember that they are both aphrodisiacs, too. Uh-oh. What is he playing at?

As he feeds me yet another spoonful of the thick syrup, I also detect a faint fishy flavour. Does it perhaps belong to stinging nettle? The thorny, flowering plant is often used in witchcraft to promote fertility. Aphrodisiac and fertility ingredients? The thought fills me with dread.

Charles turns away and takes the bowl to the kitchenette, apparently satisfied that I have had enough *medicine*. My eyes have adjusted better to the basement's darkness, and I can make out rows and rows of tiny bottles lining the shelf above the sink. Bunches of dried herbs hang from a series of hooks beside them — his little laboratory. I can't feel any effects from the tonic yet and hope it didn't contain anything sedating. The last thing I want is to lose consciousness. I am determined to get him to stop this nonsense and release me.

"Charles?" He doesn't respond. He has his back to me as he rinses the bowl and the spoon. I figure my best bet is to keep talking. Appeal to his humanity.

"Charles, these chains . . . they really hurt. Plus, they're unnecessary. I'm not going to try and run away. Why would I do that? I really like you." The lie drops out of my mouth easily. I think it's the only way I will win him over. But this is a mistake. Charles picks up a steel bowl and flings it violently across the room, where it crashes with a torrential clanging into the hard sandstone wall.

"I'm sorry," I cry. The sound of the steel bowl slamming against the wall echoes, producing an extended reverberation that feels like it penetrates my very brain. I ignore it as best as possible, trying to keep my wits about me. Oh god, I *so* have to keep my judgement unimpaired.

Charles turns around, faces me, and takes a few silent steps to my side. I meet his eyes imploringly.

"Charles."

"Don't talk." He lowers his weight to perch on the end of the bed. "You have a long journey ahead of you."

"We're going somewhere?"

The slap comes seemingly out of nowhere. Charles's hand makes contact with my cheek in an instant of pain.

"I told you — don't speak."

I press my lips together, even though all I want to do is scream at him. I meet his gaze, and I nod like a pathetic mummified doll or something. Tears spring to my eyes. I struggle to contain them. Crying might only serve to exacerbate him further.

"I will be giving you a gift," Charles says, fingers sweeping over my body. I only now register that I am still wearing my red cocktail dress. I'd been wearing it when Charles abducted me — in what feels like a lifetime ago. Its satiny softness shifts beneath his touch. The stiff peaks of my nipples rise provocatively beneath the fabric in unwanted response. It occurs to me how indelibly fear and excitement are physiologically intertwined. His fingers glide down my torso towards my sex, the movement disturbingly exhilarating. Charles cups his hands over my womanhood. His eyes are closed, in deep concentration, while his lips murmur an incantation. A spell?

I have no way to gauge Charles's supernatural abilities. For one, I don't know him well enough. For another, he is male, so his magick operates differently from mine. But I can certainly feel the effects of what he is doing, hot darts of phosphorescent lusciousness shooting from my pelvic area to saturate my whole body. It is perhaps the result of whatever was in the concoction — or may be caused by his chanting. I try to make out what he is saying, but the words are in a foreign language, possibly of Urdic origin. He flattens the palms of his hands and pushes forcefully against my vagina, channelling a flow of tantric energy through my body. I gasp. I don't want to be enjoying this, but the rush of endorphins flowing from his touch heats my inner core in a spasm of desire. Then, just as abruptly as he commenced his spellcasting, he opens his eyes and removes his hands, flicking them delicately three times in the air, dispersing any excess energy over my body. It feels like the sprinkling of fairy dust.

"My gift can only be received once you are ready for it. Your entire being must be ready. Completely ready," he says. He rises from the bed, crosses the room to the heavily inlaid wooden door, opens it with a hearty tug at its metal hinge, and leaves.

I do my best to peek at what lies beyond, but all I can see is darkness and perhaps a stairwell. Then Charles shuts the door firmly behind him, and I am left to my spiralling thoughts, his frightened and hopeless prisoner.

CHAPTER TWENTY-ONE

A nother world away, back at the KX realty office, Mia impatiently checks her phone for messages. Nothing. Almost two o'clock and still no word from Ketzia. Seriously, the girl must have completely lost her head over this Leon guy. Or maybe her recent success at work has gone to her head, and she does feel above them all now. Mia battles to control the surge of jealousy coursing through her. It isn't fair. First, Ketzia snares the attention of the head of the company, and then she has this unbelievable run of sales luck that's putting the rest of the office to shame. At that moment, Ron sticks his head out of his office and calls out to her.

"Mia, would you mind ducking down to Snap and picking up our latest batch of pamphlets?" His head disappears again to avoid the full force of Mia's rage. Great. This is what she has become, then, the new dogsbody of the organisation.

Ron sticks his head out of his office again. "You might want to take a trolley. There's going to be a heap of them. The phone's been ringing hot for information on these properties all day . . ."

The turtle head retreats into its shell. Mia mutters a swear word. No way he'd even *think* of asking his precious Ketzia to waste her time picking up promotional material. She rechecks her phone—still nothing from Ketzia. Mia wishes she didn't feel so envious of her only real office friend. If only Ketzia weren't treating her with such neglect, everything would be okay.

Frowning, she sends Ketzia another text message.

Giving up on lunch and on u! Sorry!

She then inserts an unsmiling emoticon. Hopefully, Ketzia will feel guilty enough to respond to that. Mia had been looking forward to a fancy lunch feast with Ketzia—and all the salacious gossip that goes with it. Her anger is just a way of covering up her disappointment. Oh well. She rises from her desk and goes in search of the trolley. Hopefully, there'll be a hot guy working at Snap that she can flirt with. God knows she could do with a bit of a boost.

Hours later, time zones away, Leon tries to reason with Christine Ho, the corporate head of the KX Realty Asia Pacific head office in Jakarta. The building company they had hired for the first building phase of the skyscraper that collapsed was chosen by Christine. Of course, the job had gone out to tender, but as with so many business deals in Jakarta, the process had been tempered by the low-level nepotism endemic to the business world there and the contract given to a company owned by one of Christine's relatives. The faulty pylons used in the building construction had resulted in its consequential collapse. Leon would never suspect Christine of corruption—she has an MBA from Harvard, after all—but she is being unbelievably reticent in pursuing the company for damages.

"The building could have collapsed due to any number of reasons, Mr Leon," she says, her English bearing the practised American twang of international education. Leon takes a moment to breathe deeply before responding. He must tread very carefully. Everything becomes so much more complicated when family honour is at stake.

"Christine . . ." He gently taps the insurance investigation report. "Our insurers have traced the problem with the building to faulty pylons being installed in the initial phase." These were installed by H and M Building—her relatives' company. He omits to state this overtly, knowing the shame it would cause her. He continues from where he left off, "Therefore, they are liable for the costs. All I'm asking you to do is to contact them to find out their insurance details."

Christine's face drains to an ashen hue, confirming what Leon has already suspected. The company has no insurance.

"Or if you would feel more comfortable about it, I can call them myself," he offers. He is nothing but an empathetic boss. But business is business, and he needs to recoup the money from the building's collapse. Even if that means eventually taking H and M Building to court, suing them for damages, and bankrupting a couple of Christine's relatives along the way.

"I will talk to them, Mr Leon," Christine says.

"Okay," he replies. "But I need their insurance details by close of business today. Otherwise, I'll have no option but to pursue legal action against them."

"Yes, Mr Leon." Christine sighs. She gets up and leaves the conference room, her face lined with worry.

Leon uses the opportunity to stand and stretch, staring out the 33rd-storey window at the billowing smog weighing heavily on the traffic in the street below. It's been a hell of a couple of hours. First, the flight to Jakarta had been wrought with an interminable number of difficulties. All the passengers had been strapped in their seats waiting to leave the runway in Sydney for nearly four hours before air traffic control finally gave them the okay to go. And, of course, no reasonable explanation had been provided for the delay, apart from vague murmurings of technical difficulties from the flight attendants. The plane had encountered shocking turbulence in the air that left Leon nauseous. Then he'd arrived in Jakarta to discover that his luggage had gone astray.

Leon sighs, overwhelmed with exhaustion. He'll probably have to fire Christine to keep the board happy or for legal reasons if they have to go to court down the track. It's been a shit of a day. He exhales deeply, allowing his mind to wander to thoughts of Ketzia. His lips automatically curl upwards as he visualises her delicious curves, the hypnotic pull of her eyes, and the deep sexy timbre of her voice. She's an incredible woman. Even just thinking about her fills Leon with longing. And something else, too. A cold prickle on the back of his neck. An icy stab of pain in the centre of his guts. And the unnerving sensation of being watched, not by anyone in the office or from the streets below, but rather by some omniscient and malignant presence. Leon shakes himself as though trying to rid himself of the sensation. It must be his stupid schedule—jetlag, stress, overwork—making him feel this way. He tries to focus his thoughts on Ketzia again, distracting himself from this eerie sense of foreboding by remembering her sexy body and generous smile. But the nagging, niggling feeling won't go away. It only intensifies when he thinks of her. He reaches for his mobile and dials her number without bothering to check the difference in the time zones first. Possibly it's two o'clock in the morning in Australia? He listens as her phone rings seven, eight times . . . No answer. Voicemail clicks in. Her cheery voice greets him with a prerecorded message. Then a pip. Leon takes a deep breath.

"Ketzia, it's Leon. Hi. Look, I'm in Jakarta, and I just really need to talk to you. Could you please give me a call? Otherwise, I should be back next week, and I'll be in touch then. But please call me before then." He presses the *end call* button, the nagging sense of danger still unsettling him. The woman has managed to get under his skin. Jeez. She's probably fine, and he's probably just overreacting. He will have to miss her until he gets back to Australia. He'll call her again then, take her out to dinner or something, have fun. Meanwhile, there's nothing for it but for him to attend to the business at hand. There is a lot of it.

Ketzia's mobile beeps, buzzes, and vibrates with text messages and phone calls. It is buried deep in her handbag on her living room floor and continues its dance unnoticed, except for one witness, a beady-eyed snake that lifts his head from his bed of rocks to receive the vibrations, interpreting them as interstellar messages from a prehistoric world. Bo slithers down onto the floor, sliding across the cool kitchen tiles for a drink of water. Then he freezes, perplexed. He saw Charles come and take Ketzia, of course. He has registered that what happened between them was terrible. And now his owner is gone, and he doesn't know what to do. Bo starts shedding his skin, his far-away owner oblivious to his distress.

CHAPTER TWENTY-TWO

I don't know how many hours have passed while I've been trapped in the gloomy half-light of the cellar. A few candles still flicker at the room's edges, but some have reached the base of the wick and expired. What does that mean? Three hours? Four? Impossible to tell without knowing how tall the candles were when they were lit, plus a whole host of other factors. One thing I can be sure of is that Charles would only use high-quality Wiccan beeswax candles—which have a longer lifespan.

My thoughts have shifted from tangible escape plans, rendered hopeless by the chains pillorying me to the bed, to psychic pursuits where I have mentally tried to contact Meredith and other members of the Wiccan community. Now I try to cast a binding spell to prevent Charles from causing me harm. Usually, this would involve using a white candle, sea salt, sage, rosemary, and papyrus. A chalk circle would be drawn on the ground, and the spell-caster would move between the constellations of earth, air, fire, water and spirit. But I will have to compromise on the physical aspects of the spell. Instead, I breathe deeply to enter a deep state of meditation, focusing my intent on binding Charles from any negative activities. The more specific you can be with a spell, the greater its potency, so I start to mentally note all the activities I would like to prevent him from engaging in. My list doesn't get very far, though, as fear grips me in its immobilising clutches as soon as the first item occurs to me—please don't let him kill me.

I bring myself out of the meditative trance, deciding that a more practical approach is needed. At university, I studied a range of psychology subjects before dropping out. One of the units was on psychopathology. This subject studied phenomena such as hallucinations and delusions, anxiety, somatisation, depression, dissociation, and changes in memory and cognition. I hope I have enough knowledge, apart from that it's bleeding obvious, to make a layman's prognosis — that Charles is suffering from some kind of delusional mental disorder. I wonder how he would respond to a hostage negotiation? Even though I am the hostage, it should be possible to engage him in a rapport that would eventuate in him confiding in me the cause of his imbalanced psychology and hopefully result in him releasing me. It's worth a go. Anything is. After all, my life depends on it.

My thoughts drift to other possibilities. When I fail to return to work, will Mia raise the alarm? Or will she think that I've taken off with Leon again? Probably the latter. Leon himself, of course, will be overseas by now and not concerned with my whereabouts at all. Realistically I could likely remain trapped here for at least a week without anyone getting worried. The situation is indeed dire. I close my eyes, trying to summon my spirit guides. But the sound of the thick wooden door scraping open breaks my concentration. Charles.

He enters the room with his usual silent footfall and appears at my bedside as though by magic. He has changed his clothes and wears a dark brown medieval Wiccan Midnight Ritual robe. Possibly it's nighttime, then. His face has a pale sheen to it. Perhaps he is as frightened by what he is doing as I am? Even though it caused an outburst of anger from him last time I tried it, I decide that the best tactic is still for me to continue to play along with him. Try and build some of that rapport.

"Charles," I caution, trying not to push his buttons too much.

He doesn't reply, using one hand to smooth the fabric of my dress so that it is taut across my torso. In his other hand, he holds an athame, a ceremonial Wiccan dagger. I can't control my breathing when I see it. It quickens, an involuntary reaction of alarm. He pushes the blade against the fabric of my dress, dragging downwards from the top seam. The material rips open, Charles sliding the knife downwards to the bottom hem, splicing the dress vertically down the centre. He pushes the fabric away from my body. It drops to the sides of the bed easily. I feel like a rabbit being skinned.

"Charles, why are you doing this?"

"Hush." He has a gleam in his eye that I don't like. "You'll thank me for this later."

He positions himself beside me and pushes the blade of the athame under the centre panel of my bra. The sharp edge splices the cloth easily. Charles moves the cups of my bra to the sides to expose my breasts. Then he looks at my exposed, nearly naked body and smiles. I want to thrash about, hit him, stop this. But I cannot move. The chains holding me in place restrict any movement. He focuses his attention on cutting through my lace G-string. That thing cost me nearly twenty dollars. Weird thing to feel angry about under the circumstances, I know. He snips at it twice, at the left and right hip. Then pushes the fabric out of the way, drawing it from beneath me.

I lie there, completely exposed and vulnerable. Goose pimples creep their way across my flesh, even though the room is not cold. Charles is still holding the athame in his hand. He presses the blade to the skin of my breast, circling the hard protuberance of my nipple. A thin sheen of sweat coats his upper lip, but apart from this, he appears completely calm.

"Charles —" I beg, but he cuts me off immediately.

"Silence." He turns his back to me and heads over to the kitchenette. Determined, I try again, my mind in overdrive, hoping to stumble on the key that will unlock the source of his madness and nullify it.

"Charles. You don't have to do this to me. I am your friend, and I want to help you . . ."

He turns to face me with such an expression of rage that my voice instantly dies in my throat.

"I said silence, and I meant it." His voice is lilting, almost soothing if it weren't for the palpable menace in his eyes.

"But why?" I hope my conciliatory tone won't exacerbate his anger further.

"If you can't be quiet, I'll have to gag you." With this threat, he turns his back to me again and continues with whatever he is preparing on the bench.

I lie in stunned silence, entirely at a loss as to what to do. I can hear him stirring something vigorously and then the clink of beakers. He must be creating another concoction. He appears at my side again. I must be growing accustomed to the stealthy way he moves because his sudden presence fails to surprise me this time. He holds a mug filled to the brim with a deep purple, glutinous liquid. Wisps of steam drift from the surface. It must be hot. I hope he doesn't want me to drink it. But no, it turns out he has something else planned.

Slowly he begins to pour the liquid over my naked body. It is oil—hot oil. He decants the contents of the beaker in a stream that runs in a straight vertical line from my throat to my belly button and further down to the delicate sprigs of pubic hair above my sex. The oil is thick and warm, spreading slowly like treacle across my body.

He takes the empty cup over to the kitchenette and clunks it down. Then he returns to my side. The sleeves of his cloak have generous proportions, lightly billowing as he lifts his hands to push his palms together in a prayer-like position that is at once sinister and ominous. Then he lowers his head, the dark hood of his cape casting a shadow across his face. He murmurs something, some incantation or verse. Impossible to make out the words, but again, they sound Urdic in origin. Finally, the murmuring subsides. He presses the tips of his fingers to his lips and then lowers them, ever so slowly and gently, to my stomach.

What happens next kind of starts like a massage. Charles presses his fingers to my skin and smooths the oil over my body, smearing the syrup in delicate, ever-increasing arcs over my breasts, deep into the contours of my ribs, sliding over my body with incredible detail, ensuring every part of it is covered in oil. The experience is not altogether unpleasant. As much as I hate to admit it, the truth is that the sensation of Charles's hands rubbing my body, exerting pressure on tender muscles, and stroking my limbs with energising movements is invigorating. If the circumstances were different, that is. Guiltily I allow myself to relax beneath his touch, telling myself that as a highly trained and skilled shaman, naturally, Charles would be capable of inciting or unleashing the spectacular swell of adrenaline-infused energy now coursing through my veins.

The muscles running up and down the sides of my spine spasm, pushing my back into as much of an arch as the chains allow. As the oil penetrates deeper into my skin, it unleashes a pulsating fiery force that works through my muscles to ignite a ball of heat deep within my inner core.

Lightness enters my being, a ferocious oneness with the universe that is overpowering in its illumination. In one psychedelic moment, I am at one with the past, present and future, in contact with everything I have ever experienced within my twenty-first century lifetime and in every incarnation before this. Laughter shudders through me, a cackling craziness followed by an eruption of uncontrollable screams.

I gasp as the fit wracks my body with convulsions, engulfing me in a wave of emotions as changeable as the seasons. Charles must have put something into the oil that is causing this disorientating disruption to the usual functioning of my nervous system. Already physically naked, I now feel spiritually unmasked, too, my body acting as a host to various spectres that enter me through the open pores of my skin and take over my being, unreasonable poltergeists demanding an outlet for their pains. Helplessly I look for Charles, hoping he might release me from the maniacal clutches of the wanton spirits pushing my body this way and that on the bed. I am now thankful for the chains that hold me fast, restricting the ability of the ghosts to control me physically.

Perhaps sensing my helplessness, Charles lowers me back onto the bed, releasing me from his clutches. Panic surges through me. Even though it is his fault that I am here, even though he instigated the crazy ritual I have just been subjected to, I feel reluctant for him to let go of me. I need him. I am, after all, entirely at his mercy.

"Well done," Charles says. It's the first time he's said anything nice to me since abducting me. I'm not sure precisely what he congratulates me on, but I decide to play along all the same.

"Thanks," I say, as though I know exactly what he is talking about. Thankfully my body now feels calm, possibly an after-effect of the metaphysical surges of energy it has just played host to. I let myself relax into the softness of the bed as Charles heads over to the kitchenette again, returning with a bucket of water and a sponge. Silently he washes the oil off my body, delicately stroking my skin clean with the soft loofah. He pushes the sponge into the bucket, rinsing away the oil film before pressing it again to my breasts, removing the oil pooling in the crevice of my cleavage. Then he slides the sponge over my nipples. I stifle a moan. Every inch of my body is incredibly sensitive, still aroused by the spell's effects.

"Feel good?" he asks. I close my eyes to shut him out. I feel the sponge moving over my body as he dabs at the delicate skin beneath my breasts with tiny, precise movements before circling the sponge around their circumference. I don't want to be enjoying this, but every inch of my body feels like one throbbing erogenous zone on the cusp of a torrential orgasm. He lowers the sponge to dab at the folds of my sex, and something unleashes inside of me. Every cell of my cunt feels agonizingly warm and intense. I can't hold back, and a rush of wetness gushes out of me. Charles manoeuvres the sponge to press down on my clit and anus, pushing my wetness back inside, feeding my pussy with its juices.

Sweat saturates me. Hopeless to try to calm down, to return to some semblance of normal. My brain is going crazy trying to process what happened to me. The biggest orgasm of my life but under the worst possible circumstances imaginable. I sneak a peek at Charles, but he is wholly absorbed in the task of sponging down my thighs, moving down my legs, over my knees, to my ankles. He reaches my feet and drops the sponge in the bucket for a moment, wrings it out, and then wipes the oil off each of my toes. Even this cleansing of my feet has an erotic charge to it, and when he presses the loofah against the pressure points on the inner sides of my heels, I experience a spasm of titillating awareness that cascades through my pelvic region. I hold back, biting hard on my bottom lip to distract my attention from the latent heat. Charles takes the bucket and sponge over to the sink, rinses them out, and then returns to my side with a set of keys.

"I'm going to release you from the chains," he says.

"You are?" My voice sounds stupid. Groggy and disorientated.

"When I release you from your cuffs and chains, I want you to try and stay relaxed. Don't be alarmed if your body behaves in a way that is outside your control. This will be the effects of the spell taking its natural course." He inserts the key into the keyhole of a padlock from which four chains emanate, connected with my wrists and ankles. The release of the heavy weight of the chains offers instant relief. He then unlocks my ankle cuffs and removes them, followed by the manacles binding my wrists.

I stretch, flexing my wrists and ankles to promote circulation. Strangely enough, I don't feel sore at all, just exhilarated. It is as though all the cells of my body now vibrate at a different pitch. One that is in harmonious unity with the entire universe. Charles must truly be insane and dangerous. However, apart from his angry eruptions of physical violence, he has exhibited only a warped clinical fascination for me. His obsession seems to be more about the magick he is practising on me than anything personal. I mull over his motivations for wanting me here but lose my train of thought as my body surges upwards to hover horizontally above the bed in blissful elevation. My hair flows out beneath me, the red dress left behind in torn strips of scarlet fabric on the bed.

As I hover in mid-air, Charles removes the torn dress strips from the bed and pulls down the eiderdown. He then signals with his hands, and my body slowly lowers back down. He tucks me in, the coverlet blissfully warm, the mattress soft and yielding.

"Rest now," he says.

The suggestion seems ludicrous, but the truth is I feel completely relaxed and exhausted. As sleep threatens to tide me over into dreamland, I look around and realise I am alone. Sometime during the aftermath of the ritual, Charles has done his usual silent invisibility trick and leaves the room. Alone, I must admit that the experience has been cathartic. It is the last thought to enter my head before I close my eyes and drift off to deep, impenetrable sleep.

Chapter Twenty-three

Black. *Everything is black. I am lost in a shadowy onyx-tinted vastness. A cosmos of sexual energies swirls around my spiritual sanctuary.*

I sit upon a black throne, a dais atop a mountain of black, a mound of black crushed velvet fabric beneath me, endless reams of it. At the platform's base, a snake follows the folds of fabric upwards. It is a slow, sensual journey, punctuated by the gentle, rhythmic, hypnotic pounding of a darbuka. Another snake slithers into view. The two adders intertwine — briefly — before separating and continuing their respective journeys.

They reach a pair of female feet. Naked, pale, beautiful. My feet. The snakes glide over them, orbiting upwards to encircle my ankles. And now, a camera operator would move wider, soft on the black crushed velvet fabric of my dress, visible only from the waist down. The snakes disappear upwards, under the skirt — a hand strokes my knee. The hand belongs to a centaur. He lifts the hem of my dress and dips his head to kiss my ankles, then slowly follows the trail of the snakes. I encounter heaven in the touch of his lips and surrender to his touch, languishing in pleasure.

Other exotic supernatural creatures — angels, demons, hybrids — caress and arouse every part of my body. A Leviathan teasingly sucks my left nipple while a shapeshifter who — with her long, dark hair and luminescent violet eyes — could be mistaken for my twin sister — trails its fingers up and down the length of my torso. Together they morph in and out of visibility, awakening me to the presence seated beside me on the matching dais. I immediately recognise the pallid skin, white hair, and intense blue eyes. Charles.

Recognition startles me awake. I am bathed in sweat, the duvet on the four-poster bed no longer comforting, blinking in the dreary half-light of the cellar where I am a prisoner. My recurring dream—first white, then red, now black—has left me both aroused and confused. Symbolically, of course, the colours of the dreams are significant. Trying to interpret their meaning, however, is difficult. I often use the spiritual sanctuary for meditation, so this is an easy place for my subconscious to embark on its phantasmal journeys. The prevalence of the angels, demons, hybrids and shapeshifters can be taken to mean that the spiritual cosmos is keen to communicate with me and give me pleasure. Decoding the meaning of the snakes is a little more complicated, mainly as the snakes featured in the dreams before I ever met Bo or he became my pet. Thinking of Bo, I feel a stab of longing. I wonder what he is doing in my little house, if he has had to hunt for prey, if he will still be there when I get home. *If* I ever get home. The thought rouses me from my inner ramblings, spurring me to action. I sit up in bed, pulling the sheets around my nakedness. The room temperature is warm, but I'm not too fond of the feeling of vulnerability my nakedness stirs. I knot the sheet above my breasts, then swing my feet over the side of the bed and place them on the floor. A gorgeous and soft Kilim rug covers the cold hardness of the sandstone floor—worth a fortune, most likely. Part of me can't believe Charles has left me alone in this room, unshackled.

I have to act quickly, as I have no idea when he will return. First, I rush to the door and push down on its ornate handle. Of course, the door is locked, its hinges stubbornly clamping the impenetrable heavy wood and metal door shut. I try twisting it, but it's noisy, so I abandon the effort. I don't want to alert Charles that I'm awake. I move over to the kitchenette as stealthily as possible. The view from the bed had only allowed me a fraction of visibility of Charles's private laboratory. The shelves are abundant with dried herbs, pickled insects, and bottled poisons, all neatly labelled with names and dates — for example, *batrachotoxin acquired on 24th September 2014, brodifacoum – powder form – 23rd April 2015*. My memory of high school biology classes and even my Wiccan learnings in no way assist me in deciphering the labels. However, the effervescent liquid contained within a lot of the bottles looks lethal enough for me to discard the thought of trying to use them as weapons against Charles. I wouldn't know the first thing about how to apply them and would probably end up poisoning myself in the process. Even though I am frightened by the contents of Charles's witchcraft facility, I can't help but marvel at the precision with which he has perfectly labelled and positioned everything. Several vials of blood neatly flank each other on the top shelf, their labels far more ominous than the bottles below them. One is labelled *Celeste – 2008*, another *Daphne – 2012*. I'm hoping I haven't stumbled on the secret lair of a serial killer and that I am not his next intended victim. A voice from behind me makes me jump.

"Impressive, isn't it?"

I didn't hear Charles come in. He has that silent stealth thing down pat. Or perhaps he has been in the room all along, watching me, waiting to see what I'll do. Maybe there is a secret panel in the room that I haven't discovered? I don't know which thought is the creepier. I turn and face him guiltily, hoping that the bottles against my back will act as deterrents and that he won't try to attack me.

"Ketzia." He smiles, an expression peculiar in its normality.

"What do you want from me?" My voice sounds far stronger than I feel. He keeps smiling. I am tempted to reach behind me, grab a bottle of arsenic or something, and splash it all over his face. Charles sits down on the edge of the bed, placating me with distance.

"I'm not going to hurt you, Ketzia, so you don't need to think about hurting me," he says.

"What is this place?" Perhaps the best tactic is to play along with his friendly tone.

"This is the place where you will come to know yourself — truly — in a deeper sense than you ever have before."

"What if I don't want to know myself? Like that?"

"You cannot run away from your gifts."

Charles stares at me intently. I avert my gaze, suspicious that he is attempting to hypnotise me. There is definite pulling power there, and it takes all my self-control to keep my eyes firmly focused on a little whorl in the rug, just to the left of Charles's feet. Maybe it would be best to attempt honesty with him? After all, the guy used to be my friend.

"Charles," I begin. "I'm scared. What you're doing here is scaring me."

"No need to be frightened," he says. "I'm not going to hurt you."

"Then why . . ." Nothing makes sense. My brain feels hungover, sluggish and unable to keep up with the danger of the situation, probably because it's taking all my concentration to stay focused on the knot in the carpet. Whatever Charles is doing with his eyes is undeniably powerful. It takes all my strength not to give in to the potency of his gaze.

"Look at me," he says. I shake my head. No way.

"Look at me," he repeats, and his words draw me in, the syrupy softness of his tone lulling me over the precipice, and I can no longer resist his power. I look at him — and gasp. He is still seated on the bed, but all around him swirls a menagerie of mystical beasts. A tremendous winged eagle rises behind him, spreading its wings in a magnificent show of shiny black plumage. Its sharp yellow eyes scrutinise me as though deciding whether I am edible prey. It feels like it is weighing up the very matter of my soul in the process. Behind the eagle—floating in and out of smoky transparency—are angels, demons, and hybrids. A jolt courses through me as I recognise them as the creatures from my dreams. To Charles's left, a centaur balances a bow and arrow in its muscled arms. I am immobile as I take it all in—frozen to the spot. The centaur raises the arrow and positions it against the string of the bow, aiming the arrow straight at my heart.

"No!" I manage, just before the centaur releases his grip and fires, the arrow shooting straight at my heart. I duck, just in time. It passes over my head with a fine whistle before disintegrating in a burst of combustible light. Cautiously, I gaze to see the centaur readying another arrow for flight.

"Charles," I implore, "make it stop." But Charles just smiles at me, the benign contortion of his mouth hiding the menace of everything he represents to me.

"Don't be afraid," he says as the centaur launches another missile which I sidestep by a hairsbreadth of a second.

"Embrace your destiny," he continues, his voice infuriatingly soft and calm. Anger courses through me—I have no intention of embracing any destiny designed by Charles.

"Destiny cannot be forced," I shout. My anger finally gets through to him, and he places a hand over the centaur's grip, just in time to prevent another arrow from being fired in my direction.

"It's true," he replies, still maddeningly calm. "Destiny cannot be forced. Nor can it be denied." He releases his grip on the centaur's hand. And I have no chance of escaping the arrow this time. It hurtles towards me at speed, striking my body below my collarbone, piercing the skin beneath which rests my heart. Its impact is immediate and phenomenal. A giddying, universal understanding overwhelms me. I stagger backward, slowly descending onto the floor, feeling my entire reality shifting as I do so.

Memories of past and future lives merge with experiences of this one. I am a witch being burned at the stake. I am a high school student flunking a maths exam. I am an advisor to the royal court in the 15th century. I am an antelope, running through the forest, narrowly escaping the hunter's bullet. I am a twenty-first-century real-estate agent who dabbles in witchcraft for a hobby with no idea of how dangerous this pursuit is. I am all of these things. And none of them. Everything I have ever come to believe about the world and my place within it is turned upside down. I was called to practise witchcraft and embraced the Wiccan traditions when all along, the dark arts were my true calling.

From my crumpled position on the floor, I see that all the ephemeral beings and entities have disappeared. It is now just me and Charles in a dark cellar. Alone together. Maybe I've just been tripping out all along and the mythical creatures were something I imagined? After all, who knows what he's been putting in those tincture cocktails?

"Now do you understand?" he asks. Comprehension slowly dawns on me. There is logic here. Everything in my life has brought me to this point. Now.

"Come." He pats a space on the bed beside him. "Sit with me."

The kindness in his voice prompts unheeded tears to well in my eyes. As I edge my way toward him, they spill over. By the time I reach his side, I am crying uncontrollably.

"It's okay, angel, it's okay." He says this so tenderly that I momentarily forget his violence. I forget all my misgivings about him and his obscure motivations. I allow myself to be comforted by his arms wrapping around me.

"It's time to embrace the mystery, Ketzia," he murmurs.

I swallow, thinking I am somehow still under his spell but enjoying the safety his arms seem to offer.

We sit there on the bed for a while, Charles hugging me while quietly murmuring about my greater purpose. When my tears finally stop flowing, he strokes my hair and places a hand under my chin, tilting my face to meet the mesmerising cast of his eyes.

"I need you to do something for me," he says. His blue eyes are a startling crystalline. I feel an overwhelming sense of blessedness and gratitude to this High Priest for being chosen to partake in his act of magick.

"Anything," I finally agree. "Anything." Thousands of other unheard voices from millennia of forgotten spirits join with mine.

CHAPTER TWENTY-FOUR

Days pass. They are filled with anxiety for Bo as he waits in futile hope for his new owner to return home. Many people don't realise that snakes have a sharply tuned homing instinct, easily as keen as that of a dog or homing pigeon. This reflex finally motivates Bo to push his diamond-shaped head against the cat-flap and ease his way outside. He journeys up the tree trunk before dropping in a coil onto the top of the paling fence, tumbling down to the street on the other side. He travels soundlessly along the gutters—apart from the occasional rustling when his body encounters a bunch of dead autumn leaves or some other obstacle. In this way, he inches forward, metre by metre, unseen and unnoticed, lying still at times to avoid detection in the busier parts of town.

It takes him almost two days of backtracking before he finally finds his way back to the Wiccan headquarters in Castanna Street. It is nighttime. The front doors are closed, but not averse to trespassing, Bo slides his way up the wooden panelling and squeezes his way through the letterbox.

Aboard flight 174 from Jakarta to London, Leon flicks through the in-flight movies aimlessly, an un-eaten dinner tray beside him. Usually, he would be using this time to get on top of the endless emails constantly bombarding his inbox, devising strategic plans for the business, and reading through the reams of contracts he must sign off on. On this flight, however, his heart isn't in it. Instead, he's clicking on the trailer for Maleficent, starring Angelina Jolie. Halfway through, he realises his chief motivation in selecting the film is that the lead actress reminds him of Ketzia. *Wow.*

He'd tried fruitlessly to get in touch with her again before leaving Jakarta. She hadn't replied to his calls, texts or emails. Leon wonders if their last conversation upset her. Admittedly he had avoided any talk of commitment or emotional involvement. It wasn't something he felt comfortable with. But now, here he is, missing her. Watching a Disney film for the mere reason that it makes him feel closer to her. Sad.

Hopefully, the rest of his business in London and New York won't take too long, and he can return to Australia soon. See her in person. Meanwhile, he can't quite let go of the nagging sensation that perhaps the real reason she isn't responding to his calls is that something has happened to her. Leon decides that the first thing he'll do when he gets to London is call the Sydney office. Catch her at work and placate his fears that way. Meanwhile, there is Angelina Jolie to take his mind off things and a flight hostess with a glass of brandy headed his way.

Mia is late-night shopping after work. Already she's bought several pairs of new kitten heels, a figure-enhancing taupe skirt for work, and a polka-dot dress just for the hell of it. She pauses to admire the window display of a sky-blue midi dress with a contrasting collar and cuffs that would look simply perfect on Ketzia. She reaches for her phone and takes a snapshot of it, looking forward to showing it to Ketzia in the office tomorrow. That is if Ketzia shows up. Her heart drops at the thought. The truth is, Mia misses her friend terribly, and she can't understand why Ketzia has not been in touch with anyone. Even Ron had started to ask after her. Ketzia hadn't shown up for work since she stood Mia up for lunch. Mia isn't one to hold a grudge. She is well over that by now. It all seems a bit mysterious. If Ketzia had run off with Leon, why hadn't she called first?

Mia's stomach rumbles. Loudly. At first, she thinks it's because she's concerned about Ketzia, but then she remembers she hasn't had dinner yet. She spots a sushi restaurant and heads inside. While waiting for her order of sashimi and rice, she texts the photo of the midi dress to Ketzia with a cheerful message. She is hoping that it will entice her back from wherever she is.

In the solitude of the library, Meredith has an ancient grimoire open on the table in front of her. Besides it, her laptop is open on a webpage dedicated to *cyber witchcraft*. She studies the ancient tome and the website carefully, dutifully taking notes for a seminar she will soon be running on how to make Wicca accessible in the digital age. She barely registers the already ajar door slowly creaking further open, assuming Velveteen Slips is bringing her a cup of tea and some delicious chocolate-coated figs. But when she looks up, there's no one there. She glances downwards to discover a snake slithering towards her on the floor. And then all hell breaks loose in the Wiccan headquarters.

CHAPTER TWENTY-FIVE

I don't remember falling asleep or losing consciousness or whatever state I now foggily emerge from. I vaguely remember kissing Charles on the bed before eating a bowl of soup and then? A blank. Maybe the soup was laced with sedatives? Either that or the after-effects of all that magic just wiped me out. Anything is possible in this place.

I start to get out of bed only to realise that Charles has chained me up again, the cuffs heavy on my wrists. I am still naked, but the room's warmth had made me unaware of this until now. Charles has tightened the chains so I can't budge more than an inch. The cold knot of fear returns as I wonder what the hell he has in store for me. Last night I could quite possibly have escaped. He'd untied my shackles, after all. But then I'd stupidly let myself become entrapped by his mystical powers, seduced by them, if I was to be honest with myself. The powerful esoteric encounters I've had in Charles's presence have far defied the boundaries of any magical experience I've ever had. Black magic is like that. This is why it is so dangerous and potent. It corrupts your inner core, bypasses your values, to take you to a place of almighty omnipotence. But now, here I am, shackled naked to a bed in Charles's private dungeon. I curse my weakness in not escaping when I had the chance. And make a determined vow not to let that happen again.

I try to think of a spell for strength. Inner armour is what's needed. I visualise white copper plates solidly protecting my breastbone. White steel supports grow from the plates, reaching up to form a halo of white light above the crown of my head. I am just about to conjure a swirling vortex of reflective energy for myself when I feel something damp pressing against my stomach. Charles has done his silent movement thing again. He stands beside me, dabbing at my body with a wet sponge. Immediately I recoil, but the shackles around my wrists prevent me from moving.

"Charles?" He doesn't stop what he is doing. He is concentrating so hard that I wonder if he even heard me. On the bed beside him lies an old-fashioned tan leather doctor's satchel. It has fallen on its side, and various implements and surgical tools spill out.

"Charles," I plead, unable to mask my rising panic. Charles nods his head. Smiles.

"Don't worry, Ketzia, this won't hurt a bit," he says, reaching his hand into the satchel. He pulls out a jar of oil, opens it, and lubricates his finger.

"Charles. *Charles!*" I screech, terrified beyond belief. In vain, I pull my hands against the metal of the cuffs, thrashing my body around as much as the constraints allow. It's useless. I am trapped. Charles barely registers my struggle, touching his fingers to my body.

"Charles, what are you doing?" I figure reasoning with him must be worth a shot. But he ignores me, tracing his finger in a circular motion around my navel. He dips his fingers back into the jar again, smiling to himself.

"This is a special oil, Ketzia. One I have created myself— especially for you." He speaks with the clipped professionalism of a surgeon, his detachment only enhancing my panic. He smooths the oil down my torso.

"This oil is designed to awaken and stimulate all your nerve endings and the magnetic pathways that flow from them."

Little explosions of pleasure start to spark from inside my body, as though the oil has penetrated my skin to my core. Mentally I focus on my inner armour, trying to resist surrendering to the undeniably good sensations flowing through me. I look down at my body, noticing the taut points of hardened redness of my tits. It is as though he has sparked a white-hot fire of arousal that courses through my entire body. No, not white-hot—my rational mind corrects. Black. For Charles's potency lies only in darkness. I remind myself that I want no part of it, desperately suppressing the urge to arch my back and surrender to the electrifying arousal of my body.

He dips his fingers back into the jar of lubricant again, returning them to my body and smearing the oil over the sensitive skin of my breasts. What the hell does Charles want with me? Horrible thoughts flow through my mind, renewing my determination to fight him every step of the way. Trying to break free from the cuffs on my wrists or the stirrups my feet are firmly locked into would be useless. Outsmarting him is still probably my best option.

I'm going to attempt to hypnotise him—in much the same way that he hypnotised me earlier. I feel strong, perhaps a result of my earlier meditation session.

"Charles," I command. "Look at me."

"I am looking at you," Charles replies. But not at my face. It's not so much that he is avoiding looking into my eyes. Just that he is completely engrossed with my body, which starts trembling, so intense is my trepidation at what will happen next.

"Charles." The last vestiges of my strength push my voice into animal territory. My cry sounds like the call of a wildebeest. It seems to do the trick, for he finally moves his attention to my face.

"Ketzia." His voice has an infuriating and chillingly reasonable quality about it. "Ketzia, you will come to thank me for what I am doing."

"If that's the case" — I try to keep the tremor out of my voice — "why not release me from these chains and do whatever it is that you need to do with my permission?"

"It can't be done that way."

"Why not?"

"Tsk. Because you'd never let me. I've tried in the past, and you didn't respond to my advances . . ."

"What advances? What are you talking about?"

"The flowers, for instance."

"What flowers?"

"The roses I had delivered to your office."

"Those roses were from *you*?"

Even in my dire situation, part of me feels more upset that Leon didn't send those flowers than that they came from Charles. I'd even thanked Leon for them. Hadn't I? I'm pretty sure I did, but what does any of that matter now that I'm Charles's prisoner and — I suspect — about to become his victim, too.

He goes over to the kitchenette. From the bed, I have a clear view of him setting up a Bunsen burner on the bench, attaching its rubber hose to a tap on the wall that must supply gas. Charles lowers a lever — the tap — then strikes a match. Instantly a flame spurts from the spout of the Bunsen burner. A blue-green scientific laboratory flame, not a warm cosy amber to warm your cockles by. He carefully balances a steel tripod over the flame, resting a mat on its woven mesh surface. Onto the mat, he places a beaker containing a reddish liquid. As the liquid heats up, it releases a delicious aroma of cinnamon, cloves, tea, vanilla, and lavender. The concoction starts to bubble, and Charles fiddles with the dial, lowering the force of the flame. Moving with agility and speed, he reaches up to the shelf above the bench and deftly starts adding things to the mixture — sprinklings of what must be herbs or extracted elements. He uncorks an old bottle, pouring a small amount of its contents into the beaker. The substance in the beaker clouds over, darkening to a black, lethal-looking liquid. Charles swizzles it with a small metal rod before turning off the gas supply, killing the flame instantly. Soundlessly he moves back to the bed again, stares intently at me, and smiles.

"I have made something special for you," he says, his voice slightly husky and . . . emotional? He is tough to read, but gaining an insight into his emotional state and hopefully being able to manipulate him is pretty much the only hope of freedom I've got.

"What is it?" I hope that the fear trembling my voice will pass muster as excitement. I have to make him believe that I'm on his side. It must work, for Charles laughs.

"Oh, Ketzia!" he exclaims. "You're like a child at Christmas, so eager to unwrap your present."

He chuckles again, and I nod my head vigorously. This seems like the first time I've managed to build a genuine rapport with him. Then he becomes more serious.

"But this gift is a special kind of gift. There is no . . . how shall I put it? There is no instant gratification. In fact, when you first receive this gift, there may be an element of pain involved." His words send a spasm of terror through my body, contracting every single one of my muscles into hard knots of steel.

Thankfully, Charles seems oblivious to my adverse physical reaction to his news. His eyes have a zealous glint as he heads back to the kitchenette, stirring the beaker's contents again with the swizzle stick. He presses his fingertips to the side of the beaker, testing the temperature. The black liquid must still be too hot for whatever purposes he wants to use it, for he silently moves back to my bedside without the beaker.

This will probably be my only chance to appeal to his gentler nature. He seems in such a good mood, so I force myself to smile at him.

"Charles," I coax. "I'm really looking forward to your present. But I want to be able to enjoy it properly . . . without these constraints." I shake my hands, indicating the cuffs binding my wrists.

"Oh?" He looks genuinely surprised. "Do they hurt?"

"Yes. They really hurt. And I don't need them. I promise I won't run away."

He leans forward, his hands reaching for my wrists. He's going to unclasp the cuffs. I inhale, ready to punch him as soon as I'm free. But he just tenderly strokes the skin on my wrists, planting a chaste kiss on my forehead.

"I can't let you go—yet. Trust me. You'll be thankful for the shackles. They will help keep you in place if your lesser self feels the need to struggle against the power of the dark magic we will be invoking." He smiles fondly as he says this, as though we are about to embark on a grand adventure together. I wrack my brain for some way to get through his fervent veneer, to reach that part of him that is real and sane.

"I thought you were only into good magic?" I'm careful to keep my voice low and controlled. Charles smiles wistfully. It appears I have finally gotten through to him. Then he turns away from the bed, pads silently over to the kitchenette, and tests the temperature of the beaker again.

"I think we're ready now," he says, still smiling. Reverently he carries the beaker to my side. Before I can protest, he pours the dark contents of the beaker all over my body.

At first, I don't feel anything—apart from the horror and shock I am starting to associate permanently with Charles. The liquid makes a swishing sound as it enters the recess of my navel, dripping into the cavity like hot wax. Charles watches me affectionately.

"I'll leave the magic to do its work," he says. I'm too frightened to protest. I am too flummoxed by everything that has gone on even to attempt to influence him anymore. Silently he leaves the room, and I am left to absorb the dark juices entering my body through my skin.

CHAPTER TWENTY-SIX

Meredith's screams reverberate through the Wiccan headquarters, her soprano shrieks alerting every Wiccan in the building to her distress. Velveteen Slips is the first to arrive at the open library door, a dough-coated whisk momentarily forgotten in her hand, dripping chocolate batter onto the carpet.

"Don't move," Meredith says, pointing at the snake, which has curled itself into a compact pile on the floor. Velveteen nods her head silently.

What is it and *what's going on* can be heard from several other Wiccans gathered in the corridor behind her. Velveteen turns around.

"It's a snake," she whispers.

"Perhaps — can I take a look?" Jacinta asks. She is a young woman dressed entirely in tweed. Her Wiccan speciality is animal telepathy. Velveteen steps aside to allow her to enter the room. Jacinta takes one look at the snake and then turns to Velveteen.

"Does anyone have a shawl or a jumper I can borrow?" she asks.

There is fumbling in the corridor as someone finds a shawl and passes it into the room. Jacinta crouches down, making a quiet clucking sound with her mouth. She doesn't look at the snake directly but mesmerises it with a series of rocking movements, gently swishing her hands on the floor. Soon, the snake and Jacinta move their necks in tandem, performing a strange, choreographed, snake-charming dance. Meredith watches from the far side of the library, petrified. Finally, Jacinta wraps the placid snake in the shawl.

"There," she says, holding the bundle close to her chest and patting it softly. "Nothing to be afraid of."

"Phew," Meredith says, sinking onto an armchair. Safe now, the other Wiccans enter the library from their congregation point in the corridor outside, a cacophony of questions heralding their arrival.

"How on earth did a snake get in here?"

"Meredith, are you all right?"

"Where did it come from?"

Jacinta signals for them to keep their voices down. A hush descends on the room. Finally, Meredith speaks. "Thank you," she says quietly, acknowledging Jacinta with a rueful smile. "How the snake came to be here is as much a mystery to me as to any of us. Do you have any ideas, Jacinta?"

Momentarily Jacinta closes her eyes as though hoping for telepathic communion with the reptile. Then she opens them again and shakes her head.

"Sorry, no idea."

"Maybe," Velveteen suggests, "maybe it's one of Countess Gretha's snakes?"

The possibility causes a murmur to ripple through the witches. Countess Gretha was renowned for using snakes in witchcraft, and she had been here recently, after all. Not all of those present had participated in the Orgiastic Love ritual — or even knew about it. Or that Countess Gretha had convened it. So Meredith is careful with her answer.

"If it's one of Countess Gretha's, why would it come here?" As she asks the question, she remembers Gretha giving Ketzia one of her snakes to keep on the night of the ritual. Perhaps this is Ketzia's snake?

"I think it's best if we find somewhere safe to put it while we work out what to do. Jacinta? What would you recommend?"

"Do we have a glass tank anywhere? And some wood shavings or bark for the floor?" Her words instigate a flurry of activity as the Wiccans try to find the items necessary to make a lovely temporary home for the asp.

"Meanwhile," Meredith continues, "I might just try and give Countess Gretha a call. See if she has any ideas about what to do with it . . ."

Picking up the library phone, Meredith dials Gretha's number, hoping the countess can shed some light on the matter. And, going by the dark precognitive intuition that has niggled her ever since the appearance of the snake, light was what would be needed.

Bright, magical, light.

In the Sydney KX Realty office, Mia does her best to ignore the insistent ringing of the phone on Ketzia's desk. She stares intently at a spreadsheet on her computer showing her sales figures for the last few weeks. A smile passes across her lips as she realizes she has already exceeded her monthly sales target. Maybe Ketzia's not the only one capable of success, she thinks. Part of her is still sore about Ketzia forgetting about her as soon as she started fucking Leon. She feels like her friend has dumped her.

Ring. Ring.

The sound of the phone on Ketzia's desk is getting quite antagonizing. Mia considers simply taking the receiver off the hook. But what if it was a potential sale? Mia doesn't want to miss that opportunity.

"KX Realty, this is Mia," she says in her most professional voice. She looks sensational, wearing the new figure-enhancing taupe skirt she bought last night, teemed with a crinoline blouse.

"Uh. Yes. I was actually after Ketzia—Ketzia Knowles." The gravelly voice at the other end of the line sounds vaguely familiar to Mia, but she can't quite place it.

"I'm afraid she's not here right now. Is there anything I can help you with?"

"Do you know when she'll be back?"

"I'm sorry, I don't know. But I'm sure I can help you. Is there a particular property you are interested in?"

There is a moment of silence. Then a sigh.

"Listen. It's err . . . it's Leon Furness here."

Of course! That was how Mia recognised the voice. Her hand grips the phone more tightly.

"Good morning, Mr Furness," she says quickly, hoping she doesn't sound too gushy.

"Mia," he replies, clearly remembering her name from her phone greeting. Leon's voice sounds like butter in her ear. No wonder Ketzia's been so besotted by him.

"Mia," he repeats as though collecting his thoughts. "I haven't been able to get hold of Ketzia for quite a few days now . . ."

"Really?" Mia blurts out. "I thought she was with you!"

"What do you mean?" Leon's voice has turned serious. Mia hopes she's not getting Ketzia into trouble but can't see any way to backpedal now.

"She hasn't been into the office since Tuesday . . ."

"The day I left." Leon finishes the sentence for her. "I'm actually calling from Heathrow airport. In transit back to Australia. I haven't been able to get a hold of her for days."

"So, where is she?" They both ask the question at the same time, startling each other into a moment's silence.

"I think it's time to find out," Leon finally breaks the silence. She can hear his voice tremble.

Meredith had spent several hours the night before trying to get hold of Countess Gretha. Innumerable messages later, she had finally collapsed in an exhausted heap on the couch in the library, only to awaken again with the daylight hours seeping in through the open corridor door this morning, the phone clanging away insistently beside her. Countess Gretha. She was finally returning her call.

Fifteen minutes later, Meredith sets the phone down, her mouth set in a determined line. Gretha had been able to account for all her snakes, so the slithery invader of the Wiccan headquarters did not belong to her — unless it was the snake she had given to Ketzia the night of the Orgiastic Ritual. Gretha had told Meredith that Ketzia's snake bore a distinct marking on its belly of a mandala-like swirl. It would be easy to identify it by flicking it onto its back. If, that is, one didn't have an intense fear of snakes.

Meredith sticks her head out of the library, scanning the activity in the corridor outside. Morning meditation was just about to commence in the meditation room.

Accosting one of the Wiccans in the corridor, Meredith asks, "Is Jacinta there?"

"No. Sorry, Meredith. Jacinta's at work this morning," a junior Wiccan replies.

"Oh. Anyone else with an interest in snakes present?" Meredith asks, a worried frown mark creasing her brow.

"I'll ask," the junior says, entering the meditation room. She emerges a short moment later, shaking her head.

"No one expressed an interest in snakes. Meditation's just about to begin, and Angelina is instructing us today, so . . ." she trails off. Angelina is renowned for being a stickler for time and taking her classes extremely seriously. So Meredith understands when the door is closed, and she is left with the snake problem still firmly in her court.

Taking a deep breath, she heads back up the corridor to the kitchen, where the snake had been placed in a tank the evening before. The kitchen is deserted, except for the reptile, snuggled cosily on a bed of rice and cushions—the impromptu bed Velveteen had made for it. Meredith treads quietly up to the tank, willing herself to overcome her fear in order to inspect it closely. It's curled in a tight swirl, and it is impossible to see its belly. And there is no way Meredith is prepared to open the tank and flip it over. She decides to give Ketzia a call instead. Ask her if her snake has disappeared.

Relieved by this solution, Meredith heads to her office, where she locates Ketzia's file. All members of their Wiccan chapter must complete a personal details form upon joining, even casual attendees of the workshops the centre runs throughout the year. Ketzia's file is easy to locate, and Meredith dutifully dials the mobile number. Unfortunately, the phone goes straight through to voicemail, with a pre-recorded message stating that as the message box is full, she'll have to *please try again later.* She sighs. This snake problem just isn't going to go away in a hurry. Aside from this, she's been experiencing a lot of tingling along her spine—a distinct indicator of referred telepathic messaging. It's pretty distracting, especially with the snake in its glass incubator in the kitchen, lying quietly as though waiting for action on her behalf.

Summoning all her courage, calling upon all her spirit guides for help, she treks back to the kitchen, determined to get a look at the snake's belly. Meredith breathes a sigh of relief. The snake has uncoiled itself and is stretched out, its head reaching upwards to butt the tank's roof, the white scales of its belly exposed, pushing against the side of the glass—a white belly bearing the distinct marking of a mandala.

"Ron?" Mia knocks on the open door of her manager's office, unsure exactly how she will run through this with him. Ron tears his attention away from his computer screen.

"Look at this, Mia!" he exclaims, swivelling the screen for her benefit.

Mia throws a cursory glance at the screen, the latest real-estate stats splayed in a grid across the monitor. The Sydney KX Realty office seriously trumps all the other offices in sales for the month. She meets Ron's grin with a reciprocal smile of her own.

"That's great, Ron," she says, biting her lip. "But I need to talk to you about something else."

"Oh?" Ron sounds taken aback by her worried voice.

"It's about Ketzia. Do you know where she is?" Mia figures the best approach will be to cut to the chase with this. After getting off the phone to a distraught Leon Furness, she'd taken a moment to realise that the last time she had spoken to Ketzia had been last Tuesday. After that, it was as though Ketzia had disappeared into thin air.

"Ketzia?" Ron replies uncertainly. "She's . . . oh, well, she's . . . Right now?"

"Ron, Ketzia hasn't been in the office since last Tuesday. I've tried calling her, messaging her, but I haven't been able to get in touch with her at all."

"Okay. Well. I assume she's just . . ." Ron trails off. Presumably, he knows about Ketzia and Leon and is reluctant to admit his assumption that the pair have disappeared somewhere together. So Mia will just have to do it for him.

"Initially, I thought Ketzia was with Leon — Leon Furness," Mia says. Ron blinks, saying nothing. Obviously not keen to admit knowledge of the pair's liaison. Mia continues, "But I just got off the phone with Leon Furness, and he doesn't know where she is, either."

"You did?" Ron can't hide his disbelief that the head honcho of their company had been speaking to Mia. Kind of humiliating, but concern for her friend overrides this, and Mia continues.

"He's asked me to make sure she's all right. So I thought, with your okay, I'd drop by her house. See if she's there."

"Oh? Oh. Sure. Of course, you can." Ron finally seems to understand the possible seriousness of the situation. He stands up, pulling on his blazer.

"Better yet, I'll come with you."

"You will?" Mia replies. This wasn't what she'd been expecting.

"Yep. That's what a good boss would do, isn't it? Do you know where she lives?"

"Yes, I do."

"Great. We'll go together, then. Let's take my car."

Five minutes later, they are pulling out of the car park in Ron's late-model Honda Accord, Mia hoping her friend is okay and that she hasn't done the wrong thing by her in instigating this impromptu search party.

A couple of hours have passed since Meredith identified the snake as belonging to Ketzia. Since then, she's tried to reach Ketzia on the phone innumerable times with no luck. Meanwhile, her sixth sense has been functioning in overdrive, pulsing intensely through her whole body — something it always does when there's danger. Her intuition tells her the alerts have something to do with Ketzia and the mystery behind the snake's appearance at the Wiccan HQ.

Meredith heads to the kitchen, hoping for a cup of dandelion coffee to help soothe her jangling nerves. As soon as she enters the brightly lit room, her ears are bombarded with Beethoven's Symphony no five blasting from the radio, while her nostrils are met with the sweet scent of freshly baked muffins. Velveteen grins proudly at Meredith as she bangs a tray of the lovelies down on the stainless-steel counter running the room length. Each muffin has risen to perfection, little mounds of luscious deliciousness.

"I've been hoping you'd show up," Velveteen says to Meredith.

"Oh really?" Meredith replies, her nerves still unseasonably unsettled.

"I need to know, what are we going to do with *him*?" With a jerk of the head, Velveteen indicates Bo, staring at them intently from behind the glass panel of the tank. Velveteen launches into a tirade of injustice, piping vanilla custard cream onto a slab of mille-feuille pastry.

"This is actually classified as a commercial kitchen. Lucky for me, no health inspectors have popped in while I've been accommodating this little unhygienic pet. He can't stay here any longer. You know that, Meredith?"

"I'm sorry," Meredith says, her eyes welling with tears. Usually, dealing with one of Velveteen's little outbursts doesn't bother her, but today her lousy night's sleep, coupled with the ominous premonitions she's been trying to ignore, has left her completely depleted and unable to deal with any conflict. The tears stream down Meredith's cheeks. Velveteen immediately drops the piping bag onto the counter.

"I'm sorry, I didn't mean to upset you," she apologises, wrapping Meredith in a hug.

"No," Meredith replies through her tears. "You're right. He shouldn't be here. And I'm sorry for dumping him on you. It's just that I didn't know what to do with him . . . and I'm shit-scared of snakes."

There. She's said it. A sob is released from her body with the relief of it. Velveteen holds her tighter.

"What, you think your Wiccan credentials are compromised because you're afraid of snakes?" Velveteen asks, unable to suppress a giggle. Meredith shrugs her shoulders, managing a faint smile through her tears.

"If that were the case," Velveteen continues, "wouldn't that mean that anyone in this building without warts on their nose and a broomstick for a car also wouldn't measure up?"

This last comment extracts a chuckle from Meredith, who plonks herself down on a kitchen stool with exhaustion.

"Okay, okay. I've probably been a little sensitive about my phobia," she concedes. "But it's been a stressful night. First the snake and then this terrible feeling I just can't shake."

"Really?" Velveteen pops the muffins out of their tray onto a platter, sliding the still-warm treats towards Meredith.

"Help yourself. I over-catered."

Absently Meredith picks one up, the gnawing in her stomach alerting her to how hungry she is. Sinking her teeth into the crisp gooeyness of the chocolate muffin, she finally feels herself start to relax.

"These are really good," she compliments Velveteen.

"Of course they are. I made them." Never one for modesty, at least not where her cooking is concerned, Velveteen busies herself pouring cups of dandelion coffee for them both.

"I'm pretty certain the snake belongs to Ketzia," Meredith says, getting back to business. "I've been calling her all morning but haven't been able to get in touch with her. To be honest, I have an awful feeling about the whole thing."

Velveteen knows Meredith well enough to realise that if she's having a bad feeling about something, it's worth taking it seriously.

"So, what do you want to do?" she asks.

"I think maybe we should go to her house. Take the snake with us. Hopefully, Ketzia will be there . . . Otherwise . . ."

"Otherwise?" Velveteen asks, prompting a sigh from Meredith.

"I don't know." Meredith drops her head to her hands and then looks up at Velveteen, a pleading expression on her face.

"Will you come with me?"

"Of course," Velveteen replies, giving her friend another hug. "Of course, I will."

CHAPTER TWENTY-SEVEN

Once again, in Charles's basement, time has become inexorably distorted. I have no idea how long I've been lying on the bed, in a hallucinogenic daze. All I know for sure is that it feels like I have been on a long journey, the effect of whatever was in the liquid Charles poured into my body. From the strange vortex of dreams I inhabited, I vividly recall trekking across a hyper-real landscape of mountainous terrain. The rugged territory had been teeming with symbolic wildlife. Eagles were soaring in the sky while spiders and wildebeests fought for my attention at ground level. I have little doubt that the visions I encountered on this pilgrimage all relate to ancestral memory. In my dreams, I was wearing ancestral robes of green woven hessian. And my feet were clad in strange leather sandals that protected me from the jagged edges of the rocks beneath my soles.

Intermittently a searing pain would course through my body, tearing me away from the reality of the pilgrimage to other dreams more sinister in nature. I dreamed of a snake with demonic qualities piercing the fabric of my being with sweet promises of omnipotence. And, of course, this would have been the potion's effects, trying to draw me away from the fertile imaginings of a fulfilling spiritual journey, taking me to a subliminally appealing and sensuously satisfying state of raw toxicity.

Giddiness overwhelms me, and I feel myself fall into the dream state again, choosing to return to the untrammelled hinterland of my subconscious — and history — needing to discover the true purpose of this strange journey.

I drop back into robes of green, my peculiar leather sandals making a crunching sound on the gravel driveway taking shape beneath my feet. All my senses work overtime. I am at a point of realisation. I am about to discover the purpose of my pilgrimage.

A large pair of wrought iron gates at the end of the path blocks further entry. Before I attempt to open them, they swish open automatically. Someone must have been observing my movements via surveillance or something. I spot a security camera mounted at the top of the wooden fence running the perimeter of the seemingly endless property. Cautiously I make my way up the driveway, aware of being watched, until I reach a sandstone mansion of monolithic proportions. There is an olde-worlde rope doorbell, and I tug at it hesitantly, not knowing what kind of beings will be summoned by my arrival. I don't have long to wait before the door is pulled open to reveal two Grecian beauties, a redhead and a blonde. The redhead looks stunning in a one-shouldered sage and gold Marchesa *gown, while the blonde elegantly shows off a gathered gossamer chiffon dress with a heavy band of jewellery encircling her narrow waist. The redhead wears her thick curls tied back in a goddess braid while the blonde allows her golden strands to dance about her face freely with ephemeral lightness.*

"Hi, Ketzia, we've been expecting you," the blonde announces, planting a welcoming kiss on my cheek. I can't believe this gorgeous creature seems so happy to see me, let alone that she already knows my name.

"Come in, come in," the redhead says, gesturing for me to enter.

As I enter the ancient building, its grandiosity bowls me over. Teak wall panelling abuts gold-flocked wallpaper with delicate etchings of gods and goddesses. It's difficult to make out the details of the intricate patterning because everything is lit only by candlelight.

"It's very dark in here." I instantly regret that those words are the first I utter in the presence of these magical creatures. Part of me

wants to impress them, somehow prove that I am worthy of their company. Even though I have no idea who they are. The redhead chuckles – a warm, earthy sound that has a calming effect on me.

"There's no electricity, that's why," she says.

"Oh . . ." I don't quite know what to say next. The redhead takes my hand and leads me up a long corridor.

"I'm Celeste." She smiles.

"Oh . . ." This whole experience is overwhelming, and I am completely lost for words. As though in tune with my feelings, the blonde slides a reassuring arm around my waist.

"I'm Daphne," she says by way of introduction.

"I'm Ketzia." I offer politely.

"Of course," they reply in unison. "We know."

Of course, I think, startled by a shock of reality. These women knew my name as soon as I knocked on the door. These women know my name because they are not real, nor is this house real, nor was the journey to get here, because it is all a dream.

This awareness shatters the delicate threads that bind the somatic state, and I slowly wake up. Not before I realise with a jolt that Celeste and Daphne are the names on the labels of the vials of blood in Charles's laboratory. *Celeste – 2008* and *Daphne – 2012*. Even from the reaches of my dreamtime reveries, I can recognise that this can only be an unbelievably lousy sign.

"Ho, ho, ho. Awake, are we?" Charles's laughter, even when it's genuine, always sounds forced. I open my eyes and force myself to meet his gaze without flinching.

"Yes," I reply, between clenched teeth. "I am awake."

"Did you have sweet dreams, my dear? Sweet dreams?" he asks. His mood is flippant and elevated.

"What do you care?" I am too tired to worry about tactics and strategies. All I want is to lash out at my tormentor in any way I can. He laughs as though he approves of my outburst.

"Got the fire in your belly again, then? That's what happens during this part of the process."

"What are you talking about?" My legs are killing me from being stuck in the same position for so long, my back knotted with the tightness of muscles needing to be stretched. Charles brings me a glass of water before I realise I am thirsty. As I gulp at the refreshing contents, I experience, again, a feeling of gratitude for Charles for pre-empting my needs during this time. Then I shake my head, trying to rid myself of such thoughts. I need to hold on to my rage to escape from him. It is my only source of strength.

A tapping sound interrupts my inner ramblings. Charles repeatedly knocks on the ground with a wooden staff, murmuring yet another Urdic-sounding incantation under his breath. He bangs the rod with alarming force into the ground. The top of it is decorated with a carving of two serpents that wrap around the wooden shaft. Charles moves his hand down. The handle on the staff's top is in the shape of a set of wings, growing from the serpents' backs. He notices me taking in the details and nods approvingly.

"This is a caduceus. You will come to learn, Ketzia, that everything that happens here, everything I use, has significance beyond its immediate purpose."

Inwardly I cringe, hating the sound of his voice, its wet enthusiasm. Oblivious to my dislike, Charles continues, examining the staff fondly while espousing its historical significance.

"The carving of serpents wrapped around a staff is often used in the medical field, decorating pharmaceutical packaging and hospitals and such. You might have seen it from time to time. But it is an ancient symbol, and the emblem has quite a story behind it. The caduceus is the winged version."

Charles lifts it so I can see it more clearly.

"This is actually a staff like the one that was carried by the Olympian god, Hermes. In Greek mythology, Hermes was a messenger between the gods and humans and a guide to the underworld. In one version of Hermes's myth, he was given it by Apollo, the god of healing. In another version, he received it from Zeus, the king of the gods. It was entwined with two white ribbons, which were later replaced by serpents. Hermes used it to separate two fighting snakes, who then coiled around it and remained there in balanced harmony . . ."

Charles reaches into the surgical bag still lying open on the bed. I can't see what he gets from my shackled position, but my nerves tell me it can't be anything good. Hating the sound of my voice, I resort to pleading with him.

"Please, Charles, tell me why you're doing this. Please?"

Charles smiles and places a few drops of some other kind of tincture on my forehead.

"That, my dear, would destroy the element of surprise."

"I don't want any surprises," I retort, my voice petulant and churlish. For a moment, I am frightened that my outburst has angered him. His eyes cloud to brackish darkness.

"Please," I continue, changing the tone of my voice to a more supplicating one. "Tell me, what's in the potion? Is it some sort of drug?" My thoughts and words spiral out of control, but there is nothing I can do to ebb the flow of hysteria fuelling them. But Charles smiles at me in that smarmy way of his.

"Enjoy this. It could be the greatest pleasure you'll ever know."

Then he leaves, exiting the cellar with his familiar ghostlike silence, leaving me alone to digest the horror of his intentions.

CHAPTER TWENTY-EIGHT

At noon, Ron's white Honda V6L pulls into a free parking space a few doors down from Ketzia's terrace house. Mia surprised herself by enjoying the ride in the luxury model vehicle and found Ron to be pleasant to talk to, away from the pressures of the office. Naturally, they'd discussed real estate most of the way, but then they'd moved onto other topics, discovering a shared passion for jazz music — he'd been playing Charlie Parker through the car's advanced multimedia stereo — which had kept their conversation buoyant and light for the duration of the journey. But now that they've arrived at their destination, Mia feels her anxiety about Ketzia returning. Ron parks the car and hops out, quickly moving around to the passenger door to gallantly open it for her. Mia feels a rush of pleasure at his gentlemanly attention but then quickly reminds herself that him opening the door for her is probably from the force of habit, not borne out of any genuine interest in her. After all, he's constantly taking clients to view properties and would undoubtedly open the door for them, too. However, she catches his gaze straying to the contours of her body-hugging skirt as she leaves the comfort of the leather seat and reappraises her deduction.

"Right. Let's find Ketzia then, shall we?" Ron says formally.

"Yes," Mia replies, leading the way. "Her house is this one."

They reach the front gate and stop short. Standing outside Ketzia's front door are two of the most unusual-looking women either has ever seen. One is a tall woman with extremely long, grey hair. She wears an olive-green woollen dress and a pair of Doc Martens on her feet. Her face has a transparent quality, so it is difficult for Mia to get a firm handle on what she looks like. The other woman is short and squat, with tight blonde curls. She wears a frilly white blouse teamed with what appear to be chef's trousers, the fine black-and-white chequered fabric sitting tight against her curves. She holds a large woven basket which she places gently on the ground.

"Try the bell again," the short one says. The tall one leans forward and presses her long, spindly finger to the button — Ketzia's funny honkytonk doorbell echoes from within the house.

"She's not there," the tall one says, turning to the short one, spotting Mia and Ron in the process.

"Oh, hello!" She greets them, squinting.

Ron and Mia both say hi. Then Ron asks, "Are you friends of Ketzia's?"

The two women exchange a brief, undecipherable glance before the short one answers, stretching out her hand in greeting.

"Yes, we are. I'm Velveteen . . ."

"And I'm Meredith."

"Ron . . ."

"And I'm Mia. Ron and I work with Ketzia . . ."

They all shake hands genially, surreptitiously summing each other up.

"Any idea where she is?" Ron asks Meredith and Velveteen hopefully. They shake their heads in unison.

"Hasn't she been at work?" Velveteen asks.

"Not since last week," Mia says.

"We were hoping to find her at home," Ron continues. "Can't get hold of her on the mobile."

"That's why we're here, too," Meredith says, turning back to Ketzia's front door and pressing the buzzer again impatiently. Chancing it, she twists the doorhandle.

"It's open," she announces in surprise. "Ketzia?" she calls out, opening the door.

"I think we should go in," Mia says with mounting concern.

"Yes, do let's," Ron says. "Quite a coincidence all of us showing up at her doorstep at once like this."

"No such thing as coincidence," Velveteen counters, lifting the basket from the ground. The action prompts the snake to poke his head out from under his blanket.

"Eek!" Mia screeches, spotting a snake poking its head out from under the blanket on the basket Velveteen is holding. "There's a snake!"

"Shh," Velveteen hushes. "He belongs to Ketzia. We're bringing him home to her."

"I didn't know Ketzia had a snake," Mia says, flashing Ron an expression of disbelief. Ron places a protective arm around her shoulder as the four of them — plus the snake — enter Ketzia's house.

Upon entering, they first notice that some of the furniture is in disarray. Ron is the first to say anything.

"Looks like there's been a struggle."

"Oh, look," Mia cries, noticing Ketzia's handbag on the kitchen floor, its contents — including her mobile phone — visible inside. Mia reaches down to pick up the phone, but Meredith grabs her arm and pulls her back.

"I don't think we should touch anything," she says. Comprehension slowly dawns on Mia.

"Do you think we should call the police?" she asks.

"I'll check to see if she's upstairs first," Ron volunteers bravely. He tackles the steps two at a time. They hear him stomping around up there, calling out Ketzia's name. He returns downstairs with a dejected look on his face.

"Nothing," he says, pulling his mobile out of his pocket. "I'll call the police."

While Ron is on the phone, giving the cops the address and particulars, Velveteen carefully places the snake's basket on the floor. She inspects the dregs of the half-drunk coffee curiously. Her eyes grow large and luminescent as she examines the contents. Mia observes this silently, creeped out by these strange women. The tall one is sniffing the air like a bloodhound, as though her olfactory sense will enable her to glean some perfumed information about Ketzia's whereabouts.

Mia calls the office and gets the receptionist to pull out Ketzia's emergency contact details. Maybe there is someone else they can get in touch with who would be able to help find her.

As Mia and Ron talk on their phones, Mia notices Meredith taking little, dancelike steps across the room. Her movements become more frenetic until she is swirling in circles across the room.

Finished with their phone calls, Mia and Ron watch, open-mouthed, as Meredith's twirls take on the character of a whirling dervish. Just before her dance topples her over, she freezes beside the couch and stares intently at something on the floor.

"Aha!" Meredith exclaims, picking it up. She holds it up for them all to see—a big brass button bearing an insignia of a five-pointed star.

"Charles," Velveteen proclaims, "I recognise the button from the jacket he usually wears from his corporate work. He's generally wearing it when he pops into the kitchen I work at to pick up various herbs and ointments that I order in for him. But I haven't seen him for a while.

"Meredith, when did you last see Charles?" Velveteen asks breathlessly.

"Not for a while," she finally says. "He's been . . . dabbling." She whispers the last word, intending it for Velveteen's ears only, but Ron and Mia have been listening intently, and it doesn't slip past them.

"Who's this Charles person?" Mia asks.

"And what? Is he experimenting with drugs?" Ron follows her up.

Meredith and Velveteen exchange another look. Mia can see that they aren't willing to share anything more about Charles when Meredith takes the lead and shakes her head.

"We think we might know where she could be—but it's just a hunch," Meredith says.

"You two hang fire and talk to the police," Velveteen instructs as she and Meredith start heading to the door. But Ron stands in their path, blocking their exit.

"I think you should give us your details first," he says officiously.

"Of course," Velveteen replies, giving him a charming smile. She gives him their names and her mobile number, which he keys into his phone. Satisfied, Ron steps aside to allow Meredith and Velveteen an exit.

However, just before they reach the front door, Mia calls out in a panicky voice, "What about the snake?"

The snake had slithered out of the basket and nestled atop a pile of rocks.

"What about it?" Velveteen says, smiling at the snake. "He looks pretty happy there."

"You can't leave him here!" Mia exclaims.

"Why not?"

"He looks perfectly content. And this is, after all, his home," Velveteen says.

With that, Meredith and Velveteen depart, leaving a stricken Mia and Ron behind.

Chapter Twenty-nine

I have astral-travelled my way back to the mansion with Celeste and Daphne. We pick up where we left off earlier. The two paragons of beauty lead me down a candlelit corridor.

"Where are we going?" I ask.
"You'll see," Celeste says with a reassuring smile.
I don't feel nervous or excited, for that matter. More serene, calm — even mellow. Strange that this is the way I feel. Maybe it's to do with the good energy flowing through me from Daphne's arm wrapped protectively around my waist. At the end of the corridor, we arrive at a large wooden door, identical to the door in Charles's basement.

Huh? What? The recognition instantly throws me out of my dream and back to fully-fledged consciousness, back to the nightmare of my current reality, my body chained to the bed. I still have no idea what Charles's spell work is all about, but heat emanates from my inner core, and sweat saturates my body. I can't help it and start crying uncontrollably.

I try to slow my breathing down to bring back the mellow feeling of the dream. Impossible. My body contorts in a spasm as a sharp bolt of energy surges from within me. The chains cut painfully into my body with the action, and I struggle to remain still. A wave of nausea courses through me, replaced by a dull ache in every particle of my being. I fight the urge to move, instead concentrating on my breathing again. And I lull back into that strange dreamworld again.

I am transported back to the dream with Celeste and Daphne, which picks up where it left off.

We stand in front of the large oak door at the end of the candlelit hallway. Celeste places her hand on the handle. She turns the knob, smiling at me, and I am once more filled with deep serenity. She opens the door, and a rush of pure, bright, white light assaults us. It engulfs everything, its sheer intensity blinding. The three of us float into an airborne flight of fancy. Instinctively, we reach for each other's hands as we soar higher and higher across a vast landscape filled with transparent, magical beings. Angels, cupids and colourful spirits float around us as we cross the sky at speed, not pausing in our flight until we arrive at a deep valley at the base of a mountain range.

Our bodies slowly descend until our feet contact the soft mossy grass of the valley floor. I look around us to survey our surroundings. A lush forest meanders upwards to the mountains to the left while a purple lake glistens invitingly in front of us. To our right is a raggedy hut from which music can be heard. Fiddles mingle with heavy bass to create a rich and harmonious sound. The pulsating rhythm threatens to draw me in. However, Celeste and Daphne grip my hands tightly and guide me away from the hut towards the lake. The beats of old folk ballads reverberate off the water as we make our way down to the pebbled shore. Gentle waves cascade onto the beach, the violet radiance of the water inviting us in. I remember with longing the beach on Lantau Island where Leon and I first made love. The thought fills me with ecstasy, my body responding cravingly with a growing awareness of arousal. Celeste's and Daphne's hands feel silky to my touch, and I find myself longing to run my hands over the contours of their magnificent bodies. Celeste turns to me and smiles as though sensing what is going through my mind. We come to the water's edge. Celeste leans in to caress her lips with mine in a tender kiss. Meanwhile, Daphne slowly trails her fingers up my arm and beneath my breasts, touching me with coquettish sweetness. The water laps coaxingly at our feet while the temporal beats of the music continue to flow from the hut, soothing the air with its palpitating rhythms.

We strip, dream-inspired movements of unfolding revelation, clothes landing in a billowing heap on the soft pebbles. Naked, Daphne and Celeste dive into the purple water, and I follow suit, the violet-cusped waves breaking softly against my skin as my body penetrates the lake's surface. Underwater, I discover that I can see clearly and breathe easily, not needing to come up to the surface for air. The floor of the lake abounds with coral and multi-hued seaweed. Schools of rainbow-coloured fish swim around me, beautiful creatures that nudge against my body affectionately.

Ahead of me, I can make out the silvery outlines of my new friends, their skin glittery with the reflective quality of the plum-coloured water. I kick through the water to catch up to them. They reach for my hands, and we course through the water in this fashion, taking in the marine wonders with awe. Finally, they slow down, Daphne and Celeste loosening their grip on my hands, signalling to me that we have reached our destination. We are at the centre of the lake. Together we swim to the water's surface, breaking through its violet stillness with feverish excitement.

"That was amazing." My heart beats excitedly, thrilled by the aquatic life forms I've witnessed below.

"Only as amazing as you," Daphne replies, and feeling heat slowly spreading its way across my face, I know that I'm blushing.

"It's true." Celeste joins in, her hand encircling my waist beneath the water. "Everything that you encountered down there was a product of your own self . . ."

"What?" I can't quite make sense of things. Everything feels upside down. "How so?"

"This lake, the hut, the music — this world — is all yours. None of it could exist without you."

"I don't understand . . ." I trail off, enjoying Daphne's touch as she embraces me beneath the water. Their bodies are pressing against mine with exhilarating closeness.

"This whole world has been created entirely by you," Celeste explains.

"Thank you for letting us partake in it," Daphne adds graciously.

I feel a swell of pride rise with the beauty of the landscape. Then something occurs to me.

"You say everything here is . . . created by me?"

"Everything," they agree in unison.

"Does that include you?" I'm not sure if I even wish to know the answer. The truth is that I want Daphne and Celeste to be real. I need them to be.

My question causes them to exchange a brief, hesitant glance.

"Not quite *. . ." Celeste finally answers. I wish she would clarify further, but her attention is steered away from me by seeing something rising out of the water in the distance. A grey, eel-like creature emerges from the depths of the lake. And it's racing toward us.*

"What is it?" I scream, recognising the disgusting tentacled arm wrapping itself around our bodies as belonging to the sea monster I encountered at the beach in Hong Kong with Leon. But what is it doing here? *The nonsensical imposition is too big an anomaly for my subconscious to come to terms with, and I am pulled, panting with shock, out of the dream again.*

Charles's basement swirls into my field of vision with giddying clarity. The ornate bedposts of the Jacobean suite I am lying on, the perfumed air, the walls themselves — all seem to be laughing mirthlessly at my distress. Part of me is still trying to make sense of the dream, wondering if my current situation somehow has something to do with my feelings for Leon, as though our pairing ignited an underworld force now channelling its way through Charles.

And here he is beside me, a glass of water in his hands, a bendy straw pressed obligingly to my lips. Charles. My tormentor. And my only hope.

CHAPTER THIRTY

Leon's telephone conversation with Mia left him rattled. Unable to shake the nagging sensation that Ketzia needed him, he decided on an uncharacteristically emotional course of action. He is now seated on a plane again after boarding yet another flight from Heathrow to Sydney. His London appointments would just have to wait.

He flicks through yet another in-flight magazine, trying to come to grips with his emotions. Never has he felt this way about a woman before. Sure, he's had his share of beauties in the past, but he's never felt such a deep connection with them as he has experienced with Ketzia. Work had always come first for him, and now here he is, on a plane headed back to Sydney for the sole reason that he is worried about her. She will almost certainly be fine, just taking time off work for personal reasons that she doesn't want to share with her colleagues. Or something. It's the *something* that Leon doesn't like that irks him enough to spur him to this drastic return flight back to Sydney when his overseas business is far from complete.

Meredith grips the edge of her seat as Velveteen's mini-van pulls out of its parking spot outside Ketzia's house. Velveteen is not the smoothest driver in the world, her foot hitting the accelerator erratically as the car lurches into the midday traffic. The pair don't speak for a while as they drive along, the dulcet tones of the satnav giving directions to Charles's house. Velveteen knows Charles's address from a few orders he's arranged to have delivered directly to his house from time to time.

"What are we going to do when we get there?" Meredith finally breaks the silence.

"I don't know. Ask him if he's seen Ketzia, maybe?" Velveteen shrugs.

"What if he's dangerous?" Meredith asks, her face grim. Velveteen laughs then grimaces.

"Charles should never have been expelled from the senior council." Velveteen sighs.

"He wasn't expelled—" Meredith argues.

"You know what I mean." Velveteen cuts her off. They sit in silence for a moment, the tension between them weighing heavily.

"Look," Meredith reasons, "he was playing around with energies that just shouldn't be brought anywhere near the Wiccan headquarters. We tried to talk to him, make him understand the danger of his newfound interest in attack magic, but he just wouldn't listen. What choice did we have?"

"He just wanted to expand his knowledge base. He's an intelligent person."

"I know that. And if reading up on The Voynich Manuscript was all he wanted to do, it wouldn't ever have been an issue. But Charles was more susceptible to the charms of the dark side than any of us could ever have foreseen."

Velveteen slows the car down to stop at a red light. She turns to face Meredith, a frightened expression hollowing her usually full cheeks.

"So what about when we gave him our blood?" she asks before the lights turn green.

"Well . . ." Meredith falters. "That was before he developed this obsession with evil."

"True. Otherwise, we never would have let him have it. But what if he uses our blood samples now?"

"To do what exactly? I think I can speak for both of us when I say that neither of us has ever had our blood tainted by engagement with devilry . . ." Meredith reassures her.

"Therefore, if he tried to use it, only good outcomes could be achieved?" Velveteen finishes the thought.

"Exactly," Meredith replies.

"Okay."

They both fall silent as Velveteen listens to the next set of directions from the GPS. She hangs a right at the next intersection and then a swift left. They are almost there.

"You know," Velveteen admits, "I feel worse than uneasy about this whole thing."

"Nervous?"

"More than that. I've had this tingling all through my body ever since you found the button."

"Really? I've had that, too."

The GPS takes them down a suburban side street, then announces that their destination has been reached as they pull over outside an ordinary-looking brick house. White shutters frame the windows, and a neatly trimmed lawn bereft of trees or shrubbery lends the property a clipped tidiness.

"Well, this is it," Velveteen says, switching off the GPS. The two women look at the house with trepidation, reluctant to leave the car's safety.

"You know," Meredith begins, turning to Velveteen. "I'm not so sure about this anymore."

"We have to find Ketzia," Velveteen replies.

"Do you feel that?" Meredith shudders.

"What?"

"I don't know . . . just . . ." Meredith closes her eyes for a moment, reopening them to find Velveteen reaching for her phone.

"You know what I'm going to do?" she says with practical determination. "I'm going to call Headquarters and tell them where we are."

"You're calling for backup?"

"It might be a false alarm. We both know that, hope that, but what if it's not?" Velveteen's finger hovers above the call button on her phone.

"Okay," Meredith replies. "Tell them where we are and to come over. But don't give them too many details. The last thing we want is to incite satanic panic."

"Satanic panic." Velveteen guffaws, pushing the phone to her ear. "Sounds like the name of a rock band."

"Thrash metal more like it," Meredith says, shutting up as Velveteen gets through to headquarters and explains the situation.

Meanwhile, Mia and Ron wait for the cops to arrive with mounting tension at Ketzia's house.

"I really hope Ketzia's all right," Mia cries, sitting on the couch. Ron follows her lead, plonking himself down beside her.

"Ketzia's a very capable woman. I'm sure she'll be all right," he reassures her. "You know what they say — lipstick is the only difference between a female real-estate agent and a pit bull."

Mia groans, used to Ron's cheesy humour. Meanwhile, he is distracted by the buzzing of his mobile. Ron checks the readout before switching the phone to silent. Mia watches him curiously.

"That's very un-real-estate-agent-like of you," she comments wryly.

"Huh? What?"

"Turning off your phone."

"Sometimes there are more important things to deal with than real estate," Ron says, giving her an affectionate grin. Mia isn't quite sure how to react to this. It's as though she's never actually looked at Ron properly before, always just seen him as a reasonable boss with occasionally ridiculous demands and even stupider jokes. But now he's proving to be, well, brave under the circumstances. The snake chooses that moment to slide off his bed of rocks and slither his way towards them across the floor.

"Eek," Mia screeches, lifting her feet off the floor. Her shapely legs bend into Ron's lap as he shoos the snake away with the palm of his hand. At Ron's signals, the snake obediently changes his course to head for his water bowl in the kitchen.

"I'm sure it isn't dangerous," Ron soothes, his left hand resting on Mia's legs. His touch feels quite lovely, and she does nothing to change her position.

"Maybe . . ." She watches the back of the snake's body as he drinks the water. "I can't believe Ketzia has a pet snake. She never told me about it."

"I guess it goes to show how you can work with someone for a long time and never actually get to know them," Ron replies. The two smile at each other, silently acknowledging the truth of the statement.

"I can't believe those two friends of hers, either," Mia says, flustered by the intimacy developing between her and Ron. "They were so weird."

"Very weird," Ron agrees, chuckling. "Did you see the tall one doing that dance?"

"Oh my gosh! Yes! I thought she was going to, I don't know, start speaking in tongues or something." They laugh, the mood considerably lightened.

A sharp knock at the door announces the arrival of the police. Mia slides her legs suggestively off Ron's lap, allowing his hand to trail down the muscles of her calves. Then they get up to answer the door together.

My throat feels parched, and I sip at the water Charles holds obligingly to my mouth, its refreshing coolness hydrating me. Satiated, I rest my head back on the pillow, only peripherally aware of Charles putting the glass in the kitchenette sink and returning to perch on the end of the bed. My spatial awareness is distorted. The bedposts appear as tiny sticks protruding from the corners of the bed while Charles looms large. Plus, my ordeal and exhaustion have made me super groggy.

"I feel so strange."

"That's natural at this stage of the ritual. That is perfect." Charles praises, prompting a wave of disgust in me. But at this stage, I think I've kind of given up on the idea of ever escaping from him, or if my spirit guides are trying to tell me that the way to conquer him is through my dreams, but all I want is to go back to sleep. I close my eyes and let myself be transported back to the land of dreams.

However, my hope that dreaming would provide respite from Charles's torture is quickly shattered. As usual, with this on-again-off-again somnambulistic state, I am thrown back into the dream exactly where it last left off — in the lake with Celeste and Daphne, the three of us wrapped in the tight embrace of a many-tentacled sea monster.

I scream, trying to push away from the creature, but this just enables it to tighten its grip around our naked bodies. Panic-stricken, I appeal to Celeste and Daphne for help, the creature's tentacles thrashing wildly around us.

"What do we do?" My voice barely carries over the roar of churning water.

"Stay close," Daphne calls out as a tentacle rises above us. Celeste signals for us to dive. We duck down just before it comes

crashing down in annihilation. The tentacle smashes through the water to follow our descent, but we move too quickly for it, swimming downwards to the relative safety of the reeds. Underwater, the colossal size of the beast is even more apparent. Its vast body rests on the lake floor, extending far beyond visibility, while its tentacles move feverishly through the water. Daphne and Celeste grip my hands tightly, and I gain strength from the power of their touch. They help me push through the water, and we swim further into the reeds until we are well hidden. It is a temporary solution, but one that enables me a moment to calm my shaking body. The sea creature is momentarily pacified, perhaps just because we are not visible to it anymore, and we allow ourselves a moment to rest.

Celeste examines one of the reeds curiously, sliding her fingers thoughtfully along one of the blades. Then she bends it, testing for flexibility. The seaweed is tough, unbreakable, yet pliant enough to coil. Celeste lowers her hand to the sandy ground of the lake, digging around one of the reeds until she can pull it out by the root. The water makes speech impossible, so she communicates through hand signals. Celeste signals for Daphne and me to copy her, and we join her in digging up the sharp strands. I'm not sure exactly what she has in mind, but I follow suit, happy to be guided by her. At least one of us has a plan. I just hope it will turn out to be a good one.

CHAPTER THIRTY-ONE

The two cops standing on Ketzia's front step when Ron and Mia open the door don't inspire confidence in Mia. One is hopelessly overweight, carrying his paunch like a burden as it hangs over the edge of his thick black police uniform belt. He wears glasses that—for no good reason—keep fogging up. His head is bald on top, barely concealed by a few strands of greasy brown hair that he has styled in an unsuccessful attempt at a comb-over. He reaches out to shake Ron and Mia's hands in turn.

"Officer Scott Hardley and this is Officer John Bath."

Officer Bath is a weedy young guy with a crew cut and a pronounced facial tic. Ron and Mia shake hands with the officers courteously. The officers run through a list of questions about Ketzia—how long she's been missing, what she does for work, her usual social group, and whether she is in a relationship.

Ron tells them about Meredith and Velveteen and how the two women raced off—on a hunch—to see if they could find her at a guy called Charles's place. Mia and Ron answer the rest of their questions to the best of their capabilities, though it is becoming more apparent to both of them how little they know about their colleague and friend.

The cops seem satisfied with their answers, and they take themselves on a tour of the house. Neither of them flinches when they spot the snake on his bed of rocks, which impresses Mia. They take in Ketzia's handbag and phone, thanking Mia and Ron for their foresight in not touching anything.

Then they head upstairs. Ron and Mia remain in the kitchen, allowing the cops to get on with their work.

"Fine specimens," Ron whispers, raising his eyebrow at her, causing Mia to erupt in a fit of giggles.

"The fashionista in me was extremely impressed with the vintage comb-over," she replies, prompting a grin from Ron. Mia knows they both need the light relief, the seriousness of the situation not lost on either of them. Heavy footsteps can be heard from upstairs as the officers stomp around above.

"I've seen this voodoo shit before . . ." Officer Hardley's voice travels down the stairs. Mia wonders what he is looking at.

"Messes with people's heads, it does." Officer Bath picks up where Hardley left off.

"Yes, indeed . . ."

Mia had always pondered about those parts of herself that Ketzia kept private. She had a mysterious introversion that didn't fit with the rest of her personality. But was she somehow involved in voodoo or witchcraft or something? It didn't seem possible. Finally, the officers traipse down the stairs again.

"So, who did you say were the two ladies that were here when you arrived?" Officer Hardley asks.

Ron pulls out his phone and slides through his contacts as he answers. "Their names were Meredith and . . . err, Velveteen . . ."

"Okay. Velveteen."

"Velveteen gave me her number. I thought we might need it."

"Good call," Officer Bath says approvingly. Ron hands his phone over, with Velveteen's number on the screen.

At Charles's house, Meredith and Velveteen have

unsuccessfully been knocking on the front door for several minutes. It seems to Meredith like all they've been doing all day is knocking on doors that just don't want to be opened.

Velveteen's phone rings. She checks the caller ID.

"I don't know this number. But I suppose I'd better get it just in case it's something to do with Ketzia."

She answers just as the front door opens. Charles greets Meredith in his usual aloof way while Velveteen waves a greeting before stepping back apologetically to take her phone call.

"Charles, sorry to drop in on you unannounced." Meredith takes the lead. "Hopefully, it's not a bad time?"

"Actually," Charles replies, "it's not the best time for me. Of course, it's lovely to see you, but why don't we arrange a time to catch up properly?"

Meredith pays him no heed, pushing past him to make her way inside.

"This won't take a minute." She turns around to call out to Velveteen. "Coming, Velveteen?"

Velveteen raises one finger and lowers her mobile.

"I'll be right with you," she says. Meredith doesn't let her frustration show as she heads down the dark entrance hallway of Charles's home. He follows close on her heels, quickly directing her to the lounge room on the right. It is an opulent room with expensive-looking antiques and ornate Persian rugs. Charles gestures for Meredith to sit on a maroon-upholstered Victorian Renaissance Revival sofa. And just then, she has an idea. She wishes she had thought of it before coming inside, so she could have prepped Velveteen.

"What's this all about, Meredith?" he snaps, causing Meredith to squirm in her seat. The dark energy swirling around him is unbearably strong. It causes ripples of pain to rush down her sensitive spine. She briefly wonders if she would even have the power to overthrow a maleficent force of such magnitude.

"Woo, hoo." Velveteen's cheery voice floats down the hall, and a rush of relief courses through Meredith's body. She is not in this on her own. And even though Velveteen might not have the most advanced Wiccan skills in the world, the combination of both of their talents will hopefully be enough to control Charles.

"In here." Charles steps into the hall, directing Velveteen into the lounge room.

"What an amazing house, Charles. I just adore antiques," Velveteen gushes, as though this is the most normal visit in the world. He doesn't say anything, and Meredith jumps in, hoping to shut Velveteen up long enough for her to realise her plan and play along with it.

"Charles," she says, leaning forward confidingly, "the reason we've come here today is to implement the next stage of the Castanna Street Wiccan succession plan . . ."

Charles looks at her suspiciously. Velveteen stares at the carpet.

"Recently, as you know, we had to eject you from your position on the senior council. This was part of a greater plan that—unfortunately for you—we were unable to reveal to you for political reasons at the time. For some time, many Higher Order Wiccans have wanted to establish an elite circle of Higher Order Wiccans of which we would like you to be the leader. The Chief Wiccan—if you like. And, of course, this role would be impossible for you to undertake while also being active on senior council . . ."

Charles looks from Meredith to Velveteen, taking it all in.

"Velveteen, I didn't know you were part of the higher order," he finally says, still suspicious.

"Oh, I'm not," Velveteen replies sweetly. "I just cook for them."

"And are privy to all their secrets?" Charles scoffs.

"Velveteen has been serving us under a spell of shadows for a year and a half," Meredith responds. Shadow spells were sometimes used to enable lower-level Wiccans to partake in higher-order ceremonies, with all memory of the event being obliterated from their consciousness afterwards. It is a bit far-fetched to suggest that Velveteen has been under the influence of such a spell for such a long time, but Charles seems to buy it.

"So what do you say, Charles?" Meredith asks. "Are you in?"

Charles rubs his hands together, a pleased expression on his face.

"I'll certainly think about it. Can I get you, ladies, a drink?" In charm mode now, Charles seems like a different person. The witches nod their heads, and Charles excuses himself to go and make the drinks. As soon as he has left the room, Meredith turns to Velveteen.

"She's here. I can feel it. Sure as anything."

"Where?" Velveteen asks.

"In my bones."

"No," Velveteen clarifies in exasperation. "*Where* here is she?"

Charles enters the room, carrying a tray of drinks, cutting them off.

"Aperitifs, ladies?"

"Mighty fine home you have here, Charles. Is there a downstairs?" Meredith asks.

"Nope. Nothing like that. Just, you know, everything you see." Charles makes a sweeping movement with his arm.

"Everything you see," Meredith repeats, dropping her voice about an octave. Her eyes are enlarged, and she is breathing very quickly. Charles is frozen to the spot, resisting the power of her gaze.

"Charles," Meredith says, her voice rich and deep. "Charles."

Velveteen makes little popping sounds with her lips, interfering with Charles's ability to censor Meredith's voice. He looks at Meredith, and *bam* — she has him mesmerised.

"You had so much potential," she says to him with disappointment.

"My capabilities were always going to remain unrecognised," he replies disdainfully, able to talk although frozen to the spot.

"Where's Ketzia?" Velveteen demands angrily. Charles doesn't say anything, but his eyes give him away as he glances downwards.

"Downstairs?" Meredith pushes, her eyes hallucinogenic circles. Charles nods. Meredith stands up and says to Velveteen, "Let's find her."

"What about him?" Velveteen asks, pointing to Charles.

"He's frozen. I've mesmerised him," Meredith answers.

"It's not that I don't trust your magic skills . . ." Velveteen conciliates, trailing off as she scans the room. The heavy drapes on the windows are tied back with thick rope cords.

"But just to be on the safe side." Velveteen unties two of them and uses them to tie Charles's frozen hands and feet together before the pair leave the room together to try and find a way downstairs.

Mia watches Officer Bath get off the phone to Velveteen, wondering what has his brow furrowed in consternation. "We need to talk to those women in person. Sounds like they might be putting themselves in a dangerous situation."

"Right," Officer Hardley replies, hiking his pants up over his paunch. "Did you find out where they are?"

"Yep, an address in Glebe."

The officers head to the front door, turning to Mia and Ron as they exit.

"There's really little you can do but wait, now," Officer Bath says to them. "Thanks for all your assistance."

"No way!" Ron exclaims, then seems to remember himself. "I beg your pardon, officers. But we're coming with you."

The officers look at each other, unsure of the wisdom in this.

"She might need emotional support if you find her," Mia adds reasonably. Officer Bath finally nods his head.

"I can't see any harm in that. But you must follow orders when we get there."

"Of course," Ron and Mia agree.

"We can follow behind in my car," Ron suggests.

"All right. You are to stay in your vehicle while we enter the premises. Follow us, then."

They rush from Ketzia's house.

The traffic has intensified since they were last in it, but Ron is a good driver and trails the police car effortlessly.

"I can't believe what they were saying about Ketzia being into voodoo and shit," Mia says, distressed by the situation.

"I guess it's hard to really know someone. And people have all sorts of interests," Ron replies diplomatically.

"Yeah? So, what private interests do you pursue?" Mia flirts, enjoying the blush that blooms on Ron's face.

"I don't know," he says, shrugging amicably. Mia's Crazy in Love ringtone blasts from her phone, making them both jump.

"Saved by Beyoncé!" Ron laughs, and Mia laughs with him.

"Hello?" she says.

"Hello, is that Mia?" The male voice at the other end of the line is familiar. "I hope you don't mind the intrusion. I called the office and got your mobile number," the voice continues smoothly. It's Leon.

"That's quite all right, Mr Furness," Mia replies, prompting a look from Ron.

"I've just arrived in Sydney. I'm at the airport. Have you found Ketzia yet?" he asks, an impatient edge sharpening his tone.

"We went to her house —"

"Who's *we*?" Leon cuts in. From the tone of his voice, Mia can hear how worried he is.

"Me and Ron. From the office."

"Go on," Leon says.

"She wasn't at her house. We called the police, and then these other women said they might know where she is, so we told the cops —"

"What other women? What are you talking about?" Leon cuts her off again.

"Just some of Ketzia's friends. Look, I know this all proba-bly sounds a bit confusing but rest assured, Mr Furness, we are doing our best to find her." Mia feels her grip on the phone faltering, threatening to slide out of her sweaty palm as Leon's anxiety unnerves her.

"So, where do you think she is?"

"Right now, we're headed to an address in Glebe, follow-ing the police who are also on their way there."

"Please, give me the address," Leon pleads, his voice strained with worry, leaving Mia little choice but to comply. As soon as she's given him Charles's address, he hangs up on her.

"Phew. He sounded pretty stressed," Mia exclaims after putting her phone away.

"Not your type?"

"I don't know . . ." Mia says casually, making Ron chuckle.

"So, what type do you go for?" Ron asks the question jokingly but can't prevent it from sounding hopeful. Mia smiles at him, and something like electricity pulses between them.

"Let's just say I like men who open doors for women, who have a good sense of humour, and who prove themselves to be brave in difficult situations."

"I see," Ron replies thoughtfully. The rest of their journey is travelled in silence.

Downstairs, at Charles's house, Meredith and Velveteen have found the door leading to Charles's chamber of secrets. The door is heavy, lined with oak, but opens with the first turn of the handle—only locking from the inside. They carefully block the entrance with Meredith's scarf to allow an easy escape. They don't know what to expect as they enter the basement, but the sight of Ketzia, unconscious and chained to the four-poster bed, is enough to make anyone panic.

"Ketzia," Velveteen cries, rushing towards her, "Ketzia, are you okay?"

Meredith places a restraining hand on Velveteen's arm. They will have to tread gently if they are going to be of any use in this particular witchy scenario.

Ketzia doesn't respond to Velveteen's voice at all. It is as though she is in some sort of a trance—or a coma. The surreal silence of the basement is disrupted by the sound of sirens from the street above.

"What's that?" Meredith asks in alarm.

"The cops."

"Huh?"

"The cops are on their way."

"You told the cops where we are?" Meredith asks in stupefaction.

"I had to. They were very full-on about it on the phone."

"Right, well, we must work quickly then. We have to ensure Ketzia has completely recovered from Charles's demented magic before she has contact with anyone. Otherwise, she could remain permanently entrapped by it."

Velveteen nods grimly, turning her attention to Ketzia's naked body.

"Ketzia, can you hear me?" Meredith asks. Ketzia still doesn't respond. Meredith looks at Velveteen.

"We're going to have to Dream Walk."

"Dream Walk? I've never done that before," Velveteen exclaims.

"There's a first time for everything," Meredith says, lying beside Ketzia on the bed. She signals for Velveteen to lie down on the other side.

"Shouldn't we do something about this first?" Velveteen asks, inspecting the heavy chains holding Ketzia down.

"Not yet," Meredith replies. "In her current state, releasing her could prove more dangerous. She has travelled far on the astral plane. Pulling her back from there without some interventionist action could cause her serious spiritual damage."

"How can you tell?" Velveteen, obviously still not entirely convinced, lays herself down on the other side of Ketzia nonetheless. Meredith explains with clinical precision precisely what is going on.

"Her respiration oscillates between increased and reduced rates, and her eyelids are flickering—but at a speed lower than that induced by REM sleep. She has tension in her hands and muscles, indicating physical readiness for the proclivities of the dream. Aside from these physical symptoms, energetically, I can sense that she is in a supremely heightened and fragile state somewhere on the subconscious terrain. We need to join her there and help her."

Clearly bracing herself, Velveteen says, "Okay, what do I have to do?"

"Take her hand. Close your eyes. And breathe . . ."

With Ron sitting next to her, Mia watches the police from the safety of Ron's car, parked behind the police issue station wagon out the front. They've knocked on the door several times, and Officer Bath called out to announce their arrival officially but had no response from within Charles's brick bungalow. Officer Bath has already clocked Velveteen's car on arrival, so they know they've come to the right place. Officer Hardley tests the handle of the front door. Open. The police officers enter the house, hands at the ready on their hip holsters.

"I feel like I'm in some bad re-run of The Bill," Mia says, tying her copper hair back nervously.

"I feel totally useless, just sitting here . . ." Ron says.

"Well, you heard what the cops said. We have to stay here."

"At least they seem to know what they're doing. They seemed like a couple of deadbeats when they arrived at Ketzia's house."

"They didn't really make the greatest first impression." Mia chuckles at the memory of Officer Hardley's comb-over.

"I guess we're probably more critical about first impressions than most people . . ." Ron replies.

"What? Why?"

"Being real-estate agents and all."

"Oh. I guess." Mia looks at Charles's house, trying to see if she can see movement through the windows. But it's too dark inside for her to make anything out, plus it looks like the windows are covered by heavy drapes from within.

"How much do you think it would fetch?"

In disbelief, Mia stares at Ron, who's also looking at Charles's house, clearly assessing it for a different reason.

"What?"

"The house. On the market. This area's been realising some sustainable growth over the past few years." Ron pulls out his mobile, opening a real-estate app. Mia watches him angrily.

"Ron! Ketzia's life could be in danger, and all you're interested in is *real estate*? You're fucking unbelievable."

"Well, what else are we supposed to do? Sure beats sitting here doing nothing." Ron says but lowers his phone all the same. They sit in silence for a moment, watching the minutes on the clock tick over.

"I'm sorry," Ron says.

"No. I'm sorry," Mia says. "I'm just so worried about her. I didn't mean to let it out on you."

"Hey, it's fine." Ron reaches for her hand.

A black limousine pulls over on the curb directly in front of them. They watch as the driver swiftly emerges to open the back door.

"Hello. What have we here?" Ron whistles as a tall man in a dark suit gets out of the vehicle.

"Oh my gosh. It's Leon Furness," Mia squawks in awe. Ron's eyes narrow as he watches Leon head to the front door. He heads straight inside, not bothering to knock, and disappears. Mia and Ron stare at the door, waiting, not saying anything. Finally, Ron loses patience, unclasping his seatbelt.

"Stuff this. I'm going in," Ron announces.

"Ron." Mia places a cautioning hand on his arm.

"If he can — I can," he says decisively, opening his door and stepping out. On the other side of the vehicle, Mia gets out, too. Ron stops and stares at her.

"What are you doing?"

"Going in. If you can, I can . . ."

Seeing the challenge in Mia's eyes, Ron obviously knows better than to try and argue the point. He shakes his head resignedly before reaching for her hand, and they cross the lawn to the house together.

Dream walking isn't like being asleep, though a sleep-like state must be entered to do it. It's a little like going for a long-distance drive — you are in control of the car but not entirely present the whole time. Entire suburbs can slip past while you chew over the cud of life or just tune out and listen to the radio. With dream walking, the dream is the landscape rushing past the windows. The dreamer is the driver, engaged with whatever thoughts take their interest. Practised in dream walking, Meredith instantly slips into a trancelike state, holding Ketzia's left hand. On the right side of the bed, Velveteen takes longer to induct herself into Ketzia's dream. She thinks of music — Carl Orff's Carmina Burana, Alexander Borodin's Prince Igor — grand orchestral works that can elevate even the humblest soul to that of a God. While holding Ketzia's right hand, a jolt passes through her and then she is transported underwater.

I am holding a large bunch of reeds. Beside me, Celeste and Daphne have been just as busy, digging up the stalks of the seaweed with fervour. We come together, armed with bundles of rushes. Celeste directs us to braid the strands together to form thick ropes. Fearfully, I can't help glancing over my shoulder, but the sea creature lies quiet, oblivious to our activity. Celeste's hands change as they work. They appear older, more worn — more human.

Daphne, too, is changing — her voluptuousness taking on a pudgy humanoid form. The pair continue shifting between ethereal and human beings until the familiar features of Meredith and Velveteen can be identified. They smile at me, Celeste continuing to transmogrify into Meredith, while Daphne flickers into Velveteen's shape and back again in a constant, fluid process of metamorphosis.

I feel a deep-seated panic take root, that if they entirely embody these human forms, they will lose the ability to breathe underwater. But my concerns prove unwarranted. There is still no need for us to come to the surface for air — the dream, or whatever this is, has taken care of that. Relief and gratitude course through me. My Wiccan friends can have entered my subconscious for only one reason. They want to help me conquer the beast in the lake.

We manage to knit the reeds together to form twelve coils of rope, as tough and pliant as cable ties. Carrying four ropes apiece, we propel ourselves through the water towards the sea creature. Its dark contours loom menacingly beyond a sand dune on the bottom of the lake. We take shelter behind the dune, peeking over the top to assess the creature's position. It lies spreadeagled on the lake floor, its vast tentacles spiralling out voluminously in opposite directions. I can count five of them and note that the positioning of the tentacles in relation to the globular body of the beast forms an inverted pentagram, a powerful symbol. Meredith points to two of the tentacles on the beast's right side and then signals to me, indicating that I will be responsible for restraining these. She delegates the two tentacles on the creature's left side to Velveteen, who nods in agreement. This means Meredith will have to secure the centre tentacle, probably the most difficult to overcome, being visibly connected to the beast's heart line. However, there is no time for anyone to argue as the creature starts to stir. We embrace, holding onto each other for strength before swimming over the top of the dune, reeds at the ready.

I swim to the furthest tentacle on the right-hand side. The reeds prove pliant and malleable, easily wrapping around the generous folds of the beast's arm. I knot them before harnessing the other tentacle and tying the two rope ends together. In this hogtied fashion, I hope the aquatic cyclops will be stilled long enough for us to create a serious transformation to the heart of the giant squid — a change from evil to good. Velveteen has progressed similarly to me, successfully binding the two left tentacles together. Unfortunately, Meredith has not fared quite so well, though her task was always going to be the most difficult. The creature's middle tentacle must be incredibly sensitive. Every time Meredith nears the arm, it flickers nervously, whipping the water into a frenzy of bubbles. I swim over to help her, reaching for the tip of the tentacle and gripping it tightly. Velveteen grabs hold of it, further along, enabling Meredith to wind the cord of reeds around the upper part of the tentacle. I'm not a hundred per cent sure of Meredith's plan, but it seems like she wants to tie the middle tentacle to the others. I try to help her with it, but I momentarily lose my grip on the slimy tentacle tip. It whips back, causing Velveteen to lose her balance, her feet kicking up sand from the bottom of the lake, muddying the water and making it almost impossible to see her.

I grab hold of the tentacle again, using it to steady myself as I make my way up its thickening limb. I reach the creature's body, desperate to quell it. Up close, it is even more enormous than I had anticipated, its wrinkles blurring its features, making the separate components of its physiognomy indistinguishable. A beaklike protrusion lifts and expels a jet of inky-black liquid into the murky water. Possibly its mouth? Meredith has by now found her footing and joins me. She is too far away to reach the creature's body, so she reaches forward and passes her cord of reeds. The sharpness of its edge almost slices my hand open when I grasp it. I adjust my grip to avoid cutting myself. It instantly reacts by collapsing back on itself, and the mouth orifice shapes convincingly in what would translate above-water to a discernible howl. Meredith and Velveteen join my side. Instinctively it pulls back, but we press forwards, squeezing our bodies closer and reaching out to hold hands.

Involuntarily, I gag, overwhelmed by the dark energy at the creature's core. Velveteen and Meredith surge forwards, pushing their bodies tight around the cephalopod, reaching out to join hands.

Meredith clasps my hand. Velveteen joins us to form a tiny triangle of fearful hope as we watch the blubbery wreck of a marine mollusc go through some kind of transformation, changing colour to a soft rose red.

We stay a moment, watching in frozen silence, waiting for the second gasp of evil from the creature. But none comes. Meredith, pedantic and cautious as ever, swims forward, prodding the tentacles and body. They are soft and pliant. They move gracefully in the water. Satisfied, she circles back to us, nodding her head and signal-ling for us to join her, to swim upwards, towards the miraculous rainbow-shimmering surface of the water.

CHAPTER THIRTY-TWO

Mia's ears are assaulted with the sound of shouting as they enter Charles's house. Following the source of the raised voices, she enters the door to the lounge room, Ron a solid presence beside her. Officer Bath stands beside a tall, pallid man whose wrists and ankles are bound together with curtain ropes. The man does not move. His waist is angled slightly forward, and his face wears an expression of frozen supplication.

Meanwhile, Officer Hardley tries to calm a very irate Leon Furness, demanding to know where Ketzia is. Mia and Ron hover in the doorway, reluctant to participate in the room's madness. Officer Hardley spots them and signals for them to come in.

"Who the hell is this guy — and what is wrong with him?" Leon yells, pointing to the frozen man beside Officer Bath.

"We've identified this man as Charles Aynsley. At this stage, we don't know exactly what condition he is suffering from, but an ambulance is on its way," Officer Bath replies in clipped tones. Leon moves towards Charles, but Officer Hardley quickly steps in to impede his progress.

"Please identify yourself, sir," he says.

"Me?" Leon reacts, clearly taken aback by the request. "I'm Leon Furness, the head of KX Global Realty."

"Please provide positive proof of your identity," Officer Hardley persists, obviously unimpressed by Leon's assertion. "A driver's licence will do."

"He is who he says he is. I can vouch for that." Ron speaks up from his unchanged position at the perimeter of the room. Leon notices Mia and Ron then and rushes towards them, enfolding them in a tearful hug.

"Thank God you're here. Thank you, thank you!"

Mia and Ron pat his arms, unsure how to react to this incongruous display of emotion. Mia is the first to recover, disentangling herself and walking over to Charles.

"Please, let's not waste time. We need to find Ketzia. Is she here?" she says. Charles does not move, and his eyes don't even blink. Mia turns away from him in disgust.

"This is so weird . . ." she mutters.

"Was he like this when you got here?" Ron asks the officers, who both nod confirmation.

"So what about Meredith and Velveteen?" Mia asks.

"Where are they?" Ron finishes her train of thought.

Meredith, Ketzia, and Velveteen lie side by side on Charles's ornate four-poster bed in his dark basement, holding hands. No one could ever guess at the fierce underwater battle they have just been through, claiming victory over a mythical beast of paranormal proportions. As they return from their collective out-of-body experience, the women's faces contort with spasms, and their bodies lightly rock from side to side. The chains still bind Ketzia's legs, and her wrists remain locked in place by the heavy cuffs. A smattering of goose bumps across her naked skin heralds the return of life to her cells. Velveteen is the first to open her eyes, followed shortly by Meredith. Ketzia remains in a deep, trance-like state, sandwiched between them. Velveteen raises herself on one elbow and examines Ketzia.

"Is she all right?" she whispers to Meredith.

"She will be," Meredith replies, getting up and walking around to the foot of the bed.

"Who knows how long she's been chained in this position," Meredith mutters. She presses her fingertips to the skin of Ketzia's ankles, murmuring a healing spell. Meanwhile, Velveteen moves to the head of the bed and tries to prise open Ketzia's handcuffs.

"These are locked," she says to Meredith, who looks up from her work with Ketzia's ankles to engage Velveteen in a level stare.

"Leave them," she says. "The most important thing for us to do right now is to restore Ketzia to us." She is interrupted by the sound of shouting from upstairs.

"Hear that?" she asks, and Velveteen nods. "We need to perform a ritual cleansing, sweeping ceremony on Ketzia to bring her back to us — before she has any contact with anyone from the external world. Otherwise, we risk her becoming entrapped in this state forever."

"Let's get to it, then," Velveteen says. "Tell me what I need to do . . ."

Upstairs the heat is escalating. Mia has been hurling abuse at an unresponsive Charles, while Ron has been trying to explain to Leon why he didn't raise the alarm when Ketzia failed to show up at the office several days in a row. Officer Bath has been making sure everyone maintains physical distance while Officer Hardley tries to make himself heard over the CB radio, calling for backup and lodging a request to the station for any records pertaining to Charles Aynsley. But it seems the guy is clean as a whistle — that, or he's never been caught breaking the law. They have nothing on him on file.

"Where do you think you're going?" Officer Bath's strident voice stops Leon in his tracks, halfway out of the room. He swivels around on his heel to face the policeman.

"I'm going to look for Ketzia," Leon says.

"I'm going to have to ask you to remain in the room," Officer Bath responds.

"Why?"

"This is a police matter and possible investigation —"

"I don't see much evidence of any investigating going on," Leon interrupts.

"I understand this is difficult for you, sir, but I will have to ask you to remain *in the room.*" These last words are shouted as Leon continues to ignore Officer Bath, turning his back on him to leave the lounge room. Officer Bath pulls his gun, ordering Leon to freeze. At this moment, a gaggle of women swan into the house. They are all witches from Ketzia's coven, who Velveteen had called on earlier for help. With the police officer aiming his gun at Leon, the Wiccans assume he is the bad guy. Officer Bath lowers his weapon, momentarily distracted by the witches. In his determination to find Ketzia, Leon grabs the opportunity to make a run for it. He doesn't get far. One by one, the witches pounce on top of him, each clutching a hand or foot to hold him captive.

"Got him!" They shout to the unimpressed officers. Only then do they notice Charles, a petrified statue in his own home.

"Charles!" one of them shouts.

"He's had a paralysis spell cast on him," another one says. No one hears footsteps coming up the basement stairs to this unfolding chaos. They all turn in surprise as Velveteen comes rushing in.

"We've found her," she gasps breathlessly.

Meredith has shrouded my naked body with the bedsheets, shaping them into a makeshift sarong-style dress tied in a bulky knot beneath my shoulder. My wrists are still clamped, but I've managed to manoeuvre myself into a sitting position nonetheless. Everything feels as though it's shrouded in mist, as though I am emerging from a deep, mystical experience. My thoughts are foggy, though, and I'm having trouble remembering exactly what happened to me. All I know for sure is that Charles has been keeping me prisoner in his basement. Who knows how long for? Luckily, Meredith and Velveteen came along and saved me.

"Thank you, Meredith," I croak, my voice raw with gratitude.

"Oh, Ketzia." Meredith's eyes fill with tears as she gently strokes my cheek.

There is so much I don't understand. I have no idea how long it will take for me to make sense of everything that has happened. A commotion at the door of the basement breaks my musings. Leon rushes in, throwing himself at me, showering me with kisses and tears. I return his kisses, but the handcuffs impede my ability to hug him back. Leon notices them, breaking from our emotional reunion to yell out, "Get these off her. Now."

Only now do I notice the others that have entered the room behind him—Velveteen, Mia, Ron, and a police officer.

"I think Charles has the key," I manage.

"The bastard." Leon spits out, making to head upstairs.

"I'll deal with this," the officer intercedes, hot-footing it upstairs. He leaves behind a sudden silence as everyone battles to come to grips with the situation. Leon returns to my side, his elation at having found me palpable in his shimmering eyes, which narrow to quiet concern.

"Did he hurt you?" he asks, his eyes tender.

"I . . . I think I'm fine." I sound less confident than I would like, but the heavy tread of the police officer announces his return to the basement. He walks to my side, jangling a set of keys.

225

"Found these in his pocket. Think they should be a fit." He inserts the key in the lock of the handcuffs with practised ease. A barely audible click heralds success as the hinges open and the handcuffs release me. The painful ache in my bones overpowers the relief of blood flowing easily through my veins again. I rub my wrists, trying to prevent them from swelling. Leon watches my every move, patting my back with attentive care. Aware of everyone focusing on me, I put on a brave face and smile at them all.

"Hi, Mia. Hi, Ron," I manage.

"Hi, Ketzia," they murmur in unison.

"What are you doing here?" I feel suddenly self-conscious. Having my work colleagues find me naked in a basement is not something I ever imagined possible. I'm thankful for the sheets Meredith wrapped around me.

"We were worried about you," Mia says.

"We went to your house — looking for you," Ron continues. "That's where we met . . . your two friends here. Lucky for you, they knew to come and look for you here."

Obviously, there are still a lot of unanswered questions in his mind, but Meredith and Velveteen seem in no hurry to explain the situation.

"Where's Charles?" A sudden knot of fear paralyses my insides.

"Upstairs. You have nothing to worry about," Velveteen reassures me.

"He's paralysed," Meredith adds, and I know this means that she must have cast a paralysis spell on him.

"He's under arrest," the police officer clarifies. Static from his CB radio distracts him, and he responds to its garbled tones.

"The ambulance has arrived," he says. "Please, stay here," he says. "We'll get the paramedics to have a look at you before you get up and try to move around." Then he heads upstairs.

Another uncomfortable silence descends on the room. Who knows what everyone is thinking? Leon seems completely confused by everything that's happened. Meredith's eyes are half-closed, which I know from experience means she is checking her aura—probably for signs of collateral damage. Velveteen smiles calmly at me, while Mia and Ron are like two stunned mullets, not knowing where to look. Trying to lighten the atmosphere, I smooth down the folds of my make-shift sheet dress.

"I don't think I'd win any fashion awards for this outfit," I joke, extracting the faintest of smiles from Mia. I feel the need to reassure everyone that I'm okay. It seems they've all been worried about me, and even though their concern touches me, I feel surprisingly good. Even the bruising starting to surface on my wrists doesn't bother me. Mainly, I just have an over-whelming desire for everything to return to normal.

The paramedics traipse into the room, carrying a medical kit, ordering everyone to leave the room.

"Please, can Leon stay?" The paramedics allow him to stay, and everyone except Leon leaves the room. While the paramedics take my blood pressure and check my vital signs, they ask me about what happened. I answer their questions to the best of my ability, telling them that Charles brought me here and chained me to the bed. Leon listens attentively through-out, and I purposefully skimp on the details of what happened. I omitted to mention the potions Charles used on me. That is something I will have to talk to my coven about later.

Once the paramedics are satisfied with my physical condition, they give me the all-clear, advising me to drink plenty of water to rehydrate. Leon scoops me in his arms, the sheet dress billowing glamorously out beneath his firm grip. Perhaps it's not so unfashionable after all, I muse, as Leon carries me up the stairs. He pauses on the top tread and presses his lips to mine.

"Ketzia," he says, his voice husky, his eyes glossy. "I love you." My breath catches in my throat, and trembling reverberates through my inner core. It is the first time he has spoken those words to me. And it feels, it feels, like magic.

EPILOGUE

I lather myself with soap in the deliciously warm bath Leon has prepared for me, amazed at the absence of bruising on my body. Only the faintest of lines circle my ankles where the cuffs held me in place, and my wrists are only slightly chafed, thanks to a bit of magic from Meredith, who had held my wrists in her hands and discreetly applied her healing energy to their swollen redness, to the oblivion of everyone else gathered in Charles's living room. The police then took my statement, in which I repeated everything I said to the paramedics. I decided not to press charges against Charles — much to Leon's disbelief and chagrin. It was a strategic decision on my part. I know that the law would be useless in deterring Charles from practising his evil magic, so I figured the best approach would be for me to keep him in my debt by not pressing charges. But, of course, I can't expect Leon to understand that. There are so many things I cannot tell him about.

I've always known Leon is my ancestral knight, but I now realise his knowledge of witchcraft is non-existent. The witches Meredith and Velveteen had called for back-up clarified this for me, explaining that he doesn't have a psychic bone in his body. My initial disbelief was overcome after they made me realise that all those conversations we'd shared about our Wiccan ancestry had occurred solely on the telepathic plane. Or perhaps it had been my imagination, my mortal self unable to believe that I could have such a strong union with a man and for it all to be normal.

I smile as I hear Leon rattling about downstairs, making tea. He had driven me home from Charles's house, carefully carrying me upstairs and laying me on the bed while he ran me a bath. Then he'd helped me in, and I'd felt his admiring gaze on my body as I lowered myself into the steam.

I relax into the water, wondering what he thinks of my quaint little townhouse, which is so different to the usual opulent environments he inhabits. A soft bump on the door makes me look up. But it isn't Leon, only Bo, slithering into the bathroom to be close to me.

"Hello, Bo," I say, immeasurably pleased to see him. Meredith had told me that Bo had alerted them to the fact that I was missing. The bath water is going tepid, so I unhook the plug, stand up, step onto the bathmat, and reach for the towels Leon laid out for me. I wrap one around my hair and use the other to towel myself dry — my skin pulses with life. I inspect my face in the mirror, taken aback by how sparkly my eyes are, how peachy clear my skin is, and how full my lips are. It is as though my whole being is renewed, a reinvigoration beyond that possible by a bath. Something about my experience in Charles's basement has changed me, and I exude a strong inner light unnatural in its brightness. Bo coils himself around my ankle, and I reach down to pat him affectionately. Such a dear creature — I hope he's not too traumatised by my abduction. Personally, I feel completely recovered. Mainly, I'm just thankful the ordeal is over. However, I have decided to turn my back on witchcraft. I have decided to live without its magical influence and dangerous possibilities for the rest of my life.

I hear Leon coming up the stairs. I wrap a terry-towelling robe around me and pick Bo up before walking into the bedroom. Leon carries two cups of tea in his hands, setting them on the bedside table.

"You two have met, I believe?" I raise Bo slightly, bobbing his head, so it looks like he's nodding hello to Leon.

"I would never have picked you as one for having a pet snake, Ketzia," Leon says, avoiding eye contact with Bo. I grin and place Bo gently on the ground.

"I think there's a lot we still have to learn about each other," I reply, watching as Bo slithers from the room. Leon sits down on the bed and pats a spot beside him.

"Here, I've made you a cup of tea," he says, handing me a steaming cup.

"Thanks," I reply, sipping at the liquid gratefully. We are uncharacteristically shy in each other's presence and sit silently, drinking our tea.

"I still don't understand why you didn't want to press charges," Leon says. He's obviously been mulling it over.

"Leon, I don't expect you to understand, but I feel it's the right thing to do."

"I just don't want that bastard to get away with—"

"Please, Leon," I cut him off. "He's not going to get away with anything. Getting angry about it isn't going to help or change anything. I'm okay, Leon. Trust me. I'm fine."

"All right. Ketzia, I'm sorry," Leon says earnestly. I put my cup down and then grab his, placing it on the bedside table beside mine. I lean in to kiss him. His lips are so soft and tender, trembling ever so slightly as they part to allow my tongue to enter the warm wetness of his mouth. I pull back, looking deep into his eyes.

"What you said to me earlier, did you really mean that?" I ask.

He places his fingers to my lips and then strokes my cheek adoringly.

"That I love you?" he asks.

"Yes." I close my eyes wishfully.

"Yes, Ketzia. I do. I love you," he says. I open my eyes, feeling a hunger for him that surpasses any desire that I have ever experienced for him before.

"Then make love to me, Leon," I say. He trails his fingers down the length of my throat before slipping his hand inside the fold of my bathrobe to touch my breasts.

"Are you sure?" he asks, cautious about touching my body after everything I've been through.

"Please," I respond, kissing him. He slips off my robe and lays me down on the bed, showering my body with kisses. His fingertips lock onto the stiff crests of my nipples as his mouth continues moving over my stomach towards the rise of my mound. His lips hesitate above my pussy, but I urge him to continue. His tongue tests the tenderness of my moist womanhood, and I can't help but moan with pleasure. The sound spurs him on, his fingers brushing my nipples sensuously as he pushes his tongue deep inside. The sudden memory of the explosive orgasm I experienced in Charles's basement flashes through me. Indeed, some of that energy remains, for I feel my whole body sparking with hot desire. I push Leon off me and onto his back with a strength I didn't know I possessed. The need to touch him is fierce within me, and I tear his shirt off his body.

"Whoa, whoa, Ketzia," he cries, his hands trying to slow me down. But I am unstoppable. I unclasp his belt, unbuttoning his trousers and lowering his fly, pushing his pants down with his jocks. His penis is magnificently erect. I slide my lips and mouth over his ramrod shaft, sucking and licking, circling my tongue around its thickness.

I swivel around on the bed to position my arse above his mouth. I lower my pussy so he can continue where he left off, sucking and teasing my clit, his fingers reaching to stimulate me further. As I continue fucking his mouth with my cunt, I taste the pre-cum oozing out the head of his cock and decide it's time to turn starboard. I straddle him, plunging my pussy down—hard—along the blade-like length of his cock, slamming myself roughly down with urgency. Then I'm riding him, finding a smooth rhythm, his manhood pulsating deep inside me. Leon groans with pleasure, driving me on, my mounting orgasm pushing me to an out-of-body experience. Before I know it, I'm astral travelling with old familiar friends—cupids, nymphs, centaurs, shape-shifters—the spectres all nodding at me, smiling knowingly, as I feel Leon spasm with the release of an orgasm that sends us both spiralling over the edge.

We hold each other for a while, our bodies a sweaty, tangled mess of arms and legs. Leon pulls me closer, tenderly brushing his lips against mine.

"Ketzia," he says, looking at me with an expression of wonder. "Ketzia. You are amazing."

"You're the amazing one." I giggle, kissing him.

"I love you," he says.

"I love you, too," I reply.

I lie in bed, the pleasant afterglow of my orgasm saturating me, Leon's fingers tickling my spine, sending the endorphins already coursing through my body rushing. I think of the magic that brought me here, brought us together, constitutes our love, elevates our sex beyond the physical to the fantastical, and enables me to experience the most intense orgasms of my life.

I raise myself to take in the chiselled contours of Leon's face, and I think to myself how lucky I am. But is it luck that has brought him to me, or destiny? Perhaps a combination of both. A pairing brought about through Wiccan ways. I rest my head on the pillow, the tremors of ecstasy coursing through a final series of aftershocks. My body and soul are satiated. I close my eyes. My final thought, just before I drift off to sleep, is that maybe I'm not ready to turn my back on magic entirely. Not just yet.

YOU MAY ALSO ENJOY THE FOLLOWING FROM eXTASY BOOKS INC

DIVINE LUST
Sophie Love Marseilles
Release date

Excerpt

Ketzia and Leon are deeply in lust, but as their relationship becomes more serious, powerful supernatural forces threaten to tear them apart. Unless Ketzia can uncover the mystery of Leon's birthright while keeping her pagan identity a secret.

ABOUT THE AUTHOR

Sophie Love Marseilles had her first mystical sexual awakening while travelling through Europe, in a grove of ancient trees. This inspired her to immerse herself in secret ancient texts, the occult, and the art of seduction. She continues to explore her passion for writing, love, and alchemy in her erotic fiction.

To discover more please visit her website:
https://sophielovemarseilles.com/